No Egrets

A Glenn and Glenda Oak Island Mystery

(Oak Island Series Book 2)

Lance Carney

DEDICATION

For all the dedicated, caring, talented healthcare workers I have had
the privilege to work with through the years..

ALSO BY LANCE CARNEY

Ripped Tide: A Daniel O'Dwyer Oak Island Adventure (Oak Island Series Book 1)

Mantis Preying: A Daniel O'Dwyer Oak Island Adventure (Oak Island Series Book 3)

Of Vamps and Vampiros: A Finnian O'Dwyer Universal City Crime Cape(r)

With David Moss

Fin and Tonic, Talon and Tombstone (short story collection)

Pirates for a Day (short story)

Collection with Various Authors

True Wit: Stories by Humor Authors from Around the Globe

CONTENTS

ACKNOWLEDGMENTS

Cover Illustration Copyright © 2016 Jacob Howell

Editing (plus humorous additions)-Kathy Carney

Thanks to Australian humor writer, John Martin for reading the first draft and offering his insight and ideas (many of which I used).

Thanks to Whitney Hess from The Lost Cause Band for writing the lyrics to "Bela Lugosi's Blues" after I made it up in my last book (and to The Lost Cause Band for performing it!).

Oak Island, Southport, Shallotte and Wilmington are real places, faithfully described, but used fictitiously in this novel. The same is true of certain places and businesses frequented by Glenn, Glenda and the gang. The Lost Cause Band from Charleston, West Virginia is a real band (used with permission) and can be found at www.thelostcauseband.com.

ONE

Bobby's barstool had been empty for two straight days. Glenn peered down at the red vinyl seat. It was less than a year old and still looked new except for the two massive indentations left in the cushion. As far as Glenn could remember nobody had sat there during Bobby's mysterious absence, yet somehow the imprints remained, as if they were waiting for the massive gluteus maximus to return and nestle comfortably into them.

Regulars started filtering into the bar. The building had been listed as "quaint" and "cozy" with a "classic charm". To Glenn it was just the right size—bigger than a living room, smaller than a house. Perfect for entertaining but not so big you needed to hire cleaning help.

Someone fired up the jukebox and out came the beginning of an old Bobby Bare song. Eyes squeezed into slits, brows went up and ears tilted as people played a private version of *Name That Tune*.

"Will anybody know I've been here when I'm gone?" the country legend and the accompanying voices asked.

The first song always seemed to set the daily tone for the bar. It looked like this one might end in a night of group therapy, Glenn mused.

The song on the jukebox played on. The bar had a nice sound system installed where an iPod or phone could be plugged in to play music but one day Glenn had mentioned how he would love to have a jukebox to bring character to the music. The very next Saturday Bobby hauled in the old Wurlitzer. He "knew a guy" who wanted rid of it. Glenn asked no questions, just told Bobby to put it in the corner where his wife pointed. The Wurlitzer came complete with 45 records, a strange mix of old country classics and disco, and it would stop playing at the oddest times. Bobby had always been there to open the back and with the magic of a few tools make it play again.

Glenn's thoughts bounced back to the empty stool. Bobby kept a guardian's watch over the bar patrons from his perch. And perhaps out of respect, nobody had tried to claim the stool during Bobby's sudden absence. He had to smile to himself—the smashed cushion customized by Bobby's big butt was probably the reason no one else found the stool comfortable. Talk about staking out your territory.

Will anybody think about me when I'm gone;
Will anybody ever remember me when I'm gone;

1

Will they call me failure or success;
Did I really live or just exist?

Maybe it was the bar stool. Maybe it was the Bobby Bare song. Whatever sparked the thought, Glenn waxed philosophical, wondering what imprints he had left on the world and people around him.

Matilda, at the end of the bar, brought him back to reality by letting loose a large belch, leaving a foul olfactory imprint on those around her.

"Tilly, manners," Glenn sang through clenched teeth. Less than an hour ago Glenn had addressed Matilda about her public behavior.

"Wha?" Matilda yelled, wiping her mouth with her sleeve. The clueless look on her face pushed Glenn's buttons.

"We have other customers," Glenn said as if speaking to a child, motioning toward the tourists two tables from Matilda. They were scrambling for money and gathering their things. "What do you say?"

Matilda scrunched up her wrinkled face and ran a shaky hand through her thin, white hair, apparently deep in thought.

"Tilly, what do you say?" Glenn prompted again.

Her face brightened and her eyes widened. She smiled triumphantly, exclaiming, "Damn, that was a good one!" She followed it up with an after-tremor belch and hammered her empty glass on the bar.

Glenn dropped his chin to his chest in defeat. Matilda cackled like Margaret Hamilton at the height of her wicked witchiness.

Glenn looked up in time to see the three brightly attired tourists heading for the door. The two guys had ordered expensive microbrews while the woman had a strawberry daiquiri. And they were gone after only one drink, thanks to Waltzing Matilda (or in this case, Belching Matilda). Yep, this was the good life. Small-town bar owner Glenn was much better off than big city surgical practice Glenn. Sarcasm, he had been told, was *not* a positive coping mechanism.

The jukebox glided into George Jones. Matilda had chased off her first customers; the day at the bar was officially underway.

Glenn moved down the bar away from Matilda, determined to look on the bright side of life. Approaching a patron with a sunny smile, Glenn asked, "Hey Kenny, you okay, or you need another one?"

Kenny took thumb and forefinger and stroked his thick, black beard four inches below his chin. His "man beard". Kenny was prone to fads and the current one was to grow a beard so thick that insects and small rodents could nest there undetected. Never mind that temperatures sometimes approached triple digits. It wasn't about comfort.

When Kenny still didn't answer, Glenn pointed to his half-full glass (although his patrons today seemed to be pushing him to say it was half-empty).

"Oh—no, I think I'm okay for the moment, Doc," Kenny said, still stroking his beard thoughtfully. Glenn started to move on down the bar when Kenny grabbed at him.

"Wait, Doc!" He released Glenn's wrist and went for the laces on his steel-toed work boots. "Can you take a look at my toes? I think I have some kind of fungus. The nails are all yellow and peeling. Scared a bunch of teenage girls on the pier"

"Um, maybe later Kenny. I'm the only one here right now and I have to take care of the place."

Yeah right, Glenn thought. *That's what scared the teenage girls. Not the Charlie Manson beard.* Sarcasm was not a positive coping mechanism.

Glenn passed by the spot claimed long ago by the Sonora sisters. As usual the duo sat nursing their Mimosas and talking about the "Big C." They were identical twins with identical platinum blonde finger-wave updo hairstyles. Their tops and jeans were Be-Dazzled...always. The sisters had to set off every metal detector they ever walked through. They had been known to "chair dance" on those occasions when the Wurlitzer played a disco song (their version of chair dancing involved remaining seated and swaying in the chair while dancing with their arms and head). Glenn estimated they were in their early sixties. As far as he could tell from talking with them over the last year, neither had ever been stricken with any kind of cancer. But that didn't stop them from obsessing about the disease, when it would strike, and which one of them would be the unlucky one.

Pinhead Paul motioned Glenn over. He sat at the far end of the bar away from the other customers. Paul cleaned and filleted fish over at the docks at Southport, so perhaps it was the other customers who sat away from him. Glenn caught a big whiff of his aroma and choked back a retch. He mentally scanned the area for out-of-towners. None. So far his customer count was holding steady.

"Hey Doc, got any out-of-date suds ya need to get rid of? Or maybe ya need someone to test a particular brand for skunkiness?"

For some reason Glenn's attention was drawn to Pinhead Paul's fingernails. He could distinctly see fish guts beneath the nails. What was it about the caste system that had paid him so well to be up to his elbows in human intestines and Pinhead Paul so little to be up to his in fish guts?

"Sure Paul." Glenn withdrew a Milwaukee's Best can from the cooler and placed it in front of the pungent man.

"How much I owe you, Doc? Maw always said we shouldn't take no handouts."

Glenn thought back to his college days, a time when he had very little money, and to a particular bar just off campus. A smile came to his face. He and his roommates went there and drank Blatz beer for—

"A quarter, Paul. You owe me a quarter."

3

Pinhead Paul smiled broadly. It didn't matter that his teeth were brownish yellow and he was missing one of the uppers and two of the lowers. It was simply the best thing Glenn had witnessed today.

"Thanks, Doc." Paul tilted back on his stool, searching first one pocket of his dirty jeans and then the other. He plopped a quarter on the bar. "Tips was really bad at the docks today."

The front door blasted open with a hard spin on its hinges and slammed against the wall, the doorknob digging into the drywall. Plaster dust floated through the air and those nearby covered their beers. Glenn turned his attention away from Pinhead Paul. A white-haired man in a white linen suit entered the bar theatrically. Atop his head was a white fedora. The Wurlitzer had been playing Rick James' "Super Freak" but it suddenly skipped to the end and began Merle Haggard's "Mama Tried". Inexplicably the song stopped in the middle of the vinyl record with a long, sick, "Waaahhh".

Matilda squealed like a teenager at her first Beatles concert. But then her zeal turned to evil pleasure as she announced, "Ladies and gentlemen of the Academy, may I present the great actor…Dick-Weed!"

Richard Crabgrass snorted his disapproval and strode to the bar like the man of importance he believed himself to be. He gave a tip-of-the-hat to everyone at the bar, with the exception of Matilda. Richard was an actor and spent a lot of time in Wilmington at EUE/Screen Gems Studios. Rumor had it he had small parts in *Dawson's Creek*, *One Tree Hill*, *Sleepy Hollow* and *Under the Dome*, although the rumor may have started with him. He also claimed to have a speaking role in the biggest budget movie ever to film in Wilmington, *Iron Man 3*. Even in slow motion on Blue Ray and High Def, it was hard to make out the face in the crowd mouthing the word "Shit!" as Tony Stark/Iron Man flew over.

"Barkeep, please make a nice frothy cold one magically appear right here." Richard tapped the counter five times with the last one harder than the rest. Glenn pulled the tap and filled a frosty mug with PBR. He placed it in front of the actor. Pabst had won their blue ribbon in 1893 at the World's Exposition in Chicago. Glenn doubted Richard's work would ever warrant a blue ribbon or statuette, but who could really tell. There was always the possibility that anyone in the bar could overachieve and hit it big at any time.

"You is the damned prissiest fellow I ever seen!" Matilda yelled in Richard's direction.

Glenn shook his head. Anyone except Matilda. It seemed her window for achievement had been nailed shut long ago.

"Hey Richard, have you seen Bobby around?" Glenn asked, nodding his head toward Bobby's empty barstool.

Richard studied the barstool for a minute, then shook his head. "No, as

4

a matter of fact I haven't seen Robert all week." Bobby's trailer was a few lots down 1st Street Northwest from Richard's small brick house.

Deep in thought, Glenn leaned back against the liquor shelves causing an Absolut Vodka bottle to teeter and fall. With cat-like reflexes Glenn reached out and caught the bottle, but not before the bottom caught him just above the left ear. The Sonora sisters and Pinhead Paul applauded the feat. Glenn replaced the bottle and sat on the end of the cooler with his back to the others, rubbing his head. As if on cue, the Wurlitzer tried to start playing "Mama Tried" again, only to flash twice and die. Bobby was the one who knew how to fix it. And Bobby was...missing.

His concern for Bobby and his throbbing head quickly turned him gloomy. He glanced at the framed Hippocratic Oath he had received when graduating medical school and then gazed upward to the stuffed swordfish on the wall above the bar mirror. It was all the damned fish's fault! His surgery practice had been booming and he had floated from surgery suite to surgery suite, performing his little sleight of hand miracles. He had thought he was happy. Until they came to Oak Island on vacation, took the damned deep-sea fishing trip and he had caught the damned fish.

Glenn looked in the bar mirror, surveying the local band of misfits he had somehow collected over the last year. Normally he reveled in their differences, their uniqueness. But he was feeling pissy. A trick of the light turned the mirror image of the bar into an operating room. Glenn glanced around at his collection of patients. Kenny and his man beard. Kenny was thirty-something (his beard only ten months), lived with his mother, washed new cars at a luxury car dealer in Wilmington on Mondays and Thursdays and worked for a lawn mowing service on the island when needed on the weekends. Kenny had no real ambition in life; Kenny just existed. Hernias just existed until they became too painful and needed to be removed. Wha-la, Kenny became a hernia. Glenn closed his eyes, remembering the exact instruments required and imagined removing Kenny the Hernia.

Glenn opened his eyes and looked in the mirror again, savoring this new game. His gaze fell on Matilda, but he quickly moved on. The Sonora sisters—too easy as one became tumor A and the other tumor B. He closed his eyes, imagining the long, difficult operation to remove the Sonora sisters.

Pinhead Paul became an ingrown toenail. Richard, an inflamed appendix; all puffed up and rather useless.

When his wife walked in the door, Glenn had his eyes closed as he smiled wickedly. He had just started the operation to lance Tilly the Boil from the ass of humanity.

Glenda could sense her husband's moods from a hundred paces; even looking at the back of his head and half of his face in the reflection of the mirror, she knew his outlook had soured, his aura had turned black. Glenda had coined the phrase "morbidly morose" for this particular mood. And she thought she knew the cause of it.

"Glenn darling," Glenda called sweetly as she crossed the room to the bar.

Glenn jumped, opening his eyes and turning before finishing his current daydream operation. "Drat," he mumbled, too low for anyone to hear. "Now the old broad will remain here, forever."

As if to confirm she wasn't going anywhere any time soon, Matilda said mockingly, "Oh Glenn darling. Be a dear and make yourself useful for once, *you whipped wussy.*"

Glenda half-waggled an index finger at Matilda causing Matilda to purse her thin lips and bow her head. Glenda, it seemed, was the only person with an ounce of control over Matilda.

Glenda walked around the bar. The first thing she did was plug the iPod into the sound system and start the Island playlist. "Sun is Shining" by Bob Marley and the Wailers began and Glenda could almost see Glenn's shoulders relax a little. He was still looking up, however. She peered upward at the stuffed fish above his head. "Are you blaming all this on Swordy again?"

Glenn growled. "His name isn't Swordy. That's a name a five-year-old would come up with. I told you his name is DeBakey."

Pinhead Paul chimed in. "DeBakey? What kind of name is that for a fish?"

One of the Sonora sisters had money in hand and was motioning for another Mimosa. Glenn talked as he walked over and mixed the cranberry juice and champagne. "DeBakey was a famous surgeon and inventor. He performed the first successful coronary artery bypass, implanted the first successful pacemaker and worked with Jarvik on the artificial heart. The world owes a debt of gratitude to Dr. DeBakey."

Richard was distracted by a loose thread on his white jacket but felt the need to contribute to the conversation. "I don't get it. I guess DeBakey works. Could be DeBroily, DeGrilly, or DeFryie too."

Matilda's head shot up, sensing an opening. "Idiot! Your brain is the size of a pea!" she yelled at Richard. "A fruit fly has a bigger brain than you! In fact, a jellyfish has no brain; you're a jellyfish!"

"Matilda Sue!" Glenda slammed her fist down on the bar, rattling glassware.

Glenn grimaced and tried to slink away down the bar which irritated Glenda further. The only time her big, brave husband tried to run and hide was when she pulled out the dreaded middle name on someone.

Glenda trembled as she shook her finger at Matilda. "We are one big, happy family here and we don't talk that way about—"

Suddenly all the patrons (except Matilda) placed their heads down on the bar and wrapped their arms overtop, making sure to cover their ears. Matilda just scowled at Glenda as she and Glenn put their hands over their ears and closed their eyes.

The Oak Island Fire and Rescue station, located right beside the bar, had a call and the siren was blaring. It seemed to go on for an eternity, rattling the walls. DeBakey swayed to and fro on his wall hook, trying to escape. Finally the roar of engines could be heard and everyone in the bar ran to the windows, excited as little children. As they watched the fire engine and rescue squad car speed away, they all laughed and clapped. One big, happy family once again.

The teenagers on the bank of the Intracoastal Waterway near The Point were laughing and yelling at each other above the crackle of the fire. It was Friday of their Spring Break week but the weather was cool even in the late afternoon, at least by island standards. A few of them were still running around collecting driftwood and sticks for the fire; the others were passing around a bottle of George Dickel one of them had copped from their old man's liquor cabinet. The fire was dwindling when the burly Beetman brothers appeared at the top of the bank. The oldest pulled a huge wooden post from behind his back and held it over his head in triumph. The post was new wood, not weathered and gray, and the kids by the fire cheered. Not to be outdone, the youngest Beetman reached down in the weeds at his feet and pulled up a brand new, unpainted wooden door. As the others hooted, hollered and danced around the fire, the Beetman brothers felt like famous bandits, their grins resembling those of Butch Cassidy and the Sundance Kid.

Once the new post and door caught, the fire roared, emitting a line of thick smoke skyward like it was shooting from a chimney. The teens moved back from the intense heat and continued their drinking and storytelling. All were looking at the fire except one girl who was gazing at the water. None of them saw the worker appear at the top of the bank. He had been instructed by the boss to leave the current job site and check to see if materials had been delivered to the other. It was prime house-building season on the island and they were racing to finish two and start on others. The man ran back to his truck and called the boss who wasted no time in calling the police.

Just before the siren of the Oak Island Fire and Rescue truck could be heard in the distance, the girl watched a pile of debris floating lazily in the water. The current of the Intracoastal Waterway shifted with the tides and at this time seemed to be flowing down island. The debris appeared to be a tangled mass of tree limbs although she could make out something white on one end and a darker shape on the other. The girl strained to look closer. The white item seemed to be a small bucket. Yes, she could make out a wire handle on it. The darker shape was harder to see. She took a step closer, leaning forward. What was it? As the debris floated closer, she let out a small gasp.

"Hey guys!" she called without turning around.

Two policemen appeared at the top of the bank just as the fire truck siren blared in the distance. The teenagers scattered like seagulls on the beach being chased by a small child. One of the policemen tripped coming down the bank which aided the teenagers' escape. The other policeman chose to go in the direction of the fastest runners and was soon left far behind. By the time the fire engine appeared, the police officers had given up and met back at the fire. They stood and watched as the firemen quickly extinguished the bonfire.

Nearby in the Intracoastal Waterway the tangle of debris continued to float down island.

TWO

Glenda dragged her reluctant husband by the hand through an opening in the picket fence. Glenn sucked in a breath. He could feel his butt cheeks scrunch. His stomach experienced the same feeling as that first drop of a rollercoaster. The Old Smithville Burying Ground—*Classic Creepy-Land*, Glenn thought, unable to subdue a quick shiver. Right out of *Night of the Living Dead*.

Although in a residential section of Southport, the 18th century cemetery was not part of the modern world. Glenn fought off a second shiver. Live oak trees heavy with Spanish moss blocked out any natural light at dusk. Third shiver. And then there were the really, really old tombs—concrete boxes on top of the ground. Occasionally one would have a lid slightly askew. Probably the work of vandals but who could really tell? The thought was just enough to make Glenn jump when a twig snapped.

"This is not relaxing," Glenn declared. He may as well have been talking with the cemetery residents. Glenda was unresponsive. She had wanted to get him away from the bar so he could try and relax. And she had brought him here. Unbelievable. "Can't we just go down to the waterfront?" Glenn whined. No response. "You know, watch the sunset. Enjoy the calm water. Watch the boats come in." Nothing. Glenn played his last big card. "We could sit and make fun of the people who own boats but don't know how to dock."

Glenda motioned to the right, through the trees and tombstones. "If you look through there," Glenda pointed. "Across the street and through the trees on that empty lot, you can just see the blue of the water." She sounded like Miss Dalton, his matter-of-fact teacher in elementary school. Glenn craned his neck and squinted his eyes. He followed the line of Glenda's pointing finger, across Moore Street. He knew he was near the banks of the Cape Fear River but he couldn't get visual confirmation. He dared not say anything about it to Glenda/Miss Dalton.

Glenn huffed and gave up. *Damn you, genealogy web sites,* he thought. That's where Glenda caught the bug for the whole cemetery safari crap. Tracing family roots became finding their graves. Why? Glenn didn't know. The people were dead. Now Glenda journeyed to admire the headstones of *strangers*. The markers were "art" in certain circles. Not his circles. Glenn hated cemeteries. But he loved his wife. Once they had trekked through brush and weeds, squeezed through rusty barbed wire fence and down a cliff in order to find an abandoned cemetery with only a printed Google Earth map as a guide. All to find his great-great-great grandfather's and great-great-great grandmother's plot. All Glenn could think about was snakes, a hunter mistaking them for deer, falling off a cliff and those hillbillies in that scene from *Deliverance*. The last thing he wanted to do was to squeal like a pig. Glenda, on the other hand, was ecstatic when they had found the graves. She danced around in her hiking boots taking pictures of all the stones from every angle.

"At least I don't have to climb down a cliff," Glenn grumbled as he dragged his feet across the uneven ground.

Glenda looked at her husband with amazement. "You did not just say *cliff*. The cemetery where your great-great-great grandparents are buried does not have a cliff near it." She shook her head sadly. "Glenn, it was a large rock...on flat ground. You walked around it."

Before Glenn could grumble an answer, Glenda turned and moved deeper into the shadowy interior of the burying ground. Determined not to be left alone, Glenn followed. While she deftly steered an obstacle course of headstones and grave markers, his foot struck a marker and he tumbled forward, catching himself with his hands on the ground. "See, I told you cemeteries were dangerous!" Glenn cried.

"Isn't this where hands usually shoot out of the ground to grab a helpless victim?" she shot back. Glenn jumped to his feet.

The trees in the Old Smithville Burying Ground were as ancient as the graves. Huge live oak trees, bent and gnarled, looked ominous in the fading light. Glenn thought he had ducked enough to clear a large, low hanging limb when it seemed to reach down and smack him on the side of the head.

"Ah, shit!" he cried, holding the same spot where the Absolut bottle had tagged him.

Too far to hear her husband's cry, Glenda moved deeper into the shadows, immersed in the magnificent history of the area. In front of her, Colonel Benjamin Smith, who served as a personal assistant to George Washington during the Revolutionary War. And there was the Dosher family, an important name to the area; the earliest Dosher Glenda could find was born in 1821. She spotted a towering memorial. An obelisk honoring men lost either at sea or on the Cape Fear River in the 1870s. Many of the men were just in their twenties, the same age as their son and it tore at her heart. She paused to read the names and ponder how their families went on without their men. As she raised her head from the monument, she spotted in the distance one of her favorite designs—a stone tree! The markers were placed by the Woodmen of America or its predecessor, Modern Woodmen of America. Flowers and wildlife were always in wonderful detail. Again, she took her time to soak in all angles.

Glenn gave up trying to keep up with his wife and sat down on a bench in the shadows. It was actually part of the ornamentation of a grave from 1910, but even if he had known he probably wouldn't have cared at this point. He was not relaxed, not cheered up. In fact, he was grumpier than ever.

"Are you sure Ism can run the bar on his own?" Glenn called after his wife. She seemed to be too far away to hear. "Ism" was Joshua McCarthy, a young, immature college drop-out turned surfer who claimed to have gone to bartender school. Ninety-five percent of the time he was somewhat normal and great with the customers; the other five percent he claimed to be a descendant of Senator Joe McCarthy and saw the Red Menace creeping everywhere. The local customers had plenty of issues of their own, but as far as Glenn could tell, none of them were infected with communism.

Glenn took a sudden chill and clasping his hands in front of him, pulled his arms close to hug his body. This time it was a chill from the evening and not due to Classic Creepy-Land.

"Time to go home!" Glenn called to all the dead and with hope, also Glenda. No response. "We leave now or no sex for you tonight!" No response. Not even a smart-ass comment. Glenn half-smiled.

He closed his eyes to block out his surroundings. Things would be much more relaxing if he could forget where he sat...alone...in the fading light. His mind drifted to imagining what they were missing this evening: the waterfront, fruity drinks, the outside table at Provision and Company, live music, conch fritters or some appetizer wrapped in bacon, the smell of saltwater and the topper—some guy from Jersey trying to show off his docking skills to his buddies on board his boat. Glenn could almost hear the loud crack followed by the sickening scrape of the fiberglass and the laughter from the crowd.

Distant thunder rumbled. Glenn started, shaking his head in slow motion, trying to focus. *Whoa,* he thought. *How long have I been sitting here?*

It was darker now—much darker. Where had Glenda gone? He drew shaky fingers from one side of his face to the other, bending his nose unnaturally. He was still slumped forward on the bench and looking at his feet. Suddenly a glistening black racer snake appeared from beneath the bench to his right. He wanted to leap up onto the safety of the bench, but his limbs were numb. The serpent slowly turned its head and looked at him with a beady black eye, its tongue flicking spasmodically. He watched in horror as the snake made a ninety degree turn and slithered slowly across his brown Bass boat shoes. Afraid to move, he silently urged the snake on, but the snake stopped with the weight of its rear scales firmly on his left foot and wrapped its tail around his bare ankle.

That was all it took. Glenn's body was infused with adrenaline as he leaped twice as high as the bench and came down teetering, putting his arms out for balance. He looked back over his shoulder for his wife, but could see no one, no movement in the deepening shadows. Had she left him here? Driven off without him? He looked forward, searching the ground for the snake. Nothing moved in the grass. Slowly he lowered himself to a sitting position, keeping his legs up on the bench, just in case.

Maybe Glenda had circled around and was now in front of him. He squinted futilely into the darkness. A sudden bolt of lightning lighted up the graveyard like a Salem pyre. Someone was there! In the distance he could make out a dark shape, just to the side of a large stone mausoleum.

"Glenda," he called weakly. And then more forceful, "Glenda, is that you?"

The figure was enveloped in the darkness once again. Glenn strained to listen for any sound; when an owl hooted from somewhere nearby, he nearly wet himself. He laughed nervously. Then he heard another sound—something shuffling through the dried leaves and grass. And it seemed to be getting closer! His eyes played tricks, from seeing nothing in front of him to a huge black shape approaching. Thunder rumbled, closer this time, causing him to flinch.

Surely it was Glenda; there had been no one else in the cemetery when they arrived. Wait! There was the sound again—as if something was being dragged through the grass and dead leaves.

The lightning bolt this time nearly blinded him. He saw white spots in front of his eyes, but when they were finally gone, he saw something else— a huge man dressed in black ambling toward him, as if he was dragging one leg. The first thought to come to Glenn's mind was Johnny Cash. The Man in Black had risen from the grave and was coming for him! He was here to pull him down into the Ring of Fire! The man was thirty yards away when the world was plunged into darkness once again. Glenn gripped the ends of the stone bench so tight his arms went stiff. His eyes tried to adjust to the dark, tried to find the figure approaching him. He broke into a cold sweat. It was just like *Night of the Living Dead*! In the cemetery—the first zombie coming toward Barbara and her brother!

Glenn ordered his legs to run but nothing happened. Glenn and his legs were frozen to the spot. The sound of dragging through dead leaves and grass grew louder—deafening. Even though he couldn't see, the huge shape must be less than ten yards away. Had to be! Glenn felt around for a weapon but only touched the cold stone of the bench. Quickly he went through his pockets but all he had was a cell phone and plastic comb. How in the world could he fend off a flesh-eating zombie with just those? Was there a zombie killing app on his smartphone? He wanted to scream, wanted to run. Instead he waited helplessly as the huge shape and terrible noise grew closer. All he could do was let out a small whimper.

Glenda had been enjoying all the intricacies of the headstones and graves when she had heard Glenn call her name. Now she was directly behind him and taking in the situation. The psychic bond between husband and wife is strong, and Glenda knew exactly what her husband was thinking. She couldn't help herself as she bent down to his ear and did her best Karloff impression: "They're coming to get you Barbara."

Glenn shrieked about three octaves higher than his normal voice. But still he couldn't run. He turned to Glenda. "Stop it, you're ignorant!"

She kept the movie dialogue going—couldn't help herself. "They're coming for you. Look…" She took his head and turned it quickly to the front. "Here comes one now!"

Glenn let out a small girly scream this time and closed his eyes. The figure scraped to a stop directly in front of him. Breathing heavily, the (zombie?) leaned forward (hunger in its eyes?) When no sharp teeth ripped the flesh from his shoulder, Glenn slowly focused on the form. Before him stood an old, small, bent Hasidic Jewish man leaning on a cane. He was dressed in a black suit, black hat and a full beard flowing down the front.

"Can you tell me," he said with a heavy accent, "Which is the Jewish section?"

"I…um. Well…" Glenn stammered. "…don't actually…"

The old man laughed, his head and beard bobbing. He tapped his cane on the bench. "Is okay. Just a joke. There is no Jewish section in this cemetery. Jews are sprinkled all around, just like Europe."

The old man was still laughing as he teetered away from them, disappearing into the shadows.

Glenda clucked her teeth behind him. Glenn turned back to her.

"What?" he asked sharply.

She shook her head. "That's what you get for watching all those *Walking Dead* marathons."

Glenda sat down beside her husband and put an arm around his shoulders. "What's wrong, dear?" she asked, although she thought she knew the answer.

"Nothing," he answered, turning from her. "Everything," he added.

She turned his shoulders back to her. "Look, I know you are worried about the big chance we took coming here. You, leaving you surgery practice. Me…" She thought back to all the jobs she had held over the last twenty years: mom, dispatcher at a trucking company, secretary of a news department, caterer, road crew "Stop/Go Slow" sign holder and her last job, secretary at a private investigator's office. That one had been her favorite and she was actually sorry to leave. But she had followed her man here; in truth, she would follow her man anywhere.

She focused on her man again. "Dear, you know the studies have shown that once you open a business, specifically a restaurant or bar, it takes at least a couple years before you break even. Longer to show a profit. And on Oak Island you have to factor in the lean winter months."

He smiled at her weakly. "It's not that, honey. I mean, I do worry sometimes that we made a mistake, but I'm willing to stick it out awhile. Most of the time I enjoy it, so it's really not much different than before."

She pulled him even closer. "Then what's wrong?"

Glenn's mind seemed to be elsewhere when he answered. "You sure Ism can run the bar? I mean, if he goes off, he could bankrupt us and have us blackballed from our own bar."

Glenda kissed him on the nose. "I think the term is blacklisted, dear."

"Whatever." He turned and looked at her. "You know what's really bothering me? The first anniversary of the bar is coming up."

"There's nothing to fret about," she assured him. "Everything is planned. We're going to have hors de oeuvres, free draft, half-price mixed drinks—"

He was shaking his head at her. "It's not that. I'm not worried about any of that. I know you've done a wonderful job planning the party. And I'm not worried about the expense. We may get some customers in who've never been to the bar."

"Then what is it?"

Glenn thought back to the day almost a year ago when they had opened the doors to the bar. He and Glenda had gripped a bottle of champagne together and broken it just to the right of the door facing. They had cheered, laughing and dancing. Even though it had taken them two months to clean up the old building and fix it to their taste, this day seemed the real beginning. And he had appeared behind them, almost as if by magic.

"You guys finally open for business?"

They had both gasped and turned around. There he stood, all six feet eleven inches, three hundred and fifty pounds. Looking up at him, both husband and wife had nodded eagerly, smiling broadly. Bobby ducked as he walked through the door, strode over to the bar, pausing to scan the bar stools, and plopped down on one just a little left of middle. And there he had sat, six out of seven evenings of the week during the last year—until the last two nights. Maybe three if he still wasn't there tonight.

"What is it?" Glenda repeated. "Glenn, what's wrong?"

He looked up, despondent, inhaling deeply through his nose. Exhaling slowly, he said simply, "Bobby."

THREE

"Wow!" Glenda rolled over, pulling the sheet to cover her body. She smiled dreamily at her husband. "Now I remember why I married you."

Glenn collapsed onto the pillow and turned his head toward his wife. "I thought it was because I was big, hunky surgery resident."

Glenda laughed. "More like big, nerdy surgery resident."

"Hey! Admit it—the cute hospital volunteer couldn't resist the physique and suave moves of the surgeon in training." Glenn straightened his back and puffed out his chest. Eventually though, he had to let out his breath and his stomach returned to its former shape.

Glenda laughed again, patting his stomach. "Actually, you did have muscles in all the right places...then."

Glenn stuck out his lower lip in a comical pout.

"Aww, you still look good, honey. But you have missed your last couple of workouts with Daniel."

Glenn interlocked his fingers behind his head and sighed contentedly. "Now I'm relaxed. See, this is how you get me to relax. No more cemeteries, just lead me to our bed."

"Anytime," Glenda purred. "By the way, where did you learn that delicious little dip and twist move?"

"Zimbabwe."

Glenda giggled. "And what do the Zimbabweans call it?"

Glenn turned a serious face toward her. "The Zwist."

Glenda laughed so loud a little snort escaped. Finally, wiping away the tears, she rested her head on her husband's chest. She drifted off, but not before softly singing, "Come on baby, let's do the Zwist."

The bright mid-morning sun shone through the kitchen window, cutting a swath across the green linoleum floor. Glenda, humming a made-up mishmash of several tunes, flipped the ham and cheese omelets on the stovetop. Glenn had just emerged from the shower and was toweling off. Glenda called to him, "Oh, by the way, Ron called yesterday."

"What's that?" Glenn asked, sticking a wet head out the bedroom door.

"Ron called. He and Vicky are doing well and send their love."

"Good. How's his job going?"

"He said pretty good. He's not sure there's much upward mobility in the company but he seems happy starting out there. Likes his coworkers."

Ron was their firstborn and had been married now for almost two years. The young couple had moved to Rock Hill, South Carolina, shortly after their wedding.

Glenda glanced through the kitchen window into their back yard, just as the white, long-legged bird gracefully landed on a large rock by their goldfish pond.

"Hey Glenn, Ernie is back!"

Glenda watched the egret walk around the goldfish pond, its long s-neck bending back and forth. Ernie was looking for his own breakfast, maybe a nice dragonfly and lizard omelet. Ernie had been their welcoming committee, the first visitor on the first weekend they had spent in the house. After the deep-sea fishing vacation, they had searched the listings for months before finding the perfect little ranch-style home near the Intracoastal Waterway. For the first seven months they stayed mostly weekends, occasionally managing to squeeze in a full week on the island while Glenn maintained his surgery practice in West Virginia.

She watched Ernie feint his head skyward then pounce quickly down to gobble up an unsuspecting frog. She remembered the excitement when they were looking out the window that first weekend and saw a beautiful white egret. At that time, the little pond resembled a cesspool. It had taken a lot of work, money and love to get the pond to where it was today. That first day Glenn had dubbed the bird "Ernie"; he could stand at the window and watch the egret for hours it seemed. Standing at the kitchen window each morning one of them would say, "Egret?" and the other would answer, "No egrets". It became their inside joke, their rallying cry, and some days when they were blue and doubting the sudden change they had made, it became their antidepressant. When they had taken the giant step of buying the bar, there was never a squabble about the name. In fact, they never even discussed it. It was one of those magical unspoken things that seemed to happen to couples married for a long time. Smiling at the memories, Glenda left the window, walked to the bedroom door and took great pleasure in watching her man get dressed.

Glenn walked down the snack aisle of Food Lion, stopping at the pretzel section. The grocery store on the island was relatively new, built a little over a decade ago. Designed to be a convenience for the vacationers and weekenders, it was about half the size of the Food Lion near Southport and only the most desperate locals shopped there during tourist season.

"Pretzel rods, pretzel rods, pretzel rods…" he whispered over and over until spying the thick, be-salted golden rods. He took an arm and swept six of the seven bags on the shelf into his shopping cart. Turning to leave, he stopped, looking back over his shoulder wistfully at the lone bag.

"Left without a friend in this world. Didn't shower today, huh?" he asked the Snyder's of Hanover 12-ounce bag of pretzel rods "Okay, join your buddies and go for a joy ride!" He tossed the bag behind his back into the shopping cart, popped a wheelie and zoomed the cart to the next aisle.

He stopped beside the feminine hygiene products, pulled out his shopping list and marked off the top item. The snack shipment had been delayed and the pretzels were for the bar. Everything else on the list was items Glenda had told him to pick up for the house.

He scanned the second item on the list. What the heck was Chopin Spaniard? Chopin, the composer? Did he write a Spanish symphony? Did Chopin even write symphonies or only piano concertos? Glenn looked hopelessly at the signs above the aisles designating their contents for some sort of direction. Some sort of connection. Did Food Lion even have a music section?

He squinted at the list, holding it closely, slowly moving it farther away, finally turning his head sideways. It was no use. It still looked like Chopin Spaniard.

"Shit," he said, a little too loudly. He looked around sheepishly; when he didn't see anyone, he focused his attention on the third item on the list.

"Papillomavirus Germ Fresh!" he exclaimed.

Glenn wheeled his cart over to a bench beside the bakery in defeat. His good mood had spilled out somewhere between aisle four and aisle five (*"Clean up on aisle five!"*). He slumped down onto the bench, reluctantly pulling out his cell phone.

Glenda answered after one ring, running her opening sentence together without a pause. "Hello honey what can't you read?"

Glenn pulled out the list and glanced at the fourth item and on down the list.

"Everything after pretzel rod," he said disgustedly.

On the other end, Glenda put a hand over the phone and giggled. She had set poor Glenn up for this embarrassment when she didn't write out the list, instead dictating it to him. He had been distracted anyway, which made his handwriting even worse.

"What are Chopin Spaniard and Papillomavirus Germ Fresh?"

Glenda had to set the phone on the table and walk away, holding a hand over her mouth and shaking with laughter.

"Well?' she heard Glenn ask from far away.

She picked up the phone, wiping the tears from her eyes. "Can't read the good doctor's chicken scratch, hmm?" She couldn't help herself when a small giggle escaped.

"I'm glad you're enjoying this!" he exploded. "What the hell's on the list?"

Glenda tried to straighten up but she was still smiling. "I'm sorry Glenn. The second item is chopped spinach and the third item is Pepperidge

Farms Goldfish."

He grumbled and spelled out each item in careful block letters beside his indecipherable handwriting. The most highly skilled Japanese cryptographers had not been able to decipher the Navajo Code Talkers' messages in World War II, yet Glenda finished decoding the whole list in mere minutes. Glenn gave a halfhearted laugh. "Thanks dear. I'm sorry."

"It's okay honey." Glenda laughed. "I love you—even if your handwriting resembles ancient Egyptian hieroglyphics."

He certainly felt better now. Glenda often had that effect on him. In a few minutes Glenn was standing in front of the cans of chopped spinach. He took his pen, tapped it three times on the handle of the shopping cart, and swirled it in the air preparing to lead the leafy green vegetables in a rousing Chopin symphony. Rounding the corner, a very stylish senior citizen, decked out in a wind suit and matching earrings, immediately threw on her brakes. Her too white sneakers immediately went into reverse but not before slipping and guiding her cart into a cake display.

"Damn crazy out-of-towners," she mumbled as she fled Glenn and his show. "Can't go anywhere without a freak around the corner."

Could be why Glenda refuses to shop with me, Glenn thought. He could be a tad goofy at times and nobody wanted to see that in a surgeon. But he was a bar owner now. Couldn't he be a little goofy? And what did the lady mean "out-of-towner"? He had been on the island a year and surely he blended. He looked down at his bright Hawaiian shirt and flip-flops, shrugging.

Glenn consulted his shopping list and cut down the hair care aisle. His mood was good until he spotted, of all things, bobby pins. *Bobby, Bobby*, his brain echoed.

Glenda had let him talk last night and probed him, getting him to reason it out. "Why do you think something bad has happened to Bobby?"

"For the last year he has been at the bar every night except for Tuesday bowling nights when he's in Shallotte. The only exception was that one week he went home to visit his mom. Each night he drinks his two Bud Lights perched on his favorite barstool. He peels the labels off the bottles and at the end of the night sticks the labels back on the bottles before leaving. It's like clockwork."

"Glenn, he's only been gone a few nights. I'm sure there's a reasonable explanation."

Glenn had looked at her then, expecting her to provide one.

"Look, in case you haven't noticed, Karen hasn't been in the bar in three weeks…"

Karen, Glenn thought. *Thirty-something, blonde, cute, a bit of a full-figured woman. Always orders a screwdriver.*

"And," Glenda continued. "She's been missing from church the last couple of Sundays. I don't remember her ever missing church. Does that mean something bad has happened to her, too?"

Glenn could see the logic but couldn't quite let go of all his worries about Bobby, until Glenda added, "Besides, I've seen Karen casting sidelong glances in Bobby's direction and the way he sometimes watches her when she's walking across the room. Maybe they're together.'"

"What? But I never—"

"Yes, I know dear. Sometimes you don't pay attention to the subtle things. That's why you need me."

As he hurried through the organic food aisle toward the checkout, he realized that was exactly why he needed his wife. They made a good team. And he did feel better about Bobby.

Turning the corner at the end of the aisle he nearly bowled over wind suit senior citizen with his cart. Scowling, she hurried away. At the checkout, Glenn had to wait patiently behind a pale, nervous man who was arguing with the clerk about the need for Food Lion to carry organic beer. Organic beer? Glenn chuckled. What will they think of next?

Glenn climbed in his black Ford F-150 pickup, exited the Food Lion parking lot and turned toward the bar. Up ahead he could see a tiny helmeted figure on some type of motorbike. While he was straining to see the figure, he almost didn't see the large piece of metal in the road. He quickly pulled off the side of the road, ran back and picked up the rusted metal. Shaking his head in disgust, he threw the metal into the bed of the truck and continued toward the bar.

Workers at Keiffer's Luxury Car dealership in Wilmington bounced between curiosity and fear. Everyone tried to find a reason to file through the inner lobby, but no one wanted to stay or make a second pass. The salesmen, clerks, even the mechanics entered to get a glimpse of the huge man with the gruesome scar.

The office girls hurried back to their computers to pull up the FBI website, searching the most wanted list. Surely there must be a reward for information on this beast. The service manager nervously scanned the office security camera screen, certain the man had come to collect on his personal gambling debts.

Otto was not bothered by their behavior, having experienced it most of his adult life. In fact, scaring people was fun (second only to hurting people in his book). The large scar which started outside his right eye and curved down his cheek to his chin did not invite anyone to come up and ask him the time or even say hello. His bald head and pasty complexion only accentuated the scar. Once his boss had offered to find a plastic surgeon, but Otto had declined; the wound had been poorly sutured and Otto wanted to keep the scar as a reminder of the last time he had been bested in a fight. It had been twenty-four years ago.

The office girls came back to the window to steal a second look at the man to compare him to the villains on the most wanted list. The service manager nervously scanned the security image for a bulge in Otto's jacket but couldn't find one. Otto never carried a gun. Guns were loud, messy and could tie anyone to a "meeting". Instead, Otto carried brass knuckles, the only family heirloom he owned. In Russian they were called kactet, derived from French "casse-tete" meaning "head-breaker". Otto's kactet was beautifully adorned with an engraved hammer and sickle at the base.

Otto sat straight backed in the uncomfortable dealership chair, feet flat on the floor, hands resting on thighs. His eyes were trained dead ahead, looking at nothing. The office girls swore he never blinked.

Otto didn't often think of his family, but as his hand found his pocket and kactet, his mind drifted. He never knew his father and his mother had died when he was only ten years old. He rarely thought of his parents, feeling more of a connection for the grandparents he had never met. His mother told him of his grandfather who was born in Mogilev, Russian Empire, a descendant of German settlers in Courland, while his grandmother was a Latvian. Survivors-that was how his mother described his grandparents. That was the bond with his grandparents. Otto had survived the trials of growing up alone, drifting from bad situations to dreadful situations. He had learned how to survive in this world. His best quality was his intense loyalty to the boss while those who crossed the boss came into direct contact with his worst features.

The glass door from the owner's office opened slower than usual and a silence fell over the business. Workers jockeyed to get a view from the security camera monitor. The "office girls" barely breathed. The middle-aged owner stepped into the inner lobby as if being shoved. A former college football player, he was still fit, but looking at Otto turned his insides to jelly. One hand never released his office door, keeping it open for a quick escape should he need it. Rose from *Titanic* didn't clutch her floating door as tightly. The Polo shirt with the dealership logo showed sweat.

Even the owner's voice sounded sweaty. "Mis—ter…"

Otto looked up at him slowly, blinking twice and settling into a stare. "Otto. Only Otto."

"Um…Mister Otto. This is highly irregular. I just can't release a new Rolls-Royce Ghost costing in excess of 300,000 dollars to someone who isn't the owner. I'm afraid I'm going to have to call—"

Otto stood up and at nearly seven feet tall towered over the man. Unconsciously Otto put his hand in his pocket, feeling the outline of his brass kactet.

The manager gulped, surveying all that was Otto's outline.

"You will *not* bother the doctor." Otto's voice had been low and even except for the word "not" which caused the manager to flinch.

The manager backed into his office while talking. "Yes…yes. Of course you're right." He cleared his throat loudly. "Since the doctor is such a good customer, I think we can make an exception in this case. I'll just go get the keys."

FOUR

"Your hair smells...nice today," Glenda said, bracing her legs on both sides of the barstool in order to remove Matilda's helmet. As always, it stuck on her temples before pulling free with a scraping plop.

Matilda's thin white hair stood straight up, in all directions, like each strand was trying to jettison from her ancient scalp. "Don't feed me any horseshit, Glenda. Ain't warshed my hair in a coupla weeks."

Glenda sighed and moved back behind the bar. She enjoyed all the mundane tasks of opening the bar in the afternoon, from inventorying the alcohol to polishing the large mirror behind the bar. Early afternoon customers were sparse, so it also gave her time to review the financials and double-check payments. She loved Glenn dearly, but if money matters were left to him, No Egrets and their future would sink faster than a wooden sailing ship in a storm off Cape Hatteras. Besides, she had dabbled in bookkeeping in college and at a couple of her jobs and really enjoyed it. Lately she had been toying with the idea of taking accounting classes at Brunswick Community College to sharpen her skills. BCC had just opened a new campus in Southport.

"Hit me!" Matilda shouted, slamming a boney fist on the bar.

If only, thought Glenda. The old woman was lucky she was a pacifist and not taking her literally.

Matilda didn't have a regular drink; she had a drink of the day. Saturday? Glenda glanced at the calendar on the wall. Yes, it was Saturday. Now, what mind association had she used to remember Matilda's drink for Saturday? She concentrated hard for a minute and then it came to her. Saturday was at the end of a "long" week and therefore Matilda's drink for Saturday was a Long Island Iced Tea. She gathered the bottles, determined to mix Matilda's first drink of the day as weak as she could get away with.

Matilda watched her closely. "And don't try to be Glenda the Good Witch and water down my drink. I'm paying good money so make it a double. It's what lubes this old body and keeps me moving."

The bell on the front door tinkled, causing Matilda and Glenda's heads to turn. Royce, one of the firefighters from next door paused in the doorway, removed his sunglasses and waited for his eyes to adjust. If Royce had a theme song it would be a seductive saxophone solo. It played in every woman's head as he moved. Royce was dressed in his Oak Island Fire and Rescue uniform—the shirt unbuttoned halfway down, due to the heat, with

22

NO EGRETS

a white tank-top undergarment visible. He took a hand and ran it through his wind-blown blonde hair.

"Hello," he called to Glenda. A Barry White song started playing (Glenda wasn't sure if it was on the Wurlitzer or in her head).

Glenda smiled and half waved, unable to stop her heart from beating faster. She smoothed her hair into place, calling back, "Hi! What can I do for you?"

She prepared to watch the wonderful sight of the chiseled body of Royce walking toward her—when she suddenly remembered the only other occupant of the bar.

"Damn!" Matilda said loudly. "Dat's one fine man. I'll tell you what he could do for me."

Glenda took the lemon wedge she was about to put in the Long Island Iced Tea and jammed it into Matilda's mouth. Matilda spat out the lemon wedge and sputtered beside her.

Glenda could see Matilda straining to say something risqué but thankfully the words wouldn't emerge from her puckered lips.

"Well," he said, flashing a perfect smile of brilliant white teeth. "Big John sent me over. He's chef today and needs cooking sherry. He was wondering if you had something he could use."

Glenda turned to the row of bottles behind her. "Hmm, haven't had a sherry drinker in the bar yet, so don't have that. Red wine is a good substitute." She picked up a bottle and grabbed a plastic cup with a lid.

Royce placed a five-dollar bill on the bar as Glenda presented him with the filled cup.

"Oh no. No charge," she stated firmly passing the bill back toward Royce. "It's the least I can do for the station." Glenda smiled and surprised herself by batting her eyelashes. "We appreciate the sacrifice you guys make in order to keep the island safe."

Royce placed his hand on top of Glenda's and presented her with his million-dollar smile. "Thank you. You're a good woman."

Glenda felt the heat of a blush creep up her cheeks. Matilda rolled her eyes. Royce turned and began his catwalk swagger to the door. (Somewhere someone cued the saxophone and Barry White crooned.) Glenda's head snapped from Royce's exit to Matilda. Her eyes shot daggers into the old woman. Unfazed, Matilda fluttered her eyelashes and mocked, "I feel soooo safe with you, Firefighter Ken."

Both women turned to watch Royce's last few steps before he left the building. Glenn silently slipped up beside them.

"Are you sure he likes girls?" Glenn quietly asked as the front door closed on the event of the day. Both women jumped in surprise. Before heart rates returned to normal, the women began loud protests in tandem.

"Of course he likes girls!" Glenda blurted out. "He's just

very…sensual."

Matilda turned to Glenn. "Ha! You got a thing for him?" She looked back longingly toward the front door. "Too much testosterone seeping out of that man to be light in the loafers."

Matilda returned her attention to the glass in Glenda's hand. "If you take any longer making my drink, it's going to be Sunday and you'll have to change it to a Rose Kennedy Cocktail."

Glenda stirred her new "early in the day" version of Long Island Iced Tea and placed it on a coaster in front of Matilda. The old woman snatched the glass, took a big swig and slammed it down on the bar, intentionally beside the coaster. Her level stare into Glenda's eyes was enough to say she knew the drink was half-strength. Glenda glared back.

With the women silently fuming, Glenn decided to break the silence by reaching behind the bar and throwing the rusted piece of metal from the back of his truck onto the bar with a clang. "Gotta say I'm surprised to see you here, Tilly. What with parts falling off your Vespa along Beach Drive."

If the old woman was caught off guard, it didn't show. She lowered her glass and replied, "If some shit piece falls off and I keep moving, Vespy didn't need it anyhow."

The front door opened and Royce reentered. All heads turned. "I'm sorry. Can I get a little more red wine? Big John said it wasn't enough—I think he spilled some."

Glenda moved to retrieve the wine bottle.

Hey Royce," Glenn said.

"Hi Doc!"

"Royce, do you think you guys could do us a favor?"

Royce made his way back to the bar (Matilda was entranced by the front part of his trousers this time). "Sure, Doc. How can we help?"

Glenn pointed to the rusted piece of metal. "It seems Matilda's Vespa is shedding its skin again. It molts regularly. I think the guys were kind enough to fix it last time."

Perhaps the motorized scooter Matilda rode around the island *was* a Vespa (if you cleared the rust, Bondo and duct tape you might actually find the word) but now it looked more like a mechanical wasp stepped over and over by a giant boot. It didn't help that Matilda let it fall over wherever she stopped, including housing it in the front bushes of her trailer.

Royce picked up the metal, careful not to cut himself. "Sure thing. I work on my own cycle and Big John's pretty good with body work. We'll take care of it."

Glenn snickered as the ladies watched Royce walk out again. Matilda picked up her glass of Long Island Iced Tea and teetered off after him.

"Matilda!" Glenda shouted. "Where do you think you're going?"

Matilda stopped and turned to Glenda, her lower lip quivering comically. "I'm going to make sure they don't hurt poor Vespy." She sniffed back tears. "She's all I got in this world."

Glenn watched Glenda's frown turn to a glare and involuntarily took a step back. "Bull-shark!" Glenda cried.

Matilda had taken another two steps toward the front door but now stopped. Glenn saw his chance to diffuse the situation. "Besides Tilly," he said. "You know you can't leave the bar with an open container of alcohol. You told us what happened all those years ago."

Matilda looked longingly at the door—then down at her glass of Long Island Iced Tea. After one more glance to the door, she slowly turned and made her way back to the bar. After taking a long drink, she mumbled, "Gull-shit to you, Glenda. It's probably so hot in that station they'd have to strip to work on Vespy. Why do you deny a poor old lady her Shangri-La?"

Glenn smiled, taking the remaining bags of pretzel rods behind the bar and putting them with the other snack food. Matilda sulked. Glenda polished the entire bar with a rag, carefully picking up the Long Island Iced Tea glass with hand attached. Matilda sulked

Suddenly Matilda drew in a quick breath, breaking the silence. Then she spoke. "Beautiful men like Royce are a curse unto themselves. It is the 'Elvis effect'. Women swoon, women cry, women scream—put him on a pedestal." She stopped long enough to take a big swig of her shrinking beverage before continuing. "But he's just a man. Good at some things; bad at others. Fabulous and flawed. And in the end…lonely as the night."

Glenn and Glenda were stunned, frozen in place, staring at each other with wide eyes and mouths agape. In all the time they had known Matilda they had never heard her express any deep thoughts (unless "My panties are older and smarter than you" counted).

Glenn stepped toward her, trying to find the words, but instead found himself stuttering, "Ti—Ti—Tilly…"

Glenda placed her hand over Matilda's and patted it lovingly. "Matilda, that is the wisest thing I've ever heard you—"

Matilda cut her off. "Doesn't mean I wouldn't want to be his 'Hound Dog'. He can bend me over and—"

"Matilda!" Glenda cried.

"—wouldn't have to 'Love Me Tender'. Leave me spread out and 'All Shook Up'!"

Glenda's voice turned an octave lower as she bellowed, "Matilda Sue!"

The bar started filling up a little after five with the usual suspects, the regulars who considered No Egrets their social hang-out. Dotted around the room were locals who rolled in a few times a month—Glenda was still learning their names and drinks. In the back a large, loud group of middle-aged men squeezed around two small tables. Their caps, golf shirts and sunburns told everyone they were out-of-towners. Their laughs let it be known they had already had a few on the back nine.

Glenda smiled as she approached the golf buddies. Without hesitation they ordered four pitchers: two Fat Tire, one Yuengling and one Bud Light. She got a kick out of the one in the red shirt with an equally red head and neck. He was bent over a pile of golf scorecards, circling some scores on the marked card and transcribing some other numbers to a new card. Obviously he was the master of the golf gambling games for the day. He was the only non-drinker and ordered a Code Red Mountain Dew.

When Glenda reached the bar with the order, Ism had just walked in to start his shift. He was wearing a black Bob Marley Legend t-shirt and long khaki shorts. She couldn't understand why the locals made up such stories about the young man. Descendant of Senator Joe McCarthy? She didn't know if it was true or not, but she did know he was just a normal young man and refused to believe otherwise.

"Hello Joshua." (Glenda refused to call him by his nickname which she considered offensive.)

"Yo, Mrs. G! Howzit hang…um, how are you ma'am?" Ism cleared the blonde hair hanging in front of his eyes and smiled at Glenda.

"Thirsty crowd, Joshua."

Ism looked around and nodded, which caused the hair to fall over his eyes again. "Sure is an epi horde. Looks like they all trekked to the island today to worship at the Church of the Open Sky."

Glenda showed him the drink order; she filled the two Fat Tire pitchers, Ism filled the other two.

"How was the surfing today?" she asked while they were topping off the pitchers.

Ism shook his head disgustedly. "Brah, I'm losin' my religion over this flat spell. It's straight up and soggy out there."

As they carried the pitchers (plus a Code Red Mountain Dew in Ism's pocket) to the table of golfers, Glenda said, "I'm sorry the waves aren't very good, Joshua. Maybe we'll have a big storm soon."

"Shweet!"

"Perhaps a tropical storm off the coast," she added.

Ism's eyes almost rolled back in his head. "Redonculous," was his mystical reply.

Kenny was as excited as Glenn had ever seen him. The others had gathered around him in a semi-circle, pinning him on his barstool. Glenn was tending the bar while Glenda and Ism worked the tables; he moved down the bar, curious about the animation on the face of the usually sedate Kenny.

"Sir, I am aghast!" exclaimed Richard.

"I'm telling you the truth! It was all over the dealership." Kenny was so excited his man beard quivered.

"You swear on a stack of King Mackerels?"

They all turned and looked at Pinhead Paul.

"What?" Pinhead Paul frowned at them, shaking his head. "Ya'll need to get out in the real world more," he muttered.

"I swear on a stack of King Mackerels, bibles and my mother's tuna surprise," Kenny said, trying to recapture the momentum.

"And how much did you say it cost?" Richard asked and then added, "In American dollars?"

"Over three hundred grand."

Pinhead Paul snorted. "No way! I ain't paid more'n a thousand dollars for a car." They all looked his way again. "Course I have to put at least another two thousand into 'em to get 'em to run," he added proudly.

"Doctor, Doctor," Richard called to Glenn. "Surely you find that amount for a vehicle out of proportion with life here on our humble island." And then with a slight change of tone, Richard began to pry. "Have you ever invested that much in a vehicle?"

"Of course not," Glenn answered.

"Well," Kenny said. "This guy was a doctor and he paid cash!" Kenny held up the brochure of the Rolls-Royce Ghost he had lifted from the dealership.

Glenn whistled. "I don't know what kind of patients he has, but I could never afford a car like that. He must not be married or have kids."

"Not what I heard the salesman telling." Kenny gave his man beard a tug. "He said the doctor told him he would be back next week to pick out a Ferrari F12berlinetta for his wife!"

The group let out a collective, "Oooh!" just as the front doorbell jingled.

Glenn looked around the group and saw a couple enter the bar and sit at the last empty table. He saw Glenda walk over to take their order just as two men entered the front door and walked straight to the bar. Glenn felt a tad nauseous. The two men took seats at the bar; Glenn couldn't help but notice one of them sat on Bobby's barstool.

"Hey Hands. Hey Sphinx," Glenn called to them. Off duty now, they were partners on the Oak Island Police force. "Hands" was Hans Rodriguez. He had the darker features and muscular compact body of his Mexican father; as far as Glenn could tell, his first name and blue eyes were the only things his German mother had contributed (although his first name had morphed into Hands on the island). Sphinx was African American and Glenn could not recall his first name. Sphinx was built like a boxer and had to endure the endless comparisons and jokes about the famous Sphinx boxing brothers, even though he was not related. When he tried to tell people his sport in high school and college was pole vaulting, they brushed it aside like he was jesting. A boxer—he had to be a boxer.

Glenn had paused to deliver new Mimosas to the Sonora sisters. One was Juanita and the other Bonita but he could never tell them apart. They were especially miserable tonight, acting like one of them had actually contracted the "Big C" they were always talking about.

Matilda, at the other end of the bar, had visibly perked up when the younger men walked in and was busy staring in their direction.

"Hello Ms. Matilda," Sphinx said, waving four fingers in her direction. "Are you obeying the speed limit on your Vespa these days?"

"Vespy doesn't have a speed limit, copper! I run it *wide open!*" she yelled back, winking wickedly.

Hands laughed at his partner. "You walked right into that one."

Glenn placed two pint glasses of Sweet Josie draft in front of them. He knew they were both craft beer aficionados and liked their beer dark.

"How's it going gentlemen?"

Sphinx was taking a first long drink of his beer so Hands answered. "Same ol' same ol' right now. Burglaries, drugs, drunken tourists, drunken locals, drugs, domestic disturbances, drugs."

"Don't forget bonfires," Sphinx laughed, foam on his upper lip.

"Haha. Let it go," Hands said in a monotone, taking a drink of his Sweet Josie.

"You should have seen him go tumbling down that bank," Sphinx said to Glenn, still laughing. "He looked like…what was the name of that fat guy in the comedy duo with the skinny guy? You know in the old black and white movies?"

"Oliver Hardy from Laurel and Hardy," Glenn offered.

"That's it! He looked just like Oliver Hardy taking a pratfall!"

"Yeah, yeah. Laugh it up. You didn't fall and you couldn't catch the teenagers either, Mr. Track Star."

"Hey, I was a pole vaulter, not a sprinter," Sphinx said.

Hands stared into his beer. "I'm going to get those Beetman brothers," he said sullenly. "They've managed to avoid us so far, but they've got to go back to school on Monday.

Glenn moved down the bar to pull a PBR for Richard. When he returned, the two officers were quietly drinking their beer. Glenn leaned on the bar, closer to the policemen, and in a soft voice asked, "You guys ever work any missing person cases?"

Hands was taking a long drink of his beer this time, so Sphinx answered. "Sometimes. Usually turns out to be runaways or a misunderstanding."

Hands placed his beer on the coaster in front of him. He turned to look Glenn straight in the eye and leaned in toward him. "Been a cop a long time. Can tell when somebody wants to say something. So, what's up?"

"Well…" Glenn started, not sure how to continue. His mind began to toss around opening lines. None made the cut, so he just blurted it out. "You guys know Bobby Portis, don't you? Big guy, usually sits at the bar six nights out of the week." Glenn looked around the bar, hoping Bobby would magically appear before continuing. "And I haven't seen him for three nights now. I just feel…have this feeling that something bad has happened to him."

Both police officers studied Glenn closely before Hands responded. "Nobody has reported him missing. But we'd be glad to drive by Bobby's house tomorrow, or even have someone do it tonight."

Glenn's relief was visible. "That'd be great, guys. I'd really appreciate it." He pointed toward Richard. "Bobby lives on 1st Street Northwest. Richard can tell you exactly where."

Sphinx started sniffing the air and making a face. "You guys starting to serve food now? I smell fish…sushi."

Glenn hurried down the bar and slid a Milwaukee's Best can in front of Pinhead Paul.

"Thanks Doc! Business was better at the docks today. Lots of tips. Might have an Old Milwaukee next if you got it."

Glenn moved back down the bar to help Ism mix a couple pitchers of frozen Margaritas. He stopped in front of the Sonora sisters to see if they needed a refill, but they had their heads down and one had her arm around the other, comforting her.

When he returned to the policemen, Hands had wrapped up a short call. He removed his cell phone from his ear and placed it on the bar.

"Doc, I called Brim. He was already patrolling near Bobby's house, so he stopped and checked it out. All the lights are off and it doesn't look like anyone's home. Thought he could hear a muted TV, but some people leave them on when they're gone to make it sound like someone's home. Also, no car in the carport."

"Hmm," was all Glenn could manage, a frown creasing his brow.

"I see how worried you are about him," Sphinx said, eyeing Glenn's reaction. "But there's not a whole lot more we can do unless he's reported missing."

"I know, I know," Glenn muttered.

"However," Sphinx continued, "If you know someone who has a key to his house, it would be perfectly legal for a concerned citizen…"

FIVE

Everything had happened so fast. He could vaguely remember the sound of metal slamming; the darkness that enveloped him.

Why was he so cold? Flying, flying through the atmosphere. Freezing. Or floating like a dirigible—that's what it felt like. His body convulsed with a long shiver.

Everything seemed so…strange. No sounds. But he could hear his own breathing, his heart beating as this dirigible lumbered along. He must be in the sky, miles above the world. No sounds of cars, sirens, people. Just his heart beating and the inhale/exhale of his breath.

His head throbbed and his thoughts became even more jumbled. Jermaine—what would become of him and his brothers? And what was the woman's name? Girlfriend? Try as he might, he could not remember her name. Pretty, yes—but she was in danger. He could not recall what kind of danger, only that he needed to tell someone. He grew weary and released his grip just a little. Without warning something smacked him under his chin, jarring what was left of his senses.

His focus shifted from the woman and the dirigible to random scenes of his life. The time he was twelve, opening a Christmas gift from his father. A model kit of the Frankenstein Monster, arms outstretched, walking through a graveyard. Senior League baseball, trying to impress the girls, fouling the ball straight down into home plate, the ball ricocheting hard just below his belt. His mother. He could see her face. He tried to speak to her but the words would not come. He tried to reach out for her but she disappeared. She was gone—with rising panic he realized he could not remember where she lived.

Where did *he* live? He closed his eyes and the house he lived in appeared before him. He couldn't shake the feeling he had left something on—the iron, the oven, the television? Did it matter now? Was this the end for…?

What's my name? Oh my Lord! What's my name?

He hugged the hard shape closer, struggling to remember. Just a lazy dirigible floating through the atmosphere toward a single spark.

Glenn removed the ceramic cranium from Mighty Mouse and carefully placed it to the side. He flashed the limited light from the screen of his cell phone across the mighty body of the cartoon mouse and into its skull. With great precision he reached his hand in, performing an exploratory. "Please, please, please nothing gross," he begged, which made him chuckle. Most people would think absolutely nothing could tip a surgeon's gross-ometer scale to queasy, but Glenn knew better in his case.

Gritting his teeth, he delved deeper into Mighty Mouse, now up to his elbow. Just when he began to worry someone had removed it, his fingers brushed the metal object. He pulled the key out triumphantly and sang, "Here I come to save the day!"

With Ism and Glenda both working the bar, Glenn had slipped out early. He looked at his phone: 11:30 p.m. *Darn you Matilda!* He could've been here half an hour ago. For once Tilly took her time pouring alcohol down her throat, nursing that last drink as long as she could and then throwing a holy fit when he loaded her Vespa into the back of his truck to take her home. With a heavy sigh Glenn realized he had now given Matilda (and Vespy) a ride home three nights in a row. Bobby usually volunteered for the task.

Glenn stuck the key into Bobby's front door lock and turned it. The door squeaked open and Glenn took a tentative step across the threshold. A strange feeling made him freeze. During surgeries Glenn had opened chests and abdomens, coming across many unexpected nasty surprises, and he had a sudden foreboding about opening the door into Bobby's house. Perhaps he was overstepping his bounds? In spite of Hands and Sphinx giving him the go-ahead, Glenn felt like he was violating Bobby's trust. Bobby had not given him permission to enter his house this time. The last time, Bobby had asked him to check on his house when he was out of town and feed the Five/plus one.

The door actually creaked when he closed it, long and loud. Glenn shivered. (This would be the part in the slasher movie where Glenda yelled at the screen, "Get out of the house! What an idiot!") His eyes could not adjust to the dark room in the limited light. He walked his fingers along the wall hoping to find a light switch. Pausing, he gave the room the sniff test. The air was stuffy in the house. No A/C had been running, but there was no smell of death. If Bobby's lifeless body had been sprawled on the floor after three days of no air conditioning...

The sound of someone or something scurrying across the wooden floor stopped all train of thought.

Remembering his cell phone, he turned it on, wishing again it had a zombie killing app. Holding the phone close to the wall, Glenn located the family room light switch, took a deep breath and flipped it on. "Bobby," he called loudly. While his eyes adjusted, he still half expected to see Bobby's inert body wrapped up in the throw rug, but there was something else on the rug—and it was coming at him—fast! Glenn shrieked and jumped on top of an end table by the couch, knocking off a lamp in the process.

"Gross!" he screamed.

The lamp crashed to the floor, but the sound of the end table cracking was even louder. Glenn fell onto the couch just before the end table splintered and collapsed. Facing the back of the couch, he flipped himself over quickly, eyes wide, watching for movement. Nothing. Wait…there, by the chair! Glenn jumped up with his knees on the back of the couch, at first perfectly balanced, then arms spiraling out of control, trying not to fall into the front window. He grabbed a curtain with one hand; with the other hand knocked a vase to the floor where it shattered. With a quick thunk, the curtain rod bent and the curtain assembly came down on top of him.

The Chilean rose hair tarantula stopped at the front of the couch, testing the terrain with one long segmented leg. Finding the flaps at the bottom of the couch not to its liking, the spider side-stepped, turned and scurried toward another room.

Glenn let out a long breath as he watched the tarantula exit to the kitchen. Spiders! *Uuuggghhhhh…* He gave a half-hearted laugh. "Here I come to save the day," he sang (with a lot less gusto this time). Climbing down off the couch, he looked around the room. He had caused more damage than a tornadic waterspout.

Glenn walked down the hall and knocked on Bobby's bedroom door. No sound from the other side. "Bobby?" After a minute he opened the door and peered into the dark. "Bobby?" He couldn't tell if there was a shape in the bed, so he quickly turned on the light. Glenn was astonished. The bed was made, nice and neat. Why would a bachelor make his bed? And in the middle of all the pillows (including decorative pillows—entirely too many pillows for a single guy) was a giant, stuffed Mighty Mouse. Shaking his head slightly, Glenn walked over to check the small bathroom. It was empty and before the brassiere hanging from the shower rod registered, he turned, hearing a noise from the next room. It sounded like someone talking!

With his back to the hall wall, he slipped down to the next bedroom door and listened quietly. There was definitely someone in there. And what was that other sound? Water splashing? He knocked and threw open the door. It banged against the side wall. Five sets of beady eyes flashed toward him, turning away from watching a young African American girl on a television set perched on a tall pedestal.

All at once they exploded into a flurry of arms, legs and itty-bitty tails, water flying, soaking the walls and carpet.

Glenn laughed. "I'm just as surprised to see you boys," he told the five red-eared slider turtles. They had to be the most mentally unstable creatures Glenn had ever encountered. Cats were pissy. A dog could wag its tail one minute and the next lapse into an aggressive pack mentality. Hamsters?

Hamsters were freaky when they froze during an activity and stared at you. But turtles were just downright weird. Any noise and into the safety of the water; their legs cartoon-like, moving really fast but not making any forward progress.

"I see you boys didn't forget me," Glenn said as he moved closer to the turtles. Bobby had jerry-rigged a complicated, home-made turtle filter out of PVC tubing and a large utility bucket and had turned a cattle trough into a turtle tank. Turtles he'd had for fifteen years. Turtles that started out the size of golf balls. Turtles that were now the size of dinner plates.

Glenn threw some turtle food into the water and laughed as they all scrambled for food, climbing over the backs of one another. "Now Tito, quit trying to drown Marlon. Jermaine, you let Jackie eat." He looked over at the turtle with the smallest shell, lighter than the others. The turtle seemed to be swimming backwards, almost walking on water. "Yeah Michael, you bad," he said as he threw some extra turtle sticks Michael's way.

Glenn looked back to the television, remembering the first time Bobby had told him about the turtles. The turtles had been nameless for years until Bobby accidentally discovered how enamored they became during reruns of a particular television show when a specific actress appeared on screen. The turtles, Bobby had explained, normally sunned themselves on the island in the middle of the trough, under the sun lamp, or exploded into a frenzy during feeding time. Other than that, they mostly stayed underwater, bobbing up only to take in air. Until the day Bobby had the television tuned to TV Land and the old sit-com *Goodtimes* came on. The turtles could care less when Jimmy "J.J." Walker came on and delivered his catch phrase "Dyno-mite!" and cared even less when Esther Rolle and John Amos were on screen. But when the next-door neighbor's daughter appeared, the turtles lined up at the edge of the trough, craned their long turtle necks and watched the screen, mesmerized. That's when Bobby had decided to name the turtles after the Jackson 5. And when he was out of the house, Bobby always left on a television with a built in VCR that played *Goodtimes* episodes over and over, on repeat. But only episodes featuring a young Janet Jackson.

"Janet," Glenn muttered, suddenly remembering the tarantula. The turtles were the Five—the tarantula the "plus one". Bobby had named the spider Janet the same time he named his turtles. Glenn looked over to the spider's terrarium in the corner. The screen was off the top and in the floor. It must have scaled the walls, escaped over the rim and tunneled under the door on its way to freedom.

Glenn had never had to feed the tarantula. Basically it was like a pet rock in its terrarium whenever he had fed the turtles. Bobby explained he would feed it a cricket every once in a while, but sometimes it wouldn't eat for months. One time, when it was molting, Bobby said it didn't eat for almost a year and a half.

Glenn grabbed the top screen to the terrarium and bid adieu to the rowdy reptiles. Very carefully, with the hairs standing up on the back of his neck, he entered the last room in the house. He turned on the light and watched for movement on the linoleum.

"Dammit Janet!" he called. "Where are you, you hairy little arachnid?"

He looked up on the kitchen counter and saw something that made him smile, made him temporarily forget his arachnophobia. Two Bud Light bottles. One of them had the label on while the other's label was partially peeled off. He walked over to the counter and gazed at the bottles. Again he thought of Bobby at No Egrets, carefully peeling the labels off his two Bud Lights every night. Sometimes he would write messages on the backs of the labels before sticking them back on the bottle. Once he wrote, "Glenda, you are beautiful inside and out". Another time he had written, "Glenn, you is smart, you is kind, you is important". Remembering, Glenn laughed and examined the bottles. They were both warm to the touch and any condensation had dried long ago. Both had their labels removed initially and replaced. He pulled off the one that was peeling and looked it over. Nothing out of the ordinary. The one on the other bottle was harder to remove, but he managed to keep it intact. He turned it over and saw a word scribbled on the other side. Bobby must have written something, but Glenn couldn't make it out. The first four letters looked like…"Rose". Maybe. The remaining letters were harder to decipher. Rose? Rose what? And then it came to Glenn. Rosebud! Bobby must have been watching the movie *Citizen Kane* while drinking his two Bud Lights.

Suddenly something dark skittered between his shoes and Glenn forgot all about Charles Foster Kane and Kane's childhood. He squealed and it took all his willpower not to leap in the air. He was already going to have a hard time explaining the destruction in the family room, but if Bobby came back and found a squished Janet on his kitchen linoleum…

Glenn grabbed the screen, wielding it like a shield, and pretended to be brave. He placed the screen on the floor in the tarantula's path. Janet stopped at the edge of the screen, feeling it out with a hairy leg. The spider started to turn and Glenn grabbed one of the Bud Light bottles and put it down to impede the spider's progress. With only two ways to turn, the spider turned away from the screen. Glenn looked around on the kitchen counter, quickly grabbed a spatula and slid it under the tarantula. He shuddered and the involuntary movement of his hand flipped the spider through the air. It landed on top of the screen and grabbed tight with all legs. It stared at Glenn with its eight eyes, giving him a "this human be crazy" look.

With a primal scream, Glenn grabbed the screen with both hands and charged toward the spare bedroom. "Ew-ew-ew. Ew!" Glenn cried, running. Janet hung on for dear life. When he reached the terrarium, he placed one end of the screen in the bottom, trying to get the spider to release. Glenn looked around the room. Somehow he had to get the spider back to the bottom of the terrarium so he could replace the screen. Spying a No. 2 yellow pencil, he picked it up, brandishing it like a weapon. He poked ("Ew") and prodded ("Ew-ew") Janet. Finally, the spider dropped to the dirt of the terrarium floor. Glenn quickly replaced the screen on top.

And the last thing he did before locking Bobby's door and replacing the key in Mighty Mouse's cranium was get a large rock from the side of the house and place it square on top of Janet's abode.

SIX

Glenn had been captivated by the opening song, played while the acolytes lighted the altar candles. When the grizzled, bearded man stood before the congregation clutching a beat-up electric guitar and broke into a 12-bar blues version of "Nothing but the Blood", it was something Glenn knew he would never forget. In fact, it would be the only thing he would remember from the service.

Glenn let out a little half-snore and Glenda poked him in the ribs with her elbow—hard. She shifted on the pew, watching her husband blink his eyes and look around guiltily. How in the world could he be so tired? He had actually slept better than she had last night. Glenda found the preacher's sermon, "Snare of the Fowler" particularly interesting and returned her attention to the pulpit.

After twenty more minutes of preaching (and four more elbow pokes to her husband) the preacher concluded his sermon and invited members of the congregation to the altar if they desired during the prayer. Glenda watched curiously as a short haired blonde woman, head hung low, rose from three pews back on the opposite side of the church and made her way to the altar. She appeared to be a young woman, but she shuffled slowly, shoulders slumped. Glenda leaned forward, trying to get a better look. There was something familiar about the woman, but Glenda couldn't place her. A lot of tourists and summer people came to the church and it was quite possible this woman was new. The woman's black dress was baggy and Glenda wondered what kept it from slipping right off her sagging shoulders.

She moved close to her husband's ear and whispered, "The woman at the altar looks familiar. Do you recognize her?"

Glenn already had his head bowed for the prayer (which was really just subterfuge; he had drifted off again). He raised his head and opened one eye. "Nope."

The preacher began to lead the prayer and husband and wife bowed their heads and closed their eyes. It was a long prayer, focusing mainly on health and sickness, about challenges we face and how God will not abandon us.

"Amen," the preacher finished. He walked over to the side of the altar and placed a hand on the kneeling woman's head. Glenda was shocked; five women stood up and gathered behind the blonde, placing hands on her. All locals.

Glenn's head had not snapped up at the end of the prayer; his eyes were still closed and he breathed deeply. This earned him an extra hard elbow. He nearly slid from the pew to the floor. Glenda pursed her lips and tried to draw his attention to the women gathered at the altar. She turned his head toward them and he peered at them blearily.

The offering began; Glenn reached for his billfold, Glenda remained transfixed on the crowd at the altar railing. The woman stood up and one by one the others hugged her. Glenda tried to get a good look at the woman's face but each time she turned in her direction, she was embraced by another woman. Glenda could see tears streaming down the poor woman's face.

As they stood for the offertory, Glenda lost sight of the woman. Throughout the closing hymn, "Bringing in the Sheaves", she searched for the woman on the third row. She had given up by the time the preacher gave the benediction. Her husband was yawning widely and she gave him one last poke in the ribs.

The organist was still playing loudly as they shook the preacher's hand and exited Ocean View United Methodist into the bright morning sun. Glenda searched the crowd outside for the woman in the black dress but did not see her.

Giving up finding the woman, Glenda led her sleepy husband through the parking lot to their car. "Feel like a nap when we get home?" Glenda asked sarcastically.

"No, don't think so." Glenn yawned. "I feel pretty rested. Church always energizes me."

"Uh-huh. In that case you'll have enough energy to go over the books this afternoon with me."

"Well…maybe I do need a nap later."

Cars moved in a steady steam through the parking lot, lining up for a chance to shoot the gap into the traffic on the main road. Glenda, preparing to open the driver's door of her Hyundai Sonata, surveyed the church exodus. Deciding it wouldn't take too long, she slid into the hot leather seat. Glenn had already gotten in the passenger seat and was "meditating", just as he did during the church service. This time she let him sleep.

She turned on the ignition and cranked up the air conditioner. The steering wheel was too hot to grip so Glenda let it cool. Waiting for a break in the church parking lot line, she leaned over and turned on the satellite radio. It was tuned to Willie's Roadhouse. *Odd*, she thought. *I think I've heard that old country song lately.*

"Bobby Bare!" Glenda shouted, always proud to name the artist, no matter the music genre. She listened to the words.

Will they call me failure or success;

Did I really live or just exist;
Will anybody know I've been here when I'm gone?

It was the song the Wurlitzer had played. The one Glenn had morosely connected to Bobby's disappearance. Glenda was still convinced Bobby and Karen had run off for a little romance dance.

The end of the car conga line was close, so Glenda placed her bare foot on the brake and slipped the Sonata into drive. She counted four cars before she could break out. She admired a small car as it passed, a pretty blue Chevy Aveo.

Suddenly she saw the mysterious blonde woman's profile in the passenger window. The woman lifted her head and looked Glenda right in the eye as the car moved on down the parking lot.

Oh my God! Glenda looked at her with wide eyes. She *did* know her. The blonde hair was shorter, she was much thinner. There were huge black circles under her eyes; her skin pale and sickly.

The blue car drove off. Glenda turned to her dozing husband and began pounding on his left thigh. Glenn jumped awake. "What? What the hell?" He twisted his head in all directions, trying to see what had shocked or scared his wife.

"I can't believe it!" she half-screamed. "That was Karen!"

Glenn struggled to keep up. His breathing had turned to rapid fire huffing two blocks ago. In another two blocks it had the potential of becoming a desperate man's dying gasps. His arms, now made of lead instead of flesh and bone, served as anchors. His red shirt clung to his body with sweat. In his mind he could hear Glenda reminding him he hadn't even made it halfway yet and he was going to have to run back, too. *Thanks dear!* He burped and tasted the generous portions of fish and vegetables they had eaten after church at Oak Island Restaurant.

Damn, he thought. *Am I gonna be sick?* A severe headache was building, the kind that knocks you to the couch for a whole day. He was forced to drop his speed from 0.5 miles per hour to zero. With hands on knees he bent over, gasping for breath.

Daniel, his running partner, talked to Glenn like he was still running right behind him. When he finally realized Glenn had stopped, he made a wide turn in the road and jogged back where Glenn was now squatting on the edge of the road. The house where he stopped was one of the larger ones, two-stories on stilts. The lawn was neatly manicured and a deep, lush, green grass left no bare spots, indicating either a lawn service or a retired owner. The house had a huge wrap around deck with big rockers facing the Intracoastal Waterway. Just at the bottom of the stairs sat a golf cart. For an instant Glenn thought of "borrowing" it. ("Excuse me, I'm a surgeon and I need to get back to my bar stat. I'll be commandeering your cart there to save a life—my own.")

"You okay?" Daniel asked as he leaned down trying to look Glenn in the eye. Glenn made a guttural noise and fell back on the prize winning zoysia grass of the yard.

"I'm fine." Glenn forced out the words. "But I think you need more of a workout, so you go on. I'll lie here until the turkey buzzards come."

Daniel laughed. The wit was just one of the reasons Daniel and Glenn hit it off so well. Daniel O'Dwyer had walked into No Egrets just a few days after Glenn had read about him in the Southport Pilot around Christmastime. Daniel had helped break up a drug ring at the local hospital; he was a former hospital pharmacist who had also moved to Oak Island from West Virginia. Although the picture in the newspaper was grainy, Glenn had recognized him almost immediately. Daniel had been wearing a Marshall University Thundering Herd t-shirt which further identified him as a West Virginian. Glenn had stunned Daniel by calling him by name and announcing him to the bar patrons as a local celebrity. Glenn could still remember Daniel's response, "Ah, my fifteen minutes of fame. I think local slacker or perhaps local lunatic may be closer to the truth."

Both being from the mountain state, they had struck up an immediate friendship. People from West Virginia seemed to seek each other out, forming instant bonds. A few months ago they had starting running together, discussing important subjects during their exercise ranging from "last night's NBA game" to "best songs of the 70s without a synthesizer". Glenn had been faithfully exercising with Daniel until the last week or so. He struggled up to a sitting position. Daniel extended his hand and pulled Glenn to his feet.

Slowly Glenn began jogging again. His left knee hurt a little with each stride. His right knee was fine; however his right side had a wicked stitch. He placed his right hand on his side and pressed, getting momentary relief from the pain. And there was some kind of soreness in his right ribs, like someone had poked him repeatedly with an elbow. What was that all about?

Daniel turned and ran backwards, facing Glenn. "You sure you're okay? You don't look okay."

Glenn gave him a quick glare and puffed out his answer, "I'm—just—peach—y. Could—n't—be—bet—ter."

Daniel shrugged his shoulders. "Physician, heal thyself."

Daniel was still running backwards when he looked beyond Glenn, smiled and called out, "Hey Jerry!"

Oh, that's just great, thought Glenn.

An old man ran up from behind and slowed to Glenn's pace. He was wearing a white headband, a blue Obama for President 2012 t-shirt and short white vintage gym trunks (really short, as in NBA 1970s and 80s short). Black dress socks were pulled all the way up the skinny white ankles above his running shoes. He had a head full of blondish-brown hair even though Glenn knew the man was approaching eighty years old.

"Hello Daniel, Doctor!" the man crowed.

How wonderful, Glenn thought. *He's not even breathing hard.*

Jerry came into No Egrets every two or three weeks. He would sit at the bar, order a ginger ale and tell stories to anyone who would listen. The two stories he told most often were when he was a skinny kid trying to make the high school track team and when he won the 2007 Oak Island Lighthouse 5K Run 1st Place Overall Seasoned award. When he went up to accept the award, someone had yelled, "Hey Jerry, where's your gray hair?" In response he had whipped off his Long Beach Pawpaw ball cap, allowing his full head of brownish hair to flow free, and cried, "Thank you Jesus!" Since then it had become the battle cry of area runners.

Daniel was still running backward. "How's your love life, Jerry?"

"O-K-I," Jerry replied, pointing to his eyeball on the last letter. (It was one of his favorite sayings and could be seen in black letters on white oval stickers on the back of automobiles all over the island.)

Glenn took his hand off his side and immediately felt the painful stitch return, although he acted like nothing was wrong and picked up the pace a little. He wasn't going to let Mr. 1st Place Overall Seasoned show him up.

Daniel began running circles around Glenn which didn't bother him much. Daniel was in excellent shape and ran all over the island. But when Jerry joined in running circles around him, Glenn seriously considered putting out an arm and taking him down with a clothesline.

Jerry hung with them a block, finally giving Daniel a fist bump. He gave a salute to Glenn and said loudly, "See ya later, Hopalong!" Jerry turned left and started down another stretch of road. They could hear him laughing for the next half block.

Glenn made an ululating noise deep within his throat that sounded like Lurch on the *Addams Family.*

"Don't let it get to you Glenn," Daniel said. "First, it's not about winning or losing. And second, Jerry's been running for at least two and a half centuries. You are off the couch and trying. That, my friend, is what really matters. What is your wife going to say when you come home, all sweaty with muscles bulging?"

Glenn laughed in between gasps and said in a high voice, "Dar—link— don't—touch—me. You're—gross."

Daniel laughed and turned around to run beside Glenn. "That's what I'm talking about! And that can only make your marriage stronger."

Glenn felt better after Daniel's pep talk. He started to get into a running rhythm and either forgot about the pain or it actually stopped. He found it helped to focus on his surroundings. They were running on East Yacht Drive which ran along the Intracoastal Waterway. What Glenn found most interesting about Oak Island (and Glenda found most quaint) was on full display on East Yacht Drive. Huge million-dollar homes with exquisite sprinkled lawns and palm trees sat right next to drab, painted cinderblock one-story homes with rusted grills and plastic pink flamingos in the yard.

Glenn saw a colorful sign in a yard up ahead he didn't recognize. It was election season so some were for candidates, except for the one he had seen most often with "Protect Our Coast" on one side and "Don't Drill NC" on the other. As he reached the sign he read "Kathi Mangus for Mayor". That was a new one! Someone different coming in to shake up the establishment. Good for her.

Glenn looked up at the bottom of the new bridge as they ran underneath. Daniel had told him it opened in 2011 after lengthy delays due to a worker's death and subsequent investigation. The duo checked their plastic watches as they always did when they reached the bridge, pretending to keep track of their running time.

With a start, Glenn realized he was really enjoying the run, surrounded by sights landlocked people yearned for daily. The sounds around him also added to his sudden state of running nirvana. All was quiet and calm. Nothing but the smacking of running shoes on pavement. A few distant seagull cries.

A piercing, screaming fire engine siren shattered the tranquility. Glenn heard Daniel say, "Uh-oh."

Two blocks ahead a police cruiser squealed as it rounded the corner from a side street, lights flashing. Another block and it disappeared across the road on the water side of the street. Before they could process what they had witnessed, the fire engine appeared and roared over to the same spot.

Glenn and Daniel stopped in the middle of the road. Briefly they looked at each other, their attention soon returning to the area where the emergency teams had disappeared. Together they sprinted towards the spot. As they ran closer, they could see another police car, an Oak Island Fire and Rescue truck and several unmarked cars.

"Maybe we should cut down this street," Daniel said apprehensively as they approached the last street on the left before the scene. Glenn didn't respond, just kept plowing straight ahead. He had a bad feeling.

Emergency vehicles and first responders were parked on a gravel area between two lots. Glenn recognized the place because he had once walked through the lots and down the steps to look at the Intracoastal Waterway. (He specifically remembered a sign at the bottom of the steps directing him it was unlawful to take oysters, clams, or mussels from the water because shellfish may cause serious illness if eaten.)

A crowd formed on the street, just outside some hastily strung crime scene tape. Hands sat in his cruiser talking on the radio. As if in a trance,

Glenn walked past the cruiser and toward the Intracoastal Waterway. Before he could get to the steps, he saw Royce's back slowly inching up them. He was bent over and seemed to be steadying something or someone below him. Big John's head appeared below Royce as they slowly moved up the steps. Glenn studied their careful manner. They were spaced about six feet apart...about the size of a man. The firefighters were somber. Glenn knew it had to be a body.

"Oh my God!" Daniel cried, coming up to stand beside Glenn.

Royce waited at the top for Big John to finish his climb. Supported between them was the body of a man, his head lolled to one side unnaturally, water dripping from his hair. Very carefully they placed the man's body on the grass of the far house.

"No...no, no, no," Glenn murmured, heading toward the body.

SEVEN

Glenda timidly pushed the button. In the house she could hear the chimes. No backing out now. She never was any good at ding-dong ditch. She took a step back from the door so anyone using the peephole could get the full body view. Glenda nervously shifted from foot to foot. How does one usually stand waiting for someone to answer the door? Was her smile too forced? She checked her reflection in the storm door. Maybe this wasn't such a good idea.

Karen; her appearance, her apparent disease. It was all she could think about during lunch at Oak Island Restaurant. Glenn's curiosity seemed to be of a more clinical nature. Glenda could forgive her husband for this quirk because of all the disease and injuries he had seen over the years. It had a way of hardening one's heart and even though he had been away from it for a while now, he hadn't softened much. She had urged him to go run with Daniel so she could think on her own.

She looked down at the covered bowl of macaroni salad in her hands. While she had been walking around her house after church, thinking about Karen, she had stopped at the kitchen window and looked out at the goldfish pond. "Egrets?" she whispered. "No egrets," she answered. She had immediately turned to the cabinets and refrigerator and began preparing macaroni salad. At one of the potluck dinners at the bar, Glenda had brought macaroni salad. It was her grandmother's recipe and Karen had loved it, raving about it to everyone. Glenda remembered her diving into the bowl three or four times.

The door opened a crack, just enough for Glenda to see a head. It wasn't Karen's head, but there was a certain resemblance.

"Can I help you?" The voice was low, powerful, throaty. It reminded Karen of Sarah Connor *after* she was institutionalized in the Terminator movies.

Glenda was caught off guard. She was prepared to console and be a good friend. For some reason she was a little afraid of this person. "I…umm…go to church with Karen," Glenda stammered. She held up the bowl. "I brought her some macaroni salad."

The woman at the door remained stone-faced. The door stayed more closed than open. The woman spoke but didn't open the door any wider. "Church really seemed to wear Karen out so…she can't have visitors right now."

"I understand," Glenda said, regaining her composure. "Can you give her this macaroni salad? Tell her it's from Glenda."

The woman looked at the bowl. Then she looked at Glenda's face, down to her Dooney and Bourke purse and finally to her white Chanel sandals. Glenda somehow felt violated. Raising her head back to meet Glenda's gaze, the woman said, "The Dooney looks real. What about the Chanel's?" The door inched a little wider as the woman wanted to get a better look at Glenda's feet.

"They're supposed to be." Glenda twisted her feet around to show the shoes. The woman bent down as if to give them a brand name sniff test.

The woman opened the storm door for the bowl. "I'm Brandi," she confessed, low and throaty. "Karen's sister." She offered no more information. Slowly she took the bowl. "Thanks for your thoughts."

She left Glenda staring at her reflection in the storm door. It gave her a chance to see the shocked look on her face. "Well..." Glenda trailed off. "You're welcome." She turned on her real Chanel white heels and walked away from the house. She stopped on the front walk when a black cat darted in front of her. It paused and curled back behind Glenda to rub casually against her legs.

"Hello girl," Glenda said, bending to the left to catch a glimpse of the upturned tail to see if she had guessed correctly.

The cat did a figure eight around her legs while Glenda petted the silky fur first with her left hand, then her right. The purr was so loud Glenda looked around to see if there was another cat nearby. She heard the front door open behind her and twisted around to look.

"Werdegast, you stop bothering Glenda," said a weak voice.

Karen stood in the doorway. Even in a plush robe her body looked small and frail. Glenda was shocked. Karen had always been a little overweight but now she looked like she had dropped fifty or sixty pounds. Her beautiful thick, blonde hair was now short and thin. Though her eyes looked sad, she gave Glenda a tight smile and motioned her to come back to the porch.

Glenda's first instinct was to give her friend a hug, but Karen had already collapsed into a chair on the front porch. Instead, Glenda walked over to the swing and sat down.

"Karen, I've been really worried about you," Glenda blurted out. She recovered quickly, adding, "So it was really great to see you at church today."

Karen tried to smile but looked down quickly.

"I'm sorry," Glenda said, her voice dropping. "I can see you've been ill. I just want you to know if there is anything, anything at all you need, you can call me day or night."

Karen, tears in her eyes, looked up at Glenda.

It was just at this heart-to-heart moment Werdegast put a plan in motion to get the full attention of the two women. The cat had been lazily patrolling the front quadrant before Glenda set foot on the porch. Now she was perched on the porch railing, using all her cat powers to try and get someone to pet her. When that didn't happen, she pushed off with aim and power toward Glenda's lap. Great on the aim—a little too much power. The force not only surprised Glenda, it nearly knocked her on her butt. Glenda, cat and swing were close to flipping over backward. With the desperation of a drowning woman, Glenda flailed about for something to steady her. A firm hand on the wall brought order back to the porch.

A small giggle escaped Karen and she put a hand to her mouth in surprise. That caused Glenda to laugh. Werdegast was perched on Glenda's lap, trying to nudge her head under Glenda's hand for some petting time. "Holy moly!" Glenda cried.

Karen's eyes grew wide and suddenly she was belly laughing, pitching back and forth in the rocking chair. Her laugh was infectious and Glenda couldn't help joining in. When Brandi, carrying a small bowl of macaroni salad and fork, came into view they both stopped abruptly.

"Humph!" Brandi snorted. "You two are acting like a couple of skanks on a Sunday. Stop all that cackling before the neighbors hear." She turned to go back in the house when Karen stopped her. Brandi turned, frowning at her sister.

"Please leave the macaroni salad with me."

Brandi reluctantly did as she was told, putting the bowl down on a side table just out of Karen's reach. Brandi turned back to the front door, silently fuming.

"Sis," Karen called. Brandi stopped in the doorway. "I need the fork, too." Brandi handed the fork to Karen without looking at her.

"Thank you, Brand," Karen said. Brandi went back into the house.

Glenda had been petting Werdegast frantically during this exchange; suddenly the cat turned and bit her hand.

"Ouch!"

Karen laughed again. "I'm sorry Glenda—Werdegast, bad cat!" Karen pursed her lips and raised her eyebrows, looking at Glenda and Werdegast. She looked so comical Glenda couldn't help laughing again.

"Oh Glenda!" Karen cried. "You don't know how good it is to laugh again. You take laughing for granted when it's all around you, when you can laugh without thinking. But take it away and even movies you thought were hilarious are...flat."

Karen pointed to the bowl of macaroni salad. "Is that what I think it is? Granny's recipe?"

"All your very own," Glenda replied as she retrieved the bowl and carefully passed it to her friend. She scooted the table over beside the rocking chair.

Karen wiggled in her rocker with excitement as her fork took a dive into the bowl. She was still smiling when the fork made it to her mouth. She nibbled it slowly. "Mmm. My taste buds have been shot, but this is still the most wonderful food I've eaten in a long time."

The cat jumped from the swing and sat in front of Karen, hoping for a handout.

"Is it your cat?" Glenda asked.

"Oh, she's not mine. She belongs to the people next door, Vicki and Whitney." She put the fork down. "So the cat is named for a Bela Lugosi character in some old horror movie...called, um...oh, *The Black Cat*. Duh," she said looking down at Werdegast's silky black fur. "How could I forget that?" Karen touched her temple with the palm of her hand, straining to sort out the information in her brain. "There's more to Werdegast but I just can't remember it."

"Bet it's Dr. Vitus Werdegast," Glenda offered, helping to fill in the blanks.

"Oh my gosh! How did you know that?" Karen's eyes were again wide.

"Glenn. He's been hanging around with Daniel O'Dwyer and they've been watching all the Lugosi movies for some reason. He comes home and talks about them nonstop."

"That is crazy. Whitney is obsessed with Lugosi, too. He even dressed as him last Halloween." She picked up her fork again and took another small bite. "Hey, Whitney and Vicki play in a band on the weekends. Maybe they could play at No Egrets some time. I haven't had a chance to hear them yet."

Glenda smiled. "That's a good idea." She reached down and gave the cat a long stroke from head to tail. "If it wasn't for Werdegast I would have been in my car and already gone before you came to the porch."

Karen nibbled at a macaroni noodle and looked down at her feet. "Glenda...I have cancer."

Momentarily flustered, Glenda looked out into Karen's yard. Beautiful crepe myrtles were in full bloom, surrounded by small palm plants. Over to the side the large meaty blades of an Agave Americana spread out menacingly.

Glenda turned back to her friend. "Karen, I know it's hard. I am here if you ever need to talk. I would also like very much to help—that is if you ever need me. I know with Brandi here you may not need anyone else."

Glenda noticed when Karen looked up at her, the sadness had been replaced with a look of determination. "It all started with blood work and a routine check-up from my regular doctor," Karen said. "He didn't like some of the numbers, so he suggested I go to another doctor. There's a new cancer doctor over near Shallotte, he specializes in blood diseases, so I went to his office one Friday after work for an appointment."

Karen paused to nibble on another forkful of macaroni salad. She stared into the yard as she talked. "Really you go numb. You don't hear anything. That's all you can hear—you have cancer." After a long pause, she continued. "I didn't even tell anyone I had an appointment. I was alone. And then I'm sitting there wondering if I'm going to live or die. That's the scary part."

"I'm really sorry you had to go through that alone."

"Well, I did have someone…at first." Karen looked down shyly.

Glenda waited, hoping silence might draw her out.

Karen looked up at Glenda. "You know what? I think I need to tell someone. I don't like talking about it with Brandi. She thinks she knows all about men. And she just picks-picks-picks at anyone I date."

After a long pause, Karen whispered, "Bobby…Bobby Portis. Hangs out at your bar. That's where I met him."

Karen watched for Glenda's reaction. Glenda smiled and said, "I could have guessed. I've noticed Bobby stealing glances at you." Karen blushed a little, leaning forward in her chair. "And, I've seen you looking his way more than once. It was only natural you two hooked up."

Karen slumped back in the rocker. "Yeah, well that's what I thought, at least at first. Bobby was very attentive to me. Our first date, we ate at Joseph's, you know that Italian place. We walked along the water and looked at the boats. Talked. You know, very low key. Really, really nice. Comfortable."

She pushed away the macaroni salad, continuing, "We started seeing each other a lot. He even spent a few nights here; I stayed over at his house a few times."

Glenda wished she was closer to Karen so she could put a hand over hers and comfort her. What she really wanted to do was hug her. "Where is Bobby now?" Glenda asked.

"The bastard dumped me! Can you believe that? I can understand, okay, my hair will probably fall out and I'm gonna feel like shit. Hell, I may even die. But not to say anything—just disappear. Not even a 'Hey it's been great, but you have cancer and I'm a shit-heel.' Nothing." Karen's rant took a lot of energy; she collapsed back in the rocker. "Damn him."

Suddenly Glenda was glad she was not hugging Karen. She tried to figure out what was missing from the picture besides Bobby. Karen plus Bobby; Karen sick—Bobby gone. She felt like she knew Bobby well and it just didn't add up. A sickening feeling washed over her. Something's not right. She began to see things from Glenn's point of view.

Karen laughed weakly. "I did something really stupid. I checked into hiring a private investigator to find Bobby. I was hurt and I guess a little jealous. Maybe he found somebody else. But it would've cost way too much and I've got too many other bills now. So—" She looked at Glenda, shaking her head. "I gave Pinhead Paul fifty dollars to follow Bobby."

Karen laughed at the look on Glenda's face. "It is a little funny. Paul couldn't find Bobby. The last time I talked to him he told me he had to earn the fifty dollars, so he started following around all the other people at No Egrets, in case they were meeting secretly with Bobby."

Glenda started to respond but clamped her lips shut. She had overheard both Richard and Kenny talking separately about the mysterious smell of fish that seemed to follow them wherever they went.

"Bobby." Karen's voice faltered a bit as she continued, "He was the only one I told about the results of the blood work and what my doctor said. He was my rock that day, the son of a bitch."

Suddenly she laughed. Not the therapeutic kind from earlier, but a vicious, hurtful laugh, directed inward. "Half the time I can't remember the name of the cancer I've got. It's inside me claiming squatter's rights." The sad eyes turned angry and Glenda was momentarily frightened. "I can't even remember the name!"

Glenda moved to get up from the swing, but Karen raised a shaky palm in her direction. Karen hunched her shoulders, listening, with an ear turned toward the front door. "I'm sorry," she whispered. "I hope Brandi didn't hear."

They waited. When her sister didn't appear, Karen seemed composed again. "Bobby went with me to the first couple of chemo treatments at Dr. Roshberg's office. The dirtbag."

Karen paused, glancing over her body. She reached up and pulled a small strand of hair out by the roots.

"Karen," Glenda said, her heart aching for her friend. "I've only known Bobby for about a year, but I can tell he's one of the good ones."

"That's what I thought, too. But I haven't heard from him in four days now." Her hand was trembling as she rubbed the side of her face. "He won't return my calls."

For the first time, Glenda felt a foreboding twinge.

"He doesn't want to see me now…and I really don't want to see him either."

Otto dropped on top of his cot fully clothed. He hated Sundays. The office was closed and the boss was off with his family. He had nothing to do. He briefly thought of driving somewhere but there was really nowhere he wanted to go. Otto didn't have friends, didn't want friends. So he remained in his little makeshift apartment, hidden just off the doctor's main office. There was a small bathroom with a shower next to his room, so it was all he really needed. He had lived in much worse.

He rolled over, the shape of the kactet in his pocket biting into his leg. Rolling back, he removed the brass knuckles and placed them next to his pillow. A small card pulled out of his pocket at the same time fluttered next to his face. He looked at the front of the card. It was his Communist Party USA identification card.

A line from the movie *Serpico* came to him. "How come all your friends are on their way to bein' someone else?" Waldo Salt had written the movie and was perhaps the only true friend Otto had ever had.

The memories of the smells from the trash bins and dumpsters of Los Angeles flooded his senses and Otto wrinkled his nose. He had been eighteen and starving, going through Waldo Salt's trash cans when Waldo caught him. For some reason Otto had chosen not to run. Waldo had smiled and asked Otto if he would like to join him for lunch.

Otto remembered the lunch as if it were yesterday: fried eggs, ham and coffee. His mouth watered; it was probably the best meal he had ever eaten. The two became unlikely friends, Waldo taking Otto under his wing. Although Waldo Salt had still been writing at the time, he was timeworn, gray and had already written the famous screenplays that would appear in his obituary: *Midnight Cowboy, Serpico, Coming Home*. Otto learned a lot about life from the old screenwriter, soaking up all the stories, wisdom and insight. Waldo never mentioned his two Academy Awards, instead choosing to focus on the difficult chapters of his life. In retrospect, Otto thought this was to help put Otto's hard times in perspective and help the gangly teenager assimilate into an unwelcoming society. The takeaway for Otto: Waldo Salt—survivor.

"A survivor," Otto said in his raspy voice to the empty room. Just like his grandparents. And survival was the most important thing Waldo Salt had taught Otto. He looked back at the card. Otto didn't carry a wallet and the card was his only identification. Out of respect for Waldo Salt, Otto had joined Communist Party USA many years ago, an organization that evolved from the American Communist Party.

Waldo Salt had joined the American Communist Party just as many United States citizens had during the turbulent times surrounding World War II. More than a decade later, just as his career was gaining momentum in Hollywood, Waldo was blacklisted after refusing to testify in 1951 before the House Committee on Un-American Activities, a paranoid investigation of Communist infiltration in America.

Otto picked up his kactet and slid it over his knuckles. He gripped it tight. Waldo's stories of that time always made Otto furious. He lifted his fist into the air and with a sudden jab imagined decking the crazy senator responsible for blacklisting his friend.

The result of the blacklist, Waldo had carefully explained to Otto, was rock bottom, both professionally and personally. Even after the blacklist was lifted and he could write under his own name again, it took years before Waldo would write the adapted screenplay for *Midnight Cowboy* and win the Academy Award, assuring his comeback was complete. But in the end, Waldo had had the last laugh because he had survived. Survived and thrived.

Otto took the card and put it back in his pocket. Sighing, he tried to figure out something to do. He really, really hated Sundays. He thought of the last two jobs the boss had given him and tried to focus on the smile on the boss's face when he successfully completed them. Maybe the boss would have more jobs like those for him. He had enjoyed them immensely.

As he started to drift off, Otto's mind returned to the movie *Serpico*. The plot played over in his mind, gritty scenes of brutality and police corruption in New York City. As he pictured a bearded Al Pacino in the lead role, he still couldn't understand the moral convictions of Officer Frank Serpico, turning in his crooked policeman friends. Why would he do that? In Otto's mind, that was just downright disloyal.

EIGHT

"Is it...?" Even though he was fifteen feet away, Daniel took two steps back.

Glenn charged up between Royce and Big John who were kneeling on either side of a man's body.

"Doc! Didn't know you was here," Big John said, looking up. "What you think?"

Glenn was suddenly transported back to his residency. Human remains pulled from water. Once living, breathing, laughing—now dead. Glenn kneeled to start an exam, just as he did years ago in a hospital Emergency Room. That hospital sat beside a big river known for floaters, mostly druggies and the homeless. The sight of three drowning victims in a four-day period had been indelibly seared into his soul.

The doctor focused on the swollen facial features and leaned in closer for a look at the mouth. The one thing he had learned was death by drowning was neither simple nor uniform. There were many variables; autopsy and laboratory findings were not enough on their own to solve most cases. He touched the skin of the dead man. All the drownings he had examined had been pulled from fresh water. Glenn had no idea how saltwater adversely affected the victim.

Sphinx was joined by Hands behind Glenn. "EMS and the M.E. are on the way," Hands informed the small group.

"EMS not going to do this boy any good," Big John answered. "Can you tell anything, Doc?"

Glenn was thinking about all the drowning victims he had observed; some were ruled suicides, some accidental and several murder. The hard part was to prove whether the victim was alive or dead when entering the water. Glenn looked around the victim's face and mouth for any signs of vomitus. He didn't see any, but the evidence could easily have washed away. The majority of drownings when a victim entered the water before death were termed "wet" drownings. In these cases a foam or froth exuded from the nose or mouth, but it too could be washed away, especially during recovery operations. Glenn thought he could make out a small amount of foam around the nose but couldn't be sure.

"If a victim is alive before he hits the water, there will be signs of foaming around the mouth," Glenn explained. "This could be a small amount of foam around the nose but I'm not a hundred percent sure."

Glenn turned to Royce. "When you pulled him out, did his arms appear to be in rigor mortis?"

"We didn't pull him out of the water," Sphinx said. "Fisherman spotted him washed up partly on the sand during low tide. But his arms didn't seem stiff, did they Royce?"

"Nope."

Glenn looked down at the man's abdomen. It did not appear to be too distended so possibly not much water had been taken in. "It's impossible to tell this early, but some of the signs point to the possibility this man was either ill or injured prior to submersion in the water."

"Wow," Royce said. Glenn wasn't sure if Royce was impressed by his findings, his big words or the fact the man who routinely poured his beer was indeed a doctor.

"Or possibly already dead," Glenn finished.

Daniel had crept up behind Glenn, cautiously peering around his back. "Glenn, is it...?"

Daniel's eyes grew wide.

Bobby! Glenn had forgotten all about his earlier fear. He immediately dropped to his knees again and frantically started reexamining the body. The man's face was too swollen to recognize. He looked down at the clothes. Bobby sometimes wore similar clothes. Glenn stood up and surveyed the body from head to toe.

"Hey guys," Glenn said. "How tall you think this guy is?"

Hands answered, "Six foot" about the same time Big John said, "Six two."

"That's about what I was thinking." Glenn turned to where he thought Daniel was standing. "Daniel, Bobby is six foot eleven, there's no way..."

Daniel was too far away to hear. He had retreated to a yard down the street. Hands on knees, Daniel's body heaved spasmodically before vomiting into the grass. Glenn trotted toward Daniel. "Daniel, it's not—" But Daniel was retching again and did not hear. When Daniel was finally finished, Glenn steadied him. He opened his mouth to tell Daniel the body wasn't Bobby's, but the blaring siren of the Brunswick County EMS ambulance drowned out his words.

Glenda was alarmed when Glenn, supporting a pale Daniel, burst through the door of No Egrets followed by Hands and Sphinx.

"What on earth?"

Glenn pulled Daniel to the bar and deposited him on Bobby's barstool. "Fat Tire, stat!" Glenn shouted.

Glenda grabbed a pint glass and filled it half full at the tap. She slid it down the bar where Glenn caught it. Daniel grabbed it from him and downed it in one gulp.

"Oh man, thanks. I needed that," Daniel said, taking a deep breath. He wiped the perspiration from his brow with a shaky hand.

"You sure you're going to be okay?" Sphinx asked.

"Yeah, I'm good now. Thanks for the ride guys. I don't think Glenn could've piggybacked me here." He turned to Glenda. "Una mas cervaza, por favor."

Sphinx was already heading for the door. Hands turned to Glenn before following his partner. "Thanks for the help, Doc. Gotta get back to the station. It's going to be a little crazy there today."

"What on earth?" Glenda repeated.

Glenda had just opened the bar forty-five minutes earlier and the only occupants were Kenny, Richard and Pinhead Paul. Ism had just entered through the back door looking for his longboard he had left the night before. They all gathered around Glenn and Daniel to hear the big Oak Island news.

Glenda put her hand over her mouth, her eyes wide, when Glenn told about the drowning victim and the state of the body. Daniel noticed the tears forming in her eyes.

"It's okay Glenda. It isn't Bobby," Daniel said.

Glenda let out a whoosh of breath and the tears came anyway. Glenn look surprised his wife was crying. He put an arm around her. "I'm sorry. I should have started out by telling you it wasn't Bobby. Sometimes I get too—"

"Clinical," Glenda finished for him.

"Who was it?" Pinhead Paul asked excitedly.

Glenn shook his head. "I didn't recognize him, but his features were swollen so I guess it could've been a local."

"Probably a friggin' kook or co-kook," Ism said with disdain. "Those ass clowns don't know how to float let alone glide."

Glenn looked to Glenda to translate. She shook her head. "I'll explain later," she whispered.

"He didn't look familiar to me either," Daniel added. "Of course I didn't get a good look. But I have to tell you Glenda, your man here was cool, calm and collected. Me? Not so much."

Glenn put a hand on Daniel's shoulder. "You were pretty good at calling Earl though."

Daniel laughed. The others look confused.

"Calling who?" Kenny asked, stroking his man beard thoughtfully.

"Maybe it's a West Virginia saying," Daniel said. "How about spewing, blowing chunks, hurling, tossing cookies, ralphing?"

"Oh." They all nodded their heads in understanding.

"Yo brah!" Ism exclaimed, addressing Daniel. "Down at the sandy shredquarters we call that barking the dog, parking the tiger, feeding the tuna and the Technicolor yawn."

They all laughed. Richard cleared his throat and stood, taking the stage.

"I once played a part where I had to eat meat that was supposed to be tainted with E. Coli. It was a most difficult part. I had to hold some yellowish liquid in the back of my throat while taking bites of the meat. Finally, on cue, it all came spewing out."

Pinhead Paul was looking at Richard with wide eyes. The front door jingled as someone entered.

"Some said," Richard continued. "It was the greatest acting they had ever seen. My agent put it first on my audition tape."

Matilda's voice was muffled as she came up behind them, wearing her helmet. "I've heard that story before you flaming thespian blowhard."

Pinhead Paul snorted and Glenda gave him a harsh look which caused him to shrink and curl up, shrimplike. "Don't encourage her," Glenda scolded.

"You actually puked your guts out. Acting had nothing to do with it," Matilda continued heatedly. "It even came out your nose. Not even Paul Newman could make it come out his nose."

Richard had no response. Deflated, he tipped his glass back and forth, pretending to study the swirling liquid.

Glenda moved from around the bar to help Matilda out of her helmet. The room was quiet except for the satellite radio station Classic Vinyl that Glenda had tuned in when she opened. They all watched Glenda wrestle with Matilda's helmet as "The Joker" by The Steve Miller Band floated over the speakers.

Glenn moved to help Glenda with Matilda's headwear.

Daniel, his color returned, suddenly sang along with the song. "Some people call me Maurice, 'cause I speak of the pompitous of love."

Pinhead Paul's leg started bopping in time to the music; Kenny's man beard bobbed up and down. Matilda's helmet popped off right before the chorus. Richard looked up, sensing a moment. They all joined together, like a big, happy family of misfits.

"I'm a picker, I'm a grinner, I'm a lover, and I'm a sinner. I play my music in the sun."

They all gathered closer, forming a circle.

'I'm a joker, I'm a smoker, I'm a midnight toker. I sure don't want to hurt no one."

Matilda even had her arm around Richard as they all sang loudly:
"Wooo-ooo, Wooo-ooo!"

NINE

It was an old joke all twins pulled out at some point—which one is "older". The Sonora twins had turned it into a regular comedy routine, dusting it off at church functions, backyard barbecues or whenever a party seemed dull. Not too original after the first fifty times but their social circle didn't seem to mind. Both women were quick-witted and the lines could be improvised depending on the location so it was never the same show twice.

"Ah baby sister, when I was your age, I had a piece of broccoli stuck in my teeth and used the end of this bamboo drink umbrella to pick it out."

"Hey sis, when I get to be as old as you, I'm going to order another Mimosa, play KC and the Sunshine Band on the jukebox and do a little chair dancing."

Part of the exchange would include Juanita complaining their mother always made her look after Bonita because she was younger. Unspoken was what everyone could see: Bonita was smaller and much more fragile than her gung-ho twin. Through the years Juanita had definitely become the protector of her "younger" sister. Younger by a mere ten minutes.

Together, they squeezed hands in the godawful sterile waiting room. The place was surely germ free because it was free of everything else—cheerfulness, friendliness, life.

Bonita checked her watch, not for the time of day but the date. How many days had this been going on? How many days, months would it continue? How long before she had a complete and total breakdown?

Juanita tugged at her sister's hand and laced it through her own fingers. Brightly colored fingernails made their grip look like a neon zipper running up one side and down the other.

"We need to go to a happy place," Juanita said, trying to lighten her twin's mood. "How about the campfire scene from *Blazing Saddles*?"

Bonita turned to her sister and even through red-rimmed eyes managed to convey disapproval. "The campfire scene is *your* happy place, not mine. Beans and farting—that's just gross."

"What are you doing now?" Bonita asked, looking incredulously at her sister's face. Juanita had her jowls scrunched up and her lower teeth and jaw pushed out.

"I'm doing the Grumpy Puppy! It always makes you laugh."

Bonita moaned. "Please stop." The Grumpy Puppy was a cute picture making the rounds on social media and Bonita had told her sister several times her twisted face looked nothing like the cranky canine.

"Oh, I know what will make you laugh," Juanita said, her face brightening. "Remember the time when we were kids? High school, I think. Me, you, Boots? Was she with us? A few other girls. Betty was driving and we stopped to have a Chinese Fire Drill in the middle of Second Street..." Juanita stopped, unable to continue. Laughter began bubbling out of her like a shaken soda bottle. "Oh my Lord, do you remember that?" Juanita choked out. "And Betty locked the keys in the car...with the engine running!" Laughter. "And the cops came before her parents got there!" Juanita started wiping tears from her eyes. "What a time!"

Bonita's mouth started to curve at the corners. "You know, you can't say 'Chinese Fire Drill' these days. It's not politically correct."

Juanita laughed louder. Bonita's smile became a little larger. At the time the event hadn't been funny at all. Everyone involved had gotten in a lot of trouble. Especially after a boy in their class managed to use a coat hanger to get the car unlocked. The cops were keen on talking to him after that because of some nearby car thefts. Betty's car had blocked the road and angry drivers had blown their horns for what seemed like hours.

It wasn't the first time and it certainly wasn't the last time the twins were tangled in something that shocked their parents. But Juanita had always smoothed things over. She was the talker, the manager, the "handler".

"I just want to go to No Egrets for a Mimosa," Bonita whispered in her sister's ear.

Juanita looked at her sister empathetically. She would do anything for her; give her anything—one of her kidneys if necessary. But she did not know what to do for her now.

"I'm sorry Boni. I'd like nothing more than to take you to No Egrets. But it's eight thirty in the morning. They aren't open yet."

Juanita placed an arm around her sister and pulled her as close to her as the metal armrest between them would allow. She whispered to her, "I know you're scared. I am too. But we'll get through this together, just like we do everything else."

Bonita buried her face between Juanita's shoulder and chest. Juanita stroked her sister's platinum blonde hair. She had tried to help Bonita fix her hair this morning, but Bonita had shooed her away. Now her finger-wave updo curls were flat and crashing.

Juanita blinked tears away, looking around the waiting room. The doctor's office was relatively new, although when they looked it up on-line it was called an Oncology Clinic. The surroundings were immaculate, sterile and one hundred percent impersonal. The only touch of decorating was two four-foot-tall abstract watercolors. They were neither pleasing nor comforting. The longer Juanita stared at them, the more her head hurt. She could only imagine their effect on sick people.

Pulling back from her sister, Juanita jumped to her feet. Bonita's jaw dropped as she watched Juanita march over to one of the watercolors and grasp it by the frame. Juanita gave a mighty heave; it wasn't the kind of power that made East German women famous, but it showed some pretty good muscle. It certainly would have made for a spectacular story if the picture had actually left the wall.

"Bolted," a passing nurse commented.

Not convinced, Juanita tried again. This time she added a loud grunt, like Selena Williams returning a serve. Every butt in the waiting room jumped two inches off the seat. No one was prepared for the audio portion of Juanita's power. Juanita stood back from the print and looked for any evidence that the frame had budged. Nothing.

"Why is the damn thing bolted on?" she asked no one in particular.

The nurse was still nearby. "Seriously? You just tried to tear it off the wall and you wonder why it's bolted on. The doctor sent all the way to Paris for those."

With resignation, Juanita rejoined her sister at her seat in the sterile, ugly waiting room with its well-protected "art".

The waiting room had filled up since they arrived. A man reading a *Golf Digest* near them looked healthy enough but there was a couple sitting by the far wall and the man looked quite ill. He had a yellow pallor, his hands were trembling as he held onto the woman next to him and his hair was present only in patches. Juanita looked away, not wanting to stare. She surveyed the rest of the waiting room occupants with random glances. It wasn't hard to pick out the patients from their parents or partners. While the patients exhibited different degrees of illness, Juanita was struck by the different expressions on their faces. Some were grief-stricken, some scared, a few angry, and two at opposite ends of the room looked resolute and determined.

The full waiting room made Juanita feel better. They hadn't done much research on the doctor before choosing him and they certainly hadn't been referred by their family doctor. In fact, neither she nor Bonita had been to their family doctor since their mother died two years ago. Each time they had made an appointment they had come up with an excuse to cancel it. So it had been extremely brave for them to come to this office the first time. And now the doctor had specifically asked to meet with Bonita.

The door to the inner office opened and a tall man ducked his head to exit. He was dressed in green scrubs; he turned, crossed his hands in front of him and stood motionless between the glass admitting window and the door.

"Wow Boni. Look at that guy. He's as tall as Bobby but look how wide his shoulders are—look at those muscles."

Bonita raised her head just as the glass window slid open and a nasal female voice called, "Snora?"

Juanita helped her sister stand and supported her as they walked to the window. "Sonora," Juanita said as they reached the window. "Sonora. An 'O' after the beginning 'S'." The sisters could only see the top of a female head through the window. The hair was bright purple.

It was obvious the woman didn't care about pronunciations or even feel the need to apologize to a sick woman. She offered no response about their name, instead moving on to the next order of business. "Otto will take you back to Dr. Roshberg's office."

The huge, bald man beside the door looked down at them. Juanita whispered to Bonita, "Did we just climb the beanstalk?" The twins grasped the straps on their purses a little tighter. Otto opened the door and gestured them through with a sweep of a giant hand. His blank expression was scary as hell

As they waited inside the door for Otto to take the lead, Juanita gasped at the huge scar running down his face. He shot her a look.

"Oh, I...thought I saw a mouse," she stammered, trying to cover her faux pas.

They followed Otto through the labyrinth of exam rooms and mysterious closed doors. "You must be new here," Juanita said, trying to turn on the charm, hoping her gasp would be forgiven. No response. "So, um, are you single?" This time it was Bonita who shot her a look. No response from the stone gargoyle escorting them down the hall.

The twins remained quiet. Unusual for a pair who liked to gossip, to speculate and who had ultimately convinced themselves cancer would get them, just as it got their mother two years ago. After all, they had read (many times) about the genetic component to cancer. It didn't matter that their mother had been eighty-six when the breast cancer was discovered and she had suffered from congestive heart failure and chronic obstructive pulmonary disease for over twenty years. It didn't matter when her physician assured them over and over the cancer had nothing to do with her death. The fact it was written (albeit in the third spot after the other two diseases) on the Death Certificate was all the proof they needed. It was on a drive to Calabash for seafood at Boundary House Restaurant and a visit to the Christmas Shop next door when Juanita had first noticed the new doctor's office just off US 17 right outside of Shallotte. Later, it had been her idea they visit Dr. Roshberg since neither of them could seem to get the "Big C" off their mind. The idea had been to get a clean bill of health and put the matter to rest.

Otto made a right turn and then a sharp left before stopping in front of a large ornate door. Juanita imagined the door being purchased at a castle garage sale. *Free giant ogre with the purchase of a castle door*, thought Juanita, casting a glance at Otto. He looked down at her again and she got a better look at his face. Otto's blue eyes were stunning, but his chiseled features offered no warmth, no compassion. Juanita noticed scratches on the right side of his neck; his upturned palm appeared dark, stained maybe.

Otto gave three sharp knocks on the heavy door with his index knuckle. The knocks had an unusual rhythm, like they were a code. *Knock—knock, (pause—pause), knock.* A voice from the other side could be heard. "Yes Otto?"

Otto opened the door and ushered the sisters into the room without a word. Behind a giant mahogany desk, a short man in a white lab coat stood and smiled, his hands crossed in front of him. His shirt looked professionally pressed with starch in the collar. A gold chain bracelet dangled from his right wrist. A large gold watch encased his left wrist. "Come in. Please, have a seat." His voice had a pleasing tone with a slight accent.

On their first visit they had only seen an assistant and a nurse. Dr. Roshberg had made a brief cameo appearance in the exam room at the end of their second visit. Now they were in his office. Juanita found her palms were sweating. Bonita licked her dry lips nervously.

The sisters took seats in front of the desk, sinking into plush leather chairs. Juanita felt like she had dropped beneath the top of the desk, but when Dr. Roshberg sat down he was still within her line of vision, seeming to loom over them.

"Now. Ms. Sonora. May I call you Bonita?"

Bonita nodded her head weakly

"Bonita. During your last appointment we briefly discussed the results of your blood test. Do you recall?" Another weak nod.

"Your platelets are low and your leukocytes are high..." In spite of Juanita's attempt to concentrate, her mind wandered as the doctor continued his medical mumbo jumbo, throwing out large words and technical jargon. Dr. Roshberg hadn't spoken much the last time and she found his voice hypnotizing. She watched his lips move but instead of hearing the words she found herself gazing at his dark skin, jet black hair and bushy mustache. His deep, smooth voice was taking her to other places.

Behind the doctor, a huge bookshelf lined the entire back wall; medical volumes were intermingled with old classics, books of travel and of war. In the corner of the left wall stood a beautiful Japanese screen. Beside it a bust of Napoleon Bonaparte was perched atop a marble pedestal. Pictures of Dr. Roshberg in exotic places lined the wall. Dreamily, Juanita turned to her right; a large tribal mask seemed to transport her into the photograph beside it, standing beside the good doctor and the natives somewhere deep within Africa.

Juanita closed her eyes for a minute, savoring the feeling of traveling the world with this man.

"Have you ever been to Namibia?" the good doctor asked her in her daydream.

Shaking her head, Juanita couldn't help smiling.

"Maybe someday I will take you there."

Juanita opened her eyes, banishing fantasyland to the back of her mind. Dr. Roshberg was still talking to Bonita.

"So…I have consulted a very knowledgeable and celebrated colleague of mine. We agree chemotherapy is our only option."

"Whoa!" Juanita's mind snapped back to the present. "WHAT did you say?"

Bonita, who had been leaning forward to listen to the doctor, gasped and slumped to the arm of the chair away from her sister. Before Juanita could grab her, Bonita slithered off the chair and fell to the floor with a thump.

"Bonita!" Juanita screamed, jumping from her chair. Dr. Roshberg stood but remained behind his desk.

Juanita thumped to her knees beside her sister. It was a move that would surely keep her on ibuprofen for the next week, but she didn't notice the pain. Gently she cradled Bonita's head, pulling her hair away from her face. Bonita's face was deathly white and she was perspiring heavily. Juanita gently slapped her sister's cheek. "Bonita. Bonita! Are you okay?" Bonita's eyes fluttered but remained closed.

Juanita looked to the doctor who remained behind his desk. "Help her!"

Dr. Roshberg started to move around the desk but stopped suddenly, a dark look on his face. "Otto!" he called loudly.

Otto opened the door quickly. "Otto, get a nurse! Tell her to bring an ammonia inhalant."

Bonita's eyes blinked open. Juanita stroked her sister's hair and soothed her. "It's going to be okay, Boni. I will take care of you. I love you."

Bonita looked at her sister through her tears. "I love you, too."

Juanita glared up at Dr. Roshberg who still hadn't moved. She wouldn't travel to the end of the street with this man, let alone the world. His aura now screamed used car salesman, snake oil charlatan or one of those lawyers you see on commercials trying to sucker in the general public.

Otto appeared with a nurse. The nurse knelt beside the sisters with an ampoule of ammonia. Juanita pushed the nurse away.

"She's okay now. Just help me get her to the chair."

As Otto lifted Bonita into the chair, Juanita noticed two things. Dr. Roshberg still stood in the same place, a right hand tucked in between the first two buttons of his lab coat. And Otto's fingernails had dirt under them.

What in the world had she had gotten her sister into?

TEN

Outside the kitchen window the snow-white egret glided to a two-point landing on a large rock beside the goldfish pond. A quick glance toward the window (to make sure it wasn't being watched?), then a quick stab and splash of water. The goldfish disappeared just as quick down the bird's gullet. Less than a minute later the beautiful egret was gone, leaving only a telltale tail feather as a clue.

Inside, husband and wife had just sat down at the kitchen table for a late breakfast. Both had overslept and neither had looked out the kitchen window into the back yard, as per their usual routine.

Glenn was the first to speak. "I had a dream that I had dinner with Levon Helm. We had ribs."

"Who's Levon Helm? Some doctor you used to work with?"

"No, he played drums for The Band."

"Which band?"

"The Band."

"Your high school band? Was he on the drum line?"

"No! *The* Band. You know, they backed up Bob Dylan when he went electric, then they recorded on their own."

Glenda blinked once, looking at her husband blankly.

"'Up on Cripple Creek', 'The Weight', 'The Night They Drove Old Dixie Down'?"

"So, what kind of ribs did you have?"

"What?"

"Pork or beef?"

Glenn stroked his chin, thinking.

"Pork dry rub. I think we were at the Rendezvous in Memphis."

"Ooh. I'd like to go to Memphis again. I liked staying at The Peabody, with those ducks. You remember those ducks, they bring 'em down in the elevator—"

"I think you're missing the point of my dream. Levon Helm. *The* Levon Helm."

"Yeah, I get it. *The* Levon Helm of *The* Band. Maybe I'll dream about *The* George Clooney tonight."

Glenn sighed. "Never mind."

Glenn slid hanger after hanger to the left, searching through Glenda's side of the closet for his jeans. *Look at all these clothes,* he thought. *Freaking amazing!* It had only taken him two minutes to look through his side of the closet.

He started to call out to his wife when his hand came to rest on a frilly pink cashmere sweater. It was soft, so very soft. He stroked it with both hands, enjoying the texture. Without regard, he stuck his face into the fabric, rubbing it over his cheeks, inhaling the scent.

"You'd look real pretty in that. Would you like to try it on?"

Glenn turned to see his wife standing in the doorway to the closet, hands on hips.

"Would you still love me if I told you I like to wear women's clothes?" Glenn asked, teasing his wife.

"Hmm, I'll have to think about that one."

"Here, let me show you." Glenn pulled his shirt over his head and grabbed the pink sweater.

"Glenn Michael!" Glenda shouted, pulling out the dreaded middle name. "If you stretch out my good sweater for your sick joke, I'll...I'll..."

Glenn laughed. Glenda held out her hand for the pink cashmere sweater. Glenn laughed some more.

"I'm sorry, dear. I was just looking for my jeans. Do you know you have enough outfits to clothe a third world country?"

Glenda huffed. "Very funny sicko." Under her breath she said, "I'm just glad you didn't find my shoe stash."

"What? What was that last part?"

"Nothing."

Glenn pulled his shirt back over his head. He waited for his jeans. When Glenda didn't move or say anything, he cocked his head to the side, turned his hands outward and used them to draw her attention to his boxer shorts, presenting them as a model on the *Price Is Right* would present a new living room suit or new car.

"I prefer briefs," Glenda said, crossing her arms and turning away from her husband.

Glenn slid up behind her, putting his arms around her waist. Slowly he sang, "Come on baby, let's do the Zwist."

"Oh...ooo," Glenda purred. Suddenly she pulled away. "Glenn, what time is it?"

"What? I don't know. Ten, ten thirty."

She pulled her phone out of her pocket, turning it on. "Oh my gosh. It's ten forty-five. You promised Thomas you would let him and the kids in the back room at eleven."

"Kids?"

She gave him a look. A much different look than when he was about to try on her sweater.

"Oh yeah. Thomas and his class." Glenn paused, trying to think of the name of the class. When he couldn't come up with it, he looked to Glenda for help.

"Jiu-Jitsu for Jesus."

Glenn nodded his head, remembering. "I still need my jeans."

"Oh, they should be dry now." Glenda led him to the laundry room where the jeans were hanging on a line they had stretched between the walls. As she always did, she let out a long, exasperated sigh as she noticed the old X-ray Film Viewer Glenn had mounted over the washer and dryer. The viewer had become obsolete at Glenn's hospital and he had brought it home one day, beaming. Glenda had objected to him mounting the viewer in their new house, but it was one fight she had lost. She had never found a use for the antiquated viewer; she couldn't even hang wet clothes on it.

Glenn could tell what his wife was thinking. "You just wait," he said cheerfully. "I'm going to find a use for that X-ray Film Viewer. And for the X-ray film." Glenda sighed again. She had forgotten about all the boxes of X-ray film stored in the garage.

She pulled the jeans down and handed them to her husband. Suddenly she remembered something. "I always go through your pockets before I wash your pants and there was a Bud Light label in them."

Glenn frowned. Bobby's Bud Light label? In his pocket? Then he remembered Janet skittering between his feet and the sudden urge to wet his pants. He must have stuck the label in his pocket before he started spider wrangling.

"I found it in Bobby's house when I went to check on him and ended up feeding his pets. You know how he always peels the labels, writes on the back and then sticks them back on the bottle."

Glenda looked on the top of the dryer, moving aside the fabric softener bottle and the dryer sheet box. "Ah, here it is." The Bud Light emblem was face up and she turned it over.

"Yeah, I think he must have been watching *Citizen Kane* and doodled on the back of the label."

"Citizen who?"

"You know, the classic movie."

"Was Levon Helm in it?"

"Very funny. He *was* in *Coal Miner's Daughter* though. He played Loretta Lynn's father."

Glenda looked at the word scrawled on the back of the beer label. "That doesn't spell 'Citizen' or 'Kane'."

Glenn glanced at the label. "Haven't you seen *Citizen Kane*? It's the word Orson Welles says on his deathbed."

"It doesn't look like 'Arrrggh'."

Glenn laughed loudly, remembering why he loved this woman so. He grabbed her around the waist again.

"No, it says Rosebud. We'll watch the movie on Netflix later." Glenn hugged her close and kissed her neck. "I better get down to No Egrets. It might be hard to explain to Thomas and his students that I was late because I had to perform some *special* martial arts moves on my wife."

A metallic blue Astro van was already in No Egrets' parking lot when Glenn pulled in. He parked beside it. Thomas jumped out of the driver's seat and opened the passenger door on the van. One boy in a white gi/uniform jumped out. He looked about eight or nine years old. Another boy jumped out, followed by a girl. Amazed, Glenn watched as more boys and girls dressed in gis emerged from the Astro, spilling onto the parking lot.

Glenn turned to Thomas. "I haven't seen anything like that since the clown car in the circus."

Thomas, a fit young man in his early thirties, laughed and offered his hand to Glenn. Glenn took it and Thomas shook it firmly. "I really want to thank you for letting us use your room, Glenn. They are refinishing the activities floor at the church and the kids were really bummed when I told them we were going to have to cancel the class for a couple weeks."

"No problem. Glad to do it." As Glenn led Thomas and his students around the back of the building, he felt he just had to ask. "Jiu-Jitsu for Jesus?"

Thomas didn't hesitate; it seemed to be a question he was often asked. "I'm taking the principles of Jiu-Jitsu and the teachings of Jesus and melding them together."

Glenn said the first thing to come to mind and had to catch himself. "Kind of like turn the other cheek but don't take no shi...crap off anybody."

Thomas laughed. "Something like that. Jiu-Jitsu teaches one to be proactive as well as reactive—equal parts predator and scavenger. Plus the discipline teaches us to live healthy, balanced, successful lives based on the principles of efficiency, patience and control."

When Glenn opened the door to the back room and turned the light on, the kids all ran past him yelling and screaming into the room.

"Yeah, we're still working on the patience and control part," Thomas said. "Sorry about that."

"It's okay. The door to the bar is bolted so there's no way they can get into the next room."

Glenn had been working on the back room of No Egrets for some time. Bobby had started helping him build a wooden stage and Glenn hoped to have bands on weekends soon. Maybe even for the anniversary party.

"You guys can use the stage. There's not too much trouble around, except for the paint cans."

"Thanks again, Glenn. I really can't thank you enough."

Glenn was walking around to the front of No Egrets when he saw the police car pull into the lot. Hands opened the door and stood by it, waiting for Glenn to come to him. Glenn got that sinking feeling in the bottom of his gut again.

"Didn't think you'd be here yet," said Hands, closing the patrol car door. "I was surprised to see your truck in the lot."

Glenn stood before the policeman and tried to smile, tried to force some small talk, but neither would come. Finally, he just said, "What's wrong?"

"The nuclear plant called the station. Bobby didn't show up for work early this morning. He was off last week but today starts his week of twelves. He didn't call in and nobody can reach him. The supervisor said Bobby has never missed a day in more than five years and he's worried. Wanted to know if we could check on him."

Bobby worked at the Brunswick Nuclear Plant near Southport, working the one week on/one week off schedule.

"Oh," was all Glenn could manage.

"I left Sphinx at Russell's for breakfast. I'm going back to pick him up and we'll check out Bobby's house. You haven't heard from him, have you?"

Glenn shook his head, looking at his feet. "No. I went in his house like you guys suggested. It didn't look like anyone had been there for a while. And nobody at the bar has heard from him either. I'm really worried, Hands."

"I'm beginning to feel that way, too." Hands opened the door and started to get back in the police car but stopped before he sat down. "Oh, the Medical Examiner should have a report on the drowning victim tomorrow or the next day. In the meantime, we're still trying to identify him."

Glenn watched him drive off, feeling completely helpless.

Glenda returned to the laundry room and the first thing she saw was the Bud Light label. She stopped and stared. A chill ran down her spine as she thought of Karen. She had been reading terrible handwriting ever since she had known Glenn. Bobby hadn't spelled out *Rosebud*; he had most definitely written *Roshberg*.

ELEVEN

Dr. Julius Roshberg, fingers interlocked behind his head, leaned back in his office chair contentedly. He briefly thought about putting his feet up, but with his massive mahogany desk he was afraid he might topple over backward.

Things were going very well. A call from his accountant earlier this morning confirmed the money pouring into all of Roshberg's accounts. Last month's revenue as well as the year-to-date numbers surpassed even his wildest dreams. Net income for the clinic was off the charts.

It had been an excellent idea to relocate to North Carolina. The urge to brag to someone swept over him, but his hand never reached for the telephone. Colleagues? He hadn't really developed any professional relationships yet. Friends would be nice, but he spent most of his time at the office. If he called his wife, she would start whining about a vacation through Europe which would just eat into his profits. On top of that, he hadn't found anyone he could trust to cover his practice; shutting down for a week or two was out of the question. The possibility of losing existing patients or new ones referred during a vacation was a preposterous line of thought and he refused to entertain it further. Perhaps he would buy his wife a second house in Myrtle Beach; that should pacify her wanderlust and at less than an hour's travel time, he could visit her occasionally.

He glanced at his computer screen and grinned. It was a great day. He was getting an excellent response from the paper he had published on the internet: Effect of Psychological Factors in Patients with Acute Myeloid Leukemia. It was amazing how easy it was to publish these days. It was no longer necessary to pitch an idea, convince an editor and wait for external peer review. Just a click of the button and boom! It's there for the entire world to see.

A knock at the door startled him and darkened his mood. He didn't wish to see any more patients today; those sisters and their theatrics this morning had been enough patient interaction for one day. Imagine acting like that in a public place, fainting and falling on the floor.

There was a second knock.

"Come in."

Otto ducked and stepped through the doorway. Dr. Roshberg took one look at the black expression on Otto's face and knew his good day was about to come to an end. Otto's countenance didn't change often and when it did it wasn't a good sign.

"What's wrong, Otto?"

Otto took another step forward. Reflexively he put his hand into his pocket and found the kactet, carefully inserting his fingers through the holes in the brass knuckles. Otto was gripping it when he said, "One of the two problems you had me take care of has resurfaced." He squeezed the kactet until his hand hurt. "And is still a problem."

Glenn watched a tiny ghost crab move quickly by his big toe, almost as if it was gliding sideways. In an instant the creature dropped into a small hole in the sand. Two black beady eyes supported on stalks looked back out of the hole at him. The ghost crab looked almost spiderlike, but it didn't spook him. He wondered if there were people who were frightened of ghost crabs and what that phobia would be called. Spectralclawaphobia? He remembered reading about Atlantic ghost crabs and thought their genus was ocypoda. Maybe ocypodaphobia then. As a mind at rest sometimes does, that thought linked him to another phobia. Cypridophobia: the fear of contracting venereal disease from a prostitute.

Glenda placed a hand on her husband's arm. "What're you thinking about?"

"STDs."

Glenda frowned, looking closely at her husband's face. He didn't crack a smile. He seemed to be doing okay in spite of thoughts about syphilis, herpes genitalis and such. Mondays were sometimes bad days, so she tried to alternate his favorite places. Last Monday they had gone to an antique store in Wilmington and Glenn had found two old surgical instruments for his collection. This week—the beach.

Mondays were a double whammy for Glenn; the bar was closed until evening and it used to be his surgery day at the hospital. He could lapse into the granddaddy of all funks if Glenda let him.

Glenda jumped up from her chair. "Come on, let's get in the water. I'm hot."

Glenn pulled down his sunglasses and looked his wife up and down. She had on a stunning black and white bikini and hadn't lost much of her figure through the years.

"Yes my dear, you are most certainly hot."

Glenda laughed, grabbed his hands and pulled him to his feet. She ran into the ocean and he followed. The water was cold at first, but it still felt wonderful. They splashed and played in the water like kids. Glenn couldn't help dunking his wife twice for old time's sake. After half an hour, he carried her out of the surf, carefully depositing her on the sand.

They collapsed into their beach chairs, toweling off. Glenn reclined the back of his chair, put on his sunglasses and linked his hands behind his head. Soon he was snoring softly.

Glenda glanced at her husband, realizing she had forgotten to mention her epiphany about Bobby's beer label. She would have to remember to tell him later.

In the warm sun, Glenn drifted in and out of sleep. One moment he was in his beach chair, drooling slightly out of the side of his mouth, the next he was in the operating room. The first operation of the day was a straightforward laparoscopic cholecystectomy. He easily threaded the laparoscope through the small incision just below the patient's navel. Watching the screen, he carefully inserted the instruments through other incisions and swiftly removed the gallbladder. He looked down at the patient's peacefully anesthetized face and…and…

…snore-snorted himself awake. He opened one bleary eye, spying a large blue and yellow bird on what looked like a miniature swing set frame. Surely, he must be dreaming.

The second operation of the day was more challenging. The patient had been stabbed on the west side at The Thunderbird, a notorious bar where gamblers and riffraff hung out. An exploratory laparotomy needed to be performed to determine the extent of the injury and if any abdominal organs had been perforated. With a steady hand, he made a transverse incision below the wound, continuing through the subcutaneous fat, abdominal muscles and finally, the peritoneum. Watching the screen, he explored the abdominal cavity, searching for trauma. He inspected all fluid surrounding abdominal organs; nothing seemed out of the ordinary. If a gastrointestinal organ had been perforated, an abnormal smell would most likely be present. It looked like this man had been extremely lucky…wait a minute!

What was that? He moved closer to the screen to get a better look. He narrowed his eyes. A surge of adrenaline accelerated his heartbeat. He adjusted the laparoscope slightly and suddenly a large black mass blotted the screen. The patient who had been unlucky enough to be stabbed just a second earlier was now the lucky patient who had been stabbed. Quite possibly the stab wound may have saved the man's life. Otherwise the abdominal tumor the size of a golf ball may not have been found in time. He would have to take a biopsy and the patient would need worked up for an abdominal mass, including scans, blood tests, and…

A loud squawk brought about an entirely different adrenaline surge; Glenn jerked awake, grabbing the side of his chair in a comical attempt to pull himself to his feet. Glenda watched helplessly as the beach chair collapsed backward, in slow motion, pulling Glenn with it to the sand.

He rolled out of the chair and into the sand, keeping his eye on the bird. It was a brilliant blue bird with bright yellow markings. If he would've looked closer, he would have noticed a leather band around one leg with the other end attached to the perch.

"Glenn, are you okay?"

"It's a giant parrot. Watch out!"

Glenda helped her husband to his feet. He brushed off sand, all the while watching the bird.

"It's okay Glenn. It's a blue macaw. I've been talking to its owner while you slept."

For the first time Glenn noticed the woman in the beach chair on the other side of the bird. She was reading a book and ignoring the bird (and Glenn).

"Brutus is a rescue bird originally from South America. Blue macaws are endangered because of habitat destruction and illegal trapping for the pet trade. I learned a lot from the owner while you snored. Did you know that besides their large powerful beaks, their tongue has a bone inside which makes it easy for them to—"

"Kill innocent bystanders?"

Glenda backhanded her husband in the chest with a thwack. "Nonsense. Brutus is tethered to the perch in case you didn't notice. And they are known as gentle giants."

Gentle giant. Glenn remembered some of the women in the bar referring to Bobby by that name. Glenn had kidded Bobby about it one time and Bobby had just shrugged, lamenting being treated like a big brother. There was an intense loneliness emanating from Bobby that night.

Glenn adjusted the beach chair and sat back down. Glenda could tell his mood had shifted so she searched through her canvas bag. "*Drat!*" She had only brought her Sue Grafton mystery and a magazine. She had forgotten to grab anything for Glenn. She pulled out the magazine and threw it in his lap.

"Here, read this."

Glenn turned it over, surveying the cover. "*Seventeen!* You've got to be kidding me. Why do you have an issue of *Seventeen?*"

"I like One Direction."

"Who?"

"The band on the cover. I saw it in the checkout aisle in Food Lion and bought it."

Glenn gave her a sour look. "Who *are* you?"

"Just read it. There may be a drug advertisement in it or something."

Glenn flipped through the pages. Dresses, jewelry, makeup, hair products and…hot guys. Glenn didn't think they looked hot; they looked more like scruffy slobs. He thought Shaggy from Scooby Doo would look right at home in the pages of *Seventeen*. Toward the end of the magazine he came upon a feature entitled "Dude Traumas". At first he thought it might be medical related, but no, not even close. He almost threw the magazine aside when he came across the horoscope. At least he could read his horoscope. He decided to read Sagittarius aloud for Glenda.

"Your bae's BFF has been acting *weird* around you so either he doesn't like you…or he has a huge crush on you! The full moon on the 6ᵗʰ will help you figure out what's going on—and deal."

Glenda, only half listening, replied, "That's nice."

Glenn closed the magazine and pressed it to his forehead, trying to ward off the headache he felt forming. He threw *Seventeen* onto his wife's lap.

"Already finished dear? Did you learn anything?"

"Yes. The future looks bleak."

Glenda glanced at her husband; he was rubbing his temples. Uh-oh.

He stopped and turned to his wife. "Honey, about the backroom at the bar…"

She stifled a groan. Double uh-oh.

"I've still been thinking about turning the backroom into something medical. I know we've talked about it before. What do you think?"

Glenda shrugged and gave a head tilt, realizing it was best to keep mum at this point.

"We could divide it into two rooms. One room would be the consultation room and the other a small operating room suite. The hours could be before the bar opens or they could overlap a little."

Glenda could contain herself no longer. "You can't mix vodka, cranberry juice, peach schnapps, orange juice and a surgical procedure, Glenn. Nobody is going to want you to mix them a Sex on the Beach in the bar and then take them to the next room to repair their hernia. Nobody. I repeat, *nobody*."

"I don't know, honey. We've got to think outside the box here." Glenn was getting visibly excited. "Maybe just specialize in one procedure. One procedure everyone needs at one time or another. Something diagnostic…"

This time a small groan did escape but Glenda didn't care. Glenn had his hand on his chin, head bowed a little, obviously thinking. "Glenn," she said firmly. "There is no way we could get something like that zoned not to mention sanctioned by the state's medical board."

Glenn's eyes grew wide; he raised his head, a rapturous look on his face. "I've got it! Colonoscopy! Everyone needs a colonoscopy or three during their lifetime. Why, our current customers are probably years overdue. And just think of the new customers we could draw to the bar after they've had their procedure."

Glenda shook her head. It was quite possibly the most outlandish scheme in the history of marketing. She decided to try a different tact.

"Okay Glenn, but we'll have to change the name of the bar. How about Bums and Brews? Butts and Booze? Why not add a colon cleansing room as well? It could be used before procedures or just for those days when your colon feels out of whack; those days when your colon needs a little extra love. We could pipe in some existential music, some Enya perhaps."

Glenn was smiling, staring beyond the ocean at the horizon.

"Glenn, darling, I know you sometimes miss surgery," Glenda said, her tone softening. "I understand. I know at times you regret leaving your surgery practice and coming here to open the bar. If you want to go back to surgery, we can figure out a way. I can run No Egrets and we can maybe make Joshua a partner. But this idea for the back room is…it's…it won't…"

Before she could condense her million reasons why it was a bad idea into one or two, she noticed someone sprinting toward them down the beach. The man was dressed as a typical beach runner, but he was moving way too fast. As he got closer, she recognized him.

"Glenn, it's Daniel!"

Daniel O' Dwyer sprinted to a stop in front of Glenn. Breathing heavily, he put his hands on his knees, bending over, trying to catch his breath.

"Daniel!" Glenn exclaimed. "What is it?"

"Been—looking—for—you."

Glenn jumped up and helped Daniel to his chair.

Daniel took a deep breath and tried to gather himself. His rapid-fire breathing slowed just a little as he said, "Was at—The Point. Saw Hands—and Sphinx."

Daniel grabbed Glenn's arm roughly. "They found—Bobby!"

TWELVE

Glenn had never liked Intensive Care Units. He felt comfortable in the operating room and on the medical-surgical unit, but ICUs always gave him what his son at three had called the "wheebie jeebies". Serious surgeries often required a post-op period in the Surgical ICU, which Glenn now realized was not near as bad as a Medical ICU.

A nurse led the stoic duo of Glenn and Glenda by several rooms, all of them crawling with medical equipment hovering over the patients like plastic and metal vultures; each doorway representing a story of tragedy and hope. Ventilators pulsed and thumped to their own rhythm doing their part to keep the patients alive.

Along with Daniel they had rushed to Boiling Grove Community Hospital, speeding down Highway 17 and trying not to panic. Without explanation they were ushered into purgatory—also known as the ICU waiting room. Two hours had passed with Glenn's back pressed against the most uncomfortable chair he had ever encountered. Glenn noticed Daniel never took his eyes off the clock. He seemed to watch every second, every minute, every hour pass. Glenda had excused herself several times in order to escape the tight grip that misery had on the room. Other families and small groups huddled, mired in their own catastrophes. No one spoke.

Glenn resorted to mental exercises to pass the time. He counted shoes in the room with and without laces. He estimated the number of eyelets on each shoe with a shoelace and then did the math for the final count. Finally, Glenn performed a mental customer survey of the hospital. Facilities: overall clean, visually desolate, smaller community-based offerings than where he had worked. Staff: seemingly competent but so far had not been personable, friendly, helpful or comforting.

At 6 p.m. a doorbell tone sounded from the hospital's sound system. A voice, just a bit too sexy for a hospital, announced: "Visiting hours have started for Medical ICU. Patient limit for visitors is two. Please respect others in the room and on the unit. Visiting hours will end at 8 p.m." Sexy voice then fumbled with the microphone off switch, causing piercing feedback until she found the right button.

Glenn was prepared for the sight in MICU room 2, but Glenda was not. With ashen skin, Bobby didn't look like the Bobby they knew. His chin was purple and swollen. Tubes seemed coiled around him from the waist up; two IV pumps with three IV fluid bags and one glass bottle flanked the bed. A ventilator in the corner forced air into Bobby's lungs causing his chest to rise and fall with the tempo of the machine. Glenn glanced at the glass bottle of medication—propofol. One of the IV bags contained dopamine.

Glenn felt Glenda clutch him from behind, her face pressing into his back. She let out a low sob. He turned to comfort her just as a woman in a white lab coat entered the room.

"Hello, I'm Dr. Goodfeather. Are you family?"

"No, friends of Bobby." Glenn reached out his hand which the doctor grasped and shook. "I'm Glenn and this is my wife Glenda."

"Ah yes, Bobby. I'm just glad we have a name for our patient now. I hated calling him John Doe for the first day and a half." She reached out and touched Bobby's forehead, brushing stray hairs from his face.

"Dr. Goodfeather," Glenn said. "Bobby's been missing for a few days and we just heard he was here. Can you tell us what happened?"

Dr. Goodfeather put the side of her palm to her short brown hair and rubbed back and forth three times. She appeared to be in her mid-forties. Glenn thought she looked young and compassionate, but it was too early to judge her competence as a physician.

"I'm sorry," the doctor sighed. "I can only discuss the patient's case with his family."

"I don't think Bobby has any family nearby," Glenda interjected.

Glenn looked again at the propofol IV bottle. "You don't have to answer, but he's being sedated while on the ventilator and also has a pressor hanging. He either has sepsis or has suffered some kind of trauma. My hope is he is on the ventilator in order to give his body time to heal. I don't want to think about the alternative."

Glenda butted in. "He's a surgeon." She felt compelled to explain further. "He just got lured away by the lapping of the ocean waves."

Dr. Goodfeather tilted her head slightly, studying Glenn for a minute more before she finally decided to speak. "The first twenty-four hours I wasn't sure he would survive." She looked down at Bobby. "He's a fighter and strong. That's what he's got going for him right now. A weaker person would not have made it to the hospital alive."

"Prognosis?"

"Serious, but stable."

Glenn, relieved, let out a puff of air. "Good. Let me give you my contact information. Call day or night." Dr. Goodfeather led Glenn outside the room to the nurses' desk for pen and paper.

Glenda stood frozen, looking at Bobby. She inventoried all the tubes, monitors and machines. She inched her way closer, studying where each tube connected to his arms, nose and throat. Bobby's chest continued to pulse to the rhythm of the ventilator. Glenda read the numbers on every monitor, not knowing if they were good or bad. She took a closer look at the propofol IV bottle Glenn had pointed out earlier. She whipped out her phone and typed the name into the Memo app. She would look it up later.

Her gaze returned to Bobby's face and she suddenly thought of his warm smile, his laughter; the way he would walk in the bar singing *The Flintstones*' theme song.

An IV pump emitted a loud beep, causing Glenda to flinch. A nurse swooped into the room and looked at the pump. He stopped when he saw her.

"You know if you talk to him, he will most likely hear you."

Glenda took a step closer to the bedside. "Really?"

"It happens. I've had patients wake up and recite a lot of what they heard while sedated on the ventilator. A mother of one patient sang a childhood lullaby to her adult daughter just about every day and when she woke up, the daughter was singing the song."

Glenda moved closer to Bobby's bedside as the nurse finished changing out the IV bag and tubing. He nodded encouragement.

"Hi Bobby," Glenda said tentatively. Bobby's eyes were closed, his face impassive. Glenda took a deep breath. "Everyone misses you at No Egrets."

She glanced at the nurse and he smiled, turned and left the room.

Glenda felt a little silly. She forced herself to think of Bobby entering the bar. She smiled. Leaning over him, she sang quietly, "Flintstones—meet the Flintstones. They're a modern stone age family."

She thought she saw one of Bobby's eyelids twitch, which made her braver. She sang a little louder, "Let's ride with the family down the street, through the courtesy of Fred's two feet."

When Glenn and Dr. Goodfeather walked back in the room, Glenda, with her back to them, was singing spiritedly. "When you're with the Flintstones, have a yabba dabba doo time, a dabba doo time..."

Glenn joined in the chorus, surprising Glenda. "We'll have a gay old time!"

Glenda looked sheepishly at the two physicians. "It's like Bobby's theme song."

Dr. Goodfeather smiled. "It's okay. I believe talking and singing to the patient does more good than all the medicine we can pump into their body."

Glenn and Glenda were feeling a little better as they approached the ICU exit, until they heard a ruckus on the other side of the door. They immediately exchanged a horrified look and pushed through to the hallway.

On the other side Daniel tried to restrain a wild, old woman; she was kicking, biting and punching. It appeared Daniel had met his match as he struggled to keep a grip on the wildcat. Behind Daniel a befuddled security guard picked up the handset of the emergency phone.

"Psych ward?" the security guard yelled into the phone.

"What do you mean I can't see my friend, you wanker!" Matilda screamed in the direction of the security guard.

The security guard, who was three times as wide as Matilda, took an unconscious step back. "Hey!" he shouted into the phone. "We've got one of yours on MICU. A really mean one! Bring the Haldol!"

Daniel had her by the waist, but her legs and arms were flailing. "You have besmirched me!" Matilda yelled at the security guard.

"I what?" the bewildered security guard asked. Returning his attention back to the phone he shouted, "She's got to be yours! She's freaking crazy!"

Glenn and Glenda moved to rescue Daniel, getting as close as they could while staying out of reach of Matilda's thrashing arms and legs. Together they attempted to calm her.

"What the hell? The psych ward says she's not theirs!" The guard shouted as he hung up the phone.

"She's kind of ours," Glenda answered. "Uh, sorry."

"I told her only two visitors were allowed at a time and the patient already had two in there. She would have to wait. And she went ballistic," the exasperated guard explained. "I would have tased her if the pharmacist here didn't assist me," he said, nodding in Daniel's direction.

"Tase me?" Matilda shrieked as she started flailing again. "Tase *me* you son of a bitch! I dare your flat, flabby ass!"

"Get grandma out of here! And keep her out!" the guard ordered. He gave a sudden worried glance to a security camera before refocusing on Matilda. "And I said I *would* have used the Taser on you, but only if you didn't calm down."

"LAST CALL!" Glenda announced loudly. Glenn and Daniel looked at her like she had lost her mind. Matilda, on the other hand, seemed to settle down, visibly shrinking in Daniel's grip.

"Last call? Is it that late? I need a drink." Matilda turned to Daniel. "Put me down you candy-ass. Go count pills or something by fives."

"Matilda, how in the world did you get here?" Glenda asked.

"No help from no one. I did it myself. I'm not afraid," Matilda said as proudly as a child learning to potty on her own.

Daniel nodded to the waiting room where Glenda spied Matilda's helmet on a chair. The hospital was about twenty-five miles from Oak Island! Glenda shuddered, thinking of Matilda on her Vespa on the busy road.

"I want to see Bobby," Matilda demanded.

"I'll take her in," Daniel offered. He tried to take Matilda's hand, but she knocked his away.

"I don't need your help," Matilda spat. "If you want to play touchy-feely later big boy, I'm all for it. But this is not the time or place."

Glenda grabbed Matilda by the shoulders. "Look, you old fart, this is serious. They can kick you out of the hospital and not allow you back. So you better be on your best behavior. And that guard's Taser is the least of your worries if you cause trouble for me. You got that?"

Daniel and Glenn shared a glance, both slack-jawed to hear Glenda talk to Matilda in that tone. But it seemed to work. Matilda smoothed her hair with her fingers and Daniel quietly led her through the door.

Glenn and Glenda collapsed onto the waiting room chairs, Matilda's helmet to the left of them. They did not speak, both lost in their own thoughts. When Glenn looked up, he saw the back of a policeman blocking the security guard's station. He recognized the voice of Sphinx. Glenn stood and walked to the door of the waiting room.

Sphinx turned to enter the MICU and noticed Glenn. "Hey, Doc. You waiting to see Bobby?"

"We've already seen him. Daniel and Tilly are in there now."

Sphinx walked over to him. "Hi Glenda."

Glenda nodded to the policeman but remained seated.

"I was going to check on Bobby's condition. How is he, Doc?"

"He's in serious condition but the doctor said he's stable. She couldn't tell me a lot since I'm not family."

"So he's still out of it? I was hoping he was awake so I could talk to him."

"He's on the ventilator and sedated. You won't be able to talk to him until they wean the sedation and get him off the ventilator. God willing."

"Oh," Sphinx said, clearly disappointed.

Glenn grasped the policeman by the arm, gently pulling him aside. "Sphinx, what happened to Bobby?"

"A couple found him in the Intracoastal water near Lockwood Folly. He had one arm wrapped around their dock piling and the other arm was clutching a detached buoy. He was barely alive."

"But how'd he get in the water?"

"Not sure. But his jaw looks like he was in the boxing ring and he's got a nasty gash on the back of his head."

"What?" Glenn thought about this revelation for a moment. "Do you think it happened before he ended up in the water or after? He may have floated for a while and hit debris in the water."

"Dunno. That's what I was hoping to ask him."

"How did you find out he was here?"

77

"Pure luck. He didn't have any identification on him when the paramedics brought him to the hospital. He was kept in ER for more than twenty-four hours until an ICU bed opened up and then the ICU unit clerk happened to see him when he was wheeled in and recognized him immediately. She lives on the same street on the island."

"That *was* lucky." Glenn thought about the few patients he had operated on who were labeled John or Jane Doe and how surreal and heartbreaking the cases always turned out to be. Nobody knew they were there; nobody present to cry and worry when they were within a millimeter of death.

The door behind them crashed opened. Matilda ran into the waiting room, picked up her helmet and slumped in the chair. With a sickening plop she squeezed the helmet on to her head and turned her face away from Glenda, away from Sphinx and Glenn.

Daniel came running out the door. "Where'd she go? I lost her!"

Glenn pointed to the waiting room. Daniel shook his head, obviously perplexed. "I never thought she'd act that way."

Glenn grimaced and looked back at the little old fireball of a lady. "Oh no. How bad was it?"

"Bad?" Daniel's face looked blank as he considered it.

Glenda had moved to the chair beside the helmeted old woman, but Matilda would not look at her.

"I've never heard her like that," Daniel said.

Glenn groaned. He had heard Matilda rant, rave, fume, curse and go into tireless tirades. He could only imagine what had happened in the hospital room.

"No, you don't understand," Daniel said. "She was...she was..."

Glenn watched Glenda put her arm around Matilda and Matilda pull away, hiding her face.

Daniel shook his head, trying to clear it. "It was the most poignant scene since E.T. died. It was heart-wrenching and...and creepy at the same time."

Glenn's eyes were wide as he looked from Daniel to Matilda.

Daniel continued: "She lost it when she saw Bobby, starting bawling like a baby. Then she straightened up and started telling him everything was going to be okay.

"By this time a nurse had brought her tissues and she would blow her nose with a huge honk. Then..."

Daniel shivered. "Then she started singing the Tomorrow song from *Annie* to him. In between lines she would blow her nose."

Daniel changed his voice to a high croak as he sang. "The sun will come out tomorrow. *Honk!* Bet your bottom dollar. *Honk!* That tomorrow. *Honk!* There'll be sun. *Honk! Honk!*"

Glenn walked over to Matilda and put his hand on her shoulder. "Come on you tough old bird. Let's load up your Vespa and get you home."

THIRTEEN

"Bobby was a target of ISIS!"

"That's not what I heard. You know Jeb, the guy who fixes cars over in Supply? He heard Bobby was attacked by a grizzly bear on the riverbank."

Glenn shook his head and rolled his eyes. Bobby's condition remained unchanged and it seemed everyone was attempting to fill in the blanks about what happened, no matter how ridiculous the rumor. Glenn was pretty sure neither an Islamist militant group nor grizzly bears were indigenous to the region.

"Esther over at the thrift shop said it was a kamikaze drone that attacked Bobby and that other guy. It's possible. The machine could have a mind of its own like in them Terminator movies."

Glenn was wiping down the bar; he stopped so suddenly that everyone quieted and turned to him. He decided to play along. Hunching his shoulders and dropping his head, he put an index finger to his lips. He looked side to side. His voice was barely above a whisper. "I heard it was aliens."

The crowd at the bar moved closer. Glenn continued, "And it's a government cover-up. The FBI's coming to investigate; they're sending a male and a female agent that specialize in this kind of thing. The female agent is skeptical but the male agent is a believer because aliens abducted his—"

Glenda had just walked behind the bar and had heard everything. She threw a towel over Glenn's head. "Hogwash! Why don't we all wait for Bobby to wake up and then we'll know what happened."

Everyone returned to their drinks and their individual conversations. Glenn remained standing with the towel over his head. Finally, after a couple long minutes Glenda removed it, giving him a disgusted look as she walked around him.

"Is that all you're going to do today?" she asked.

"Well, I thought in between rampant rumors," Glenn said, pointing up to the stuffed swordfish above the bar, "I might polish DeBakey. After all he's partly responsible for our current state of affairs."

Glenda sighed. "What are you blaming on Swordy now?"

Glenn growled as he always did when Glenda called his swordfish by her childish name.

"Seriously now, Glenn. I've called Joshua to come in early to help you. I

79

want to go to Karen's to bring her up to date on Bobby. I've tried to call her, but she doesn't answer her phone."

"How did Ism sound when you called him? He hasn't had an episode in a while and I'm starting to get worried he's going to blow."

"*Joshua* sounded fine. You leave that boy alone."

"Me? What did I do? You weren't here that time when he turned into his ancestor McCarthy. It was…it was scary."

Glenn thought back to the one time he had seen Ism change right before his eyes. It had only been for a few minutes, but the transformation had been shocking. Glenn's logical mind tried to pigeonhole what he witnessed into a multiple personality or even demonic possession; in the end there was no good explanation. Pinhead Paul, who claimed to have been present every time Ism turned into his ancestor, swore it only happened when a communist set foot on the island. "Ism's like my old yellow dog a-layin' on my porch," Pinhead Paul had told Glenn. "He only barks at strangers I don't want comin' round my property."

Glenda scowled. "Just because Joshua's surname is McCarthy doesn't mean he is a descendent of Senator Joe McCarthy. You people have filled his head with that garbage."

"*You* people? The first time I met him the locals were calling him McCarthyism. I didn't have anything to do with it."

"No, but," Glenda said, giving him one of those looks. "You've done nothing to put a stop to it."

Glenn hung his head, defeated. He could no more put a stop to it than he could stop Matilda from belching in public.

As if on cue, Ism emerged from the back room. He was wearing a colorful Margaritaville t-shirt hanging over long, faded denim shorts which defied the laws of gravity by balancing halfway down his buttocks without falling to the floor.

"What's up Mr. G? Mrs. G?" Ism asked in his high voice.

"Hello Joshua," Glenda responded. "Thank you for coming in early."

"No problemo Mrs. G. Skunkfest today; nothing but ankle busters and a bunch of Barneys and spongers on the beach. Allie had to leave for her shift at San Felipe to sling some salsa anyway. S'all wooka."

Glenn looked to his wife to gauge her degree of comprehension of Ism's speech. Glenda just smiled at the young man and said, "That's nice. S'all's wooka here, too."

Ism moved behind the bar and began washing some glassware. Glenda turned back to Glenn. "Did that sound like 1950s Washington-speak to you? I repeat—leave that boy alone."

"Yes ma'am." Glenn walked down the bar and drew another beer for Kenny. He noticed Richard had moved to Bobby's stool beside Kenny. Today Richard was wearing a lime green leisure suit, complete with a purple cummerbund for some reason.

Glenn moved over in front of Richard. "Going to the dance at the junior high gym tonight, Richard?" Kenny looked over and snorted.

Richard was shifting his bottom around on Bobby's barstool, trying to find the most comfortable indentation. "No, had an early audition in Wilmywood. They're casting for *Welcome Back Kotter-The Movie (Throwdown at James Buchanan High)*."

Glenn surveyed Richard's leisure suit again, deciding he didn't look much like a Sweathog and doubting he would get a return call. "Can I pour you a nice, frothy PBR?"

Richard frowned, shifting on the seat again and not answering. Glenn frowned; Richard had never ordered anything but PBR since he had been coming to No Egrets.

When Richard finally settled on the barstool, he said, "Give me a Bud Light. In a bottle." Richard noticed Glenn's confusion. "I know it's silly, but I thought if I sat on Bobby's stool and ordered a Bud Light he might wake up."

Glenda came up beside Glenn. "I think that's sweet." Glenn smiled and Kenny gave Richard an affectionate slap on the back.

Glenn placed a glistening Bud Light bottle in front of Richard.

Richard grinned. "And I'm going to peel off the label, just like my friend."

"Oh!" Glenda exclaimed. "The label! I forgot all about the label."

Glenda turned to her husband. "Bobby's label that was in your pocket."

"Yeah, the one he had written Rosebud on?"

"He didn't write Rosebud; it says Roshberg."

Kenny perked up at the name and began stroking his man beard.

"What's a Roshberg?" asked Glenn.

Richard was leaning over the bar, listening intently. "Yes, what's a Roshberg?"

"Roshberg is a doctor," Glenda said. "He's Karen's oncologist."

Kenny stopped stroking his man beard. "Yes. Dr. Roshberg. I thought the name sounded familiar. That's the name of the doctor who paid cash for the Rolls Royce Ghost I told you about. In fact, he did come back and buy the Ferrari F12berlinetta for his wife. Paid cash for that one, too! I got to wash it before this tall, scary looking guy picked it up for the doctor."

"Karen's oncologist," gasped Richard. "I knew she was sick but didn't know how serious." He began absentmindedly trying to peel the label off the Bud Light bottle. "Karen and Bobby began dating before she became sick. Maybe Bobby wrote the physician's name on the beer label so he wouldn't forget it."

Glenn looked at Richard, amazed. Was he the only person in the bar that didn't know Karen and Bobby had been seeing each other?

"Most likely that's why he wrote it," Glenda said. "And Karen told me Bobby went with her to Dr. Roshberg's office a couple times."

"Hmm, I guess that makes sense," Glenn said. "But I still think it says Rosebud if you ask me."

Glenda was heading back to the office to grab her purse. She addressed her husband over her shoulder. "Uh-huh. You can't even read your own writing, let alone somebody else's."

Glenda reached Karen's house just as the blue Chevy Aveo was trying to navigate a path through the trash cans, lawn mower and unidentified boxes into the garage. Glenda coasted to the side of the road and stopped on a well-worn patch of grass across the street from the house. Unconsciously her hand went toward her purse, but she stopped mid-reach. Remembering her last encounter with Karen's sister and the remarks about her accessories, she stuffed the Dooney bag under the passenger seat instead. Glancing upward, she removed the Fendi sunglasses from the top of her head and gently put them in their case. The case was also stuffed under the seat (but with a gentler touch than the Dooney bag.)

After a quick inventory to make sure other accessories were not remarkworthy, Glenda slid off the seat and into the street. She locked the door, stopping to test the door handle and then pressed the lock button on her key fob two more times for good measure.

She walked toward Karen's house and on to the paving stone path. Even though it was light gray and not yellow, the walkway always made Glenda feel like singing, "We're off to see the wizard." She halted as a lizard darted across the path in front of her. *Oh wise and mighty lizard*, she thought, a small giggle escaping. Watching the lizard disappear into the landscaping, she noticed for the first time it was starting to look shabby. It needed pruning, weeding, mulching. Glenda knew Karen took great pride in her home's curb appeal. Just one more thing to add to her depression.

Glenda had almost reached the front door when a voice called out, "What the hell do you want?" Brandi was standing just inside the garage. Her arms were crossed and she was ready for a fight.

"I want to see my friend," Glenda said, marching toward the garage, determined to let Brandi know she could not be bullied. "I've tried calling but Karen's not answering her phone."

Brandi clucked her tongue, shaking her head. "She has caller ID. Ever think she's not answering because she doesn't want to talk to you? Why should she answer her phone? She doesn't want to talk with anyone. The chemo wipes her out."

Brandi hesitated, looking at the ground. "You got a cigarette?"

Glenda was taken aback. "No. I don't smoke."

Brandi grunted and nodded her head toward the house. "Her highness won't allow them in the house. Says it makes the furniture stink. How am I supposed to deal with her and all the stress if I can't smoke?" Brandi felt her pockets in case a cigarette had magically appeared. "You wouldn't believe the disgusting people I had to look at today while Karen had her chemo. Shit, just shoot me if I get like that."

Gladly, Glenda thought.

"Chemotherapy is scary shit," Brandi continued. "And Karen looks like hell, with a capital H."

Glenda did not respond. She had known several people who had received chemotherapy and knew there were many factors involved: the type of cancer, the chemotherapy regimen, the physical and mental state of the person. One co-worker did not seem to suffer any untoward effects. One friend had never quite recovered.

Brandi pounded her fist on the garage door frame. She pointed back into the house. "I'm not even sure who that is anymore! She resembles my sister, but the life has been sucked out of her." She paused before adding, "Damn cure is worse than the disease. She looked normal when the doctor told her she had cancer...now look at her."

Brandi straightened, eyeing Glenda's Hyundai Sonata across the street. "Can I take your car to get some cigarettes?"

Glenda was stunned. "Are you serious? No! I'm not going to help you buy cigarettes when your sister is fighting cancer."

Brandi's countenance darkened. "Fine. You know how she's doing so you can leave now."

"Thank you for the update," Glenda responded in her best "kill them with kindness" tone. She started toward her car when she stopped suddenly and turned. "Tell Karen we found Bobby. He's in the hospital and—"

A hiss escaped Brandi's lips. "I will NOT give her the message! That man has been part of the problem. As if she's not depressed enough about her cancer, he has the gall to leave her!"

Brandi slammed the button on the inside of the door and turned away. Glenda watched the garage door slide down until it banged close. *So much for finding the wizard*, she thought. In her mind, as she walked back to the car, she pictured throwing a bucket of water on Karen's sister and watching her melt.

Bonita Sonora studied the heparin lock inserted into the vein in her forearm; she had a large purple bruise forming around the area where the nurse had started the IV. She followed the IV tubing up to the intravenous bag hanging on the silver pole. Bold black letters by the manufacturer identified it as 0.9% Sodium Chloride. When she asked the nurse why she was only getting saltwater, the nurse had assured her all her chemotherapy drugs had been mixed in the bag. Bonita thought it strange there wasn't another label attached to the bag with the chemotherapy drugs written on it. She remembered being with her mother in the hospital and studying all the extra labels attached to the IV bags; some looked computer generated from the pharmacy, some handwritten by a nurse, but every IV bag had at least one additional label stuck to it.

A sudden burning sensation brought her attention back to her purple forearm. It felt like molten lava flowing into her veins. She whimpered. Why wouldn't they let Juanita come back and be with her? This was all happening so fast. It seemed like one day the doctor told her she had cancer, the next day his office had called and said they were contacting her insurance company to obtain approval for chemotherapy. And now here she sat, in this chair, alone, with fire infusing into her.

Juanita had been with her when the doctor had quickly discussed the potential side effects of the medication. Bonita had been so numb at the time she didn't remember any of them. She was sure her sister would remember every last side effect; why wouldn't they let her come back to the room? She felt lost without her sister. Juanita had been so strong throughout the whole ordeal. She had been her rock.

"Juanita!" she cried. A funny feeling swept over her and she forgot her burning forearm. Her head became hot, cold sweat breaking out; she felt dizzy. The room was spinning.

"Juanita!" she screamed.

For some strange reason, her thoughts focused on their dinner the night before—spaghetti and meatballs. Bonita had cleaned up afterward and since she hadn't had much of an appetite, she had scraped almost her whole dinner into the sink. Turning on the water and disposal she had watched the mass of food swirling down the drain. Now she was twirling with it, round and round. She leaned over the side of the chair and vomited onto the white floor.

FOURTEEN

He no longer felt like he was flying. The chill that enveloped his body was gone; breathing no longer a struggle. He could feel his chest rise and fall as his lungs filled with delicious oxygen. The fog in his brain remained however, clouding his thinking. The more he tried to reason, to make sense of his situation, the more frustrated he became.

And what the hell was the woman's name? The woman—his woman—his girl. He still couldn't remember. Danger! His girl was in danger. He had to tell someone—but tell them what?

His mind filled with random thoughts. Fred Flintstone trying to put that saber-toothed tiger out for the night, the Frankenstein Monster coming at him with arms outstretched (although this one was short, bald and the bolts were missing from his neck) and a caterwauling Annie singing about tomorrow. "Tomorrow, beep, tomorrow, beep, I beep you tomorrow." That incessant beeping! What in God's name was that beeping?

The mechanical beep was really starting to get under his skin. It sounded like the first digital alarm clock his mom bought him in junior high school. The clock wasn't really digital; it had flip numbers. And the most annoying beep. She put it in the hallway outside his room and if he wanted the beeping to stop, he had to get out of bed and turn it off. Mom's way of eliminating hitting the snooze button ten times.

Mom, he thought. *Mom, turn off the clock. I can't get out of bed.* He had tried to force the words out of his head and through his mouth without success. Frustrated, he opened his eyes to see where she had positioned the blasted, beeping clock. Maybe he could throw something at it.

For just a minute the world came into focus. The ceiling white, the walls beige. He saw tubes and tubing everywhere, seemingly floating through the air, snakelike. He tried to follow one to its end, but another crisscrossing tube caught his eye. It was a maze and he couldn't escape! Finally, he tore his gaze away and looked beyond the tubes.

Machines. A hospital? A mad scientist's laboratory? It definitely wasn't his mom's house. He could feel the pounding in his chest increase. The clock's beeping increased, too. Was this real? His eyes skimmed the room for something familiar. He tried to move his arms, but they felt like lead. He closed his eyes and opened them again. No Fred Flintstone. But someone (Wilma?) ran out of the room. He began to tire and his head started to throb. He wanted to call out, but it felt like his mouth was gagged or blocked. He realized his girl was not the only one in danger.

Someone was in the room with him again. No! It can't be—somebody help me! Karen! Karen! The last thing he saw was the short, bald Frankenstein Monster coming at him, arms outstretched.

Glenn felt right at home in the hospital cafeteria, thoughts of bad food and good fellowship with other healthcare professionals flooding back to him. Memories of swapping stories, happy and sad, hashing out diagnoses and the gossip from the hospital grapevine wrapped around him like a favorite, well-worn sweatshirt (the one you love but are afraid to drag out because your wife would trash it.)

Across the table Daniel was focused on a conversation with a pretty redhead. Daniel had introduced, "Jaclyn, the Emergency Room Clinical Director". Her title explained the scrubs she wore. Glenn began to notice little telltale signs that perhaps Daniel and Jaclyn were more than friends. Little nuances: sitting closer than necessary; holding eye contact well past the friendly limit; arm and shoulder touching. Perhaps Glenn wasn't as dense as Glenda accused him of being on certain subjects.

Glenn checked his watch with the clock on the wall. The two were in sync. He exhaled. They had arrived an hour before ICU visiting hours began and the time had finally whittled down to ten minutes. It was getting more difficult for Glenn to hide his concern for his friend's condition; Bobby hadn't shown any signs of improvement in the last twenty-four hours.

Jaclyn said she had never met Bobby but apparently she knew one of Daniel's other friends. "How's Willie?" she asked Daniel. (Glenn had never met Willie but one time he did catch a glimpse of him through the trees at Daniel's house.) Willie was a strange agent who lived in the woods on Daniel's property aboard the Silent Cow, a landlocked houseboat. The boat had started out a fixer-upper at best. (Willie had tried to get Bob Villa to do a make-over on it. The Property Brothers merely replied they "don't do watercraft". Ty Pennington never returned his call.)

Daniel paused, grimacing a little. "Willie is…Willie. The latest thing he's into is Zen golf."

"I didn't think he had clubs of his own. Did he borrow yours again?" Jaclyn asked.

Daniel twisted his mouth to the side. "No, he doesn't have clubs of his own and no, he didn't borrow mine."

Daniel sat silently without adding additional details. Jaclyn only looked at him, waiting patiently. A couple of minutes passed. Finally Jaclyn reached over, grabbed Daniel's ear and twisted.

See, a sign, thought Glenn.

"Ow! What the heck!" exclaimed Daniel, smiling a little. "What were we talking about?"

Jaclyn let go of his ear. "That unique little troll who lives on your back lot."

"Oh yeah. According to Willie, you don't need clubs for Zen golf. You visualize your swing, you visualize the club in your hand, you visualize striking the ball, visualize the flight of the ball down the fairway. And all the while you are in this relaxed meditative state."

Jaclyn laughed. "In your case Daniel, you would visualize the ball flying through the Spanish moss, going deep into the woods and coming to rest beside a large knotted root."

Another sign, thought Glenn.

"Oh, oh, oh," Daniel said, holding a hand to his heart. "You wound me so."

Glenn decided to get into the act. "And then you would throw your imaginary club into the shimmering, fabricated waters of the fairway water hazard. Meditatively speaking, of course."

Silently, they both looked at Glenn before bursting out laughing. "I like this guy," Jaclyn said. "He may be the only normal friend you have."

Jaclyn stood, giving Daniel's face a little smack with two fingers. "Lunch break is over. Have to get back to work. Can't be setting any bad examples."

Daniel stood and kissed her full on the lips.

Ah ha, I was right, thought Glenn proudly. No "little sign" there.

"Nice to meet you, Glenn." Jaclyn reached a hand over to him and he shook it. As she left, Glenn thought she either told Daniel she would see him later "stud" or "bud". Or maybe "slug".

Suddenly the overhead speaker blared, "Code Green MICU. Code Green MICU. Code Green MICU."

Jaclyn stopped dead in her tracks and looked back. At the same instant Daniel and Glenn jumped to their feet. The same thing screamed through their minds—security emergency in the Medical ICU!

Adrenaline surged as Bobby realized the man coming at him intended to harm him. The beeping sound kicked into high gear. Bobby was so confused. He didn't know the man. He was in danger. He couldn't scream out for help. It was like watching a suspenseful scene in a movie; he could tell what was going to happen next but was powerless to intervene.

The man began pulling and kicking electrical plugs out of the wall. The clock beeping finally ceased. After a minute of blessed silence, all hell broke loose. The pumps and machines around the bed started dinging and screaming, filling Bobby's head with sound.

Bobby poured all his energy into confronting the man. He tried to sit up, but the tube down his throat pinned him to the bed. The best he could do was lift a finger on his right hand, a movement that brought on the wrath of the aggressor.

"No, no, no, no," the man repeated through clenched teeth. His eyes were wild, his face a fiery, scary red. "You—can't—wake—up. Can't!"

Bobby again tried to call for help which only caused him to gag on the tube. It seemed lifting a single finger would be his only defense.

The man noticed the finger moving, reached down, grasped the IV tubing from that arm and ripped the heparin lock out. He threw it aside. Bobby's blood leaked out, staining the white sheets.

Bobby squeezed his eyes shut and tried to will his body to rise up and fight back. When he opened his eyes, his position hadn't changed and the angry man was leaning over him.

The man grabbed the tube protruding from Bobby's mouth and started yanking. He rocked it from side to side while pulling and as the tube started sliding out, Bobby felt like his insides were coming with it. With a sickening plop the tube was out, leaving Bobby gasping for breath like a fish removed from the hook and thrown on the deck.

"You will not wake up!" the wild man threatened. He snatched the pillow from under Bobby's head. Bobby could see the pillow coming at his face but was helpless. He was enveloped in blackness.

In those few seconds, Bobby remembered everything. The tall man clubbing him in the back of the head with something metal, floating in the water, grasping the buoy. And Karen! *His* girl, Karen. She was in danger and he must...must...tell...

Glenn, Daniel and Jaclyn reached the ICU double doors just in time to see the backs of two security guards storm through the opening. The heavy, steel doors dividing the intensive care unit from the rest of the world closed slowly. The trio darted to the doors, desperately trying to catch a glimpse of the action without crossing the threshold. The doors unceremoniously latched with a loud click just inches from their noses.

The three dropped their heads in defeat. Glenn stretched his palms to the wall, leaning over, head down, like he was being frisked. "Damn," he muttered.

Daniel smacked the door with an open hand. Jaclyn gathered the men and herded them to the waiting room. They grabbed seats spaced around the empty room. Jaclyn, nervously twirling a lock of red hair, was the first to break the tense silence. "Look...there are others back there besides Bobby. Maybe someone, a visitor, was asked to leave and they refused," she said with a drummed up hopeful tone.

Glenn slumped over in his chair. "I don't know why, but I think it has to do with Bobby."

"It could be anything," Daniel said. "A patient going berserk because a nurse poked him one too many times, a jealous husband after his wife's lover, an insane family member trying to do in the abusive patriarch and inherit the family fortune."

Jaclyn looked forlornly at the ICU doors. "It's against protocol for me to go in there; it's not my unit. That's spelled out in hospital policy. Code Green...security and essential personnel only."

Glenn placed a hand on her wrist. "I know. We'll know soon enough." Glenn rubbed a hand over his face as he glanced toward the ICU doors. Bobby. He wasn't sure how he knew, but it was definitely Bobby.

All three jumped from their seats when the loudspeaker blared: "Code Blue, MICU room 2, Code Blue MICU room 2, Code Blue MICU room 2."

Bobby's nurse, who ran out of the room to phone the doctor when Bobby first opened his eyes, was the first to hear the commotion and enter Bobby's room. Griselda, at five feet two inches tall, had enormous breasts and looked like John Goodman, but when she took a flying leap and landed on the assailant's back she looked as graceful as Lolo Jones clearing a hurdle in the Olympics. She even managed to pull the pillow from Bobby's face as she and the man crashed to the floor.

The man tried to rise but Griselda sat on top of him and he couldn't budge her. She was screaming and slapping his face. "What the hell, Mark? What the hell, Mark? What the *hell?*" She whacked him again.

When the security guards ran into the room, they looked at each other, not sure which one to subdue. So they chose both; one pinned the man named Mark with a knee to the back and his face pressed to the floor, the other tried to pin Griselda.

"Get the hell off me!" Griselda yelled as she pulled the security guard's head to her breasts, smothering him. As soon as the guard started gasping for breath, she flung him aside and leaped to Bobby's bedside. Another nurse was finally brave enough to poke her head in the room.

"He's not breathing!" screamed Griselda. "Call a code!"

"Bobby!" Glenn and Daniel cried together.

"That's my cue," Jaclyn announced, springing toward the door. She scanned her ID badge and ran through the doors before Glenn or Daniel could react. "I'm Code Blue essential personnel," she called over her shoulder just as the automatic doors closed.

Glenn felt helpless. He had trained for these situations, yet here he stood in the ICU waiting room while all the action occurred on the other side of those doors. With a huge sigh he dropped to an empty waiting room chair, staring at the locked doors to the ICU.

A huge commotion in the hall soon had their attention as a security guard appeared with two Brunswick County Sheriff Deputies behind him. When they disappeared through the doors, Daniel turned to Glenn, his mouth open.

"Did you see that? The guard opened the door with his card; the woman deputy edged to the door and covered them as they entered. Then the first deputy in covered for the woman to enter! What the heck is going on in there?"

Daniel poked his head out the waiting room door to see if any more cops were on their way. "Incoming," Daniel replied, backing up. A fast-moving Respiratory Therapist hit the automatic doors and made it through in record time.

Glenn groaned. He knew he could help Bobby, but if he ran in and tried, he would surely be arrested. Why had he ever left the profession? What had he been thinking?

"Griselda!" Jaclyn yelled, tearing into the room. The level of urgency in her voice was off the charts. "Where's his doctor?"

"I just talked to her and she's at a meeting in Southport!" Griselda called back.

"Where's the hospitalist?"

"I don't know!"

Jaclyn darted to the phone and called the Emergency Room, pleading with her nurse on the other end to send Dr. Facinoli, the ER physician on duty. Jaclyn checked the wall clock.

Three other ICU nurses were in the room when she returned and a Respiratory Therapist had arrived. They swarmed around Bobby like a well-oiled machine, each one performing their part flawlessly, none speaking. Griselda inserted the airway into Bobby's throat; the Respiratory Therapist grabbed an ambu bag from the crash cart, attached it to the airway and started bagging him, forcing air into his lungs. Another ICU nurse inserted a new med-lock while another broke the seal on the medication tray from the crash cart. Jaclyn, standing on a stool, with hands linked performed rhythmic compressions on Bobby's chest while counting out loud.

Glenn had just pocketed his cell phone after calling Glenda when the physician in green scrubs and a white coat ran through the ICU doors. Damn! How he wanted to follow him! What kind of medicine did he practice now? Mixing Zombies and Long Island Iced Teas for burned out broads hardly compared.

Five minutes later the ICU doors opened yet again, except this time they were being used as an exit. A short, bald man dressed in hospital whites was being escorted out by the two Brunswick County deputies. The man had his wrists cuffed behind his back. Gibbering and crying, his face was red and puffy.

"Hey!" Daniel exclaimed. "I remember that guy. I think he's a nursing assistant. He played in the basketball games out back when I worked here."

Glenn watched them walk out of sight. *What the hell*, he thought.

It was forty-five minutes before the physician who had entered earlier exited the ICU and almost an hour before Jaclyn came back out. Glenn and Daniel jumped up when they saw her.

"What happened?" Daniel asked.

"How's Bobby?" Glenn asked at the same time.

"He's going to make it. I don't know how much more punishment his body can take though. Right now he's sedated and back on the ventilator."

"Holy cow!" Daniel exclaimed. "That guy the deputies took out, doesn't he work here?"

Jaclyn sighed heavily. "His name is Mark. He's been here a couple of years. He started out in Dietary and worked his way up to nursing assistant. I don't get it."

"What did he do to Bobby?" Glenn growled.

Jaclyn looked directly at Glenn. "He tried to smother him with a pillow. If it hadn't been for Griselda, he would've succeeded."

"But...but, why? Why...would he do that?" Glenn stammered.

Jaclyn shook her head sadly. "I don't know. He just kept crying and saying, 'He can't wake up. He can't wake up'."

FIFTEEN

"Where's Glenda?" Benton asked as he looked back over his shoulder out the office door, scanning the empty bar. He was seated at the desk in the tiny office, nervously drumming his fingers between the laptop and his bottle of cold water. A ceiling fan kept the room cool. Benton, dressed in a red polo shirt and khakis was "the computer nerd with a touch of style".

Glenn glared down at the computer technician. "What does that have to do with the price of eggs in India?"

Benton grimaced, returning his attention to the screen. "Nothing wrong," he mumbled. Sweat started to run down Benton's back in a little stream despite the overhead fan. Benton's keystrokes and the scraping of a warped blade on the ceiling fan were the only sounds until Benton mumbled again, "And it's not India."

"What?"

Benton turned back to Glenn. "Price of eggs in China, not India."

It was beginning to look like the business would get a late start today. Instead of stocking the bar and doing prep work, Glenn had practically tethered himself to Benton's side. As the tech pushed buttons and called up menus and screens Glenn never knew existed, the bar owner hovered anxiously.

Benton knew the No Egrets computer well. Glenda had made desperate calls to him at all hours, but only after she had exhausted all the fixes she could find on the internet. Benton didn't mind—life of a tech. More often than not, Glenn would have been the last one to touch the computer and months ago Benton and Glenda agreed Glenn should be kept away from the computer at all costs. His knee-jerk reactions to a little problem made any wrong mouse click into a major issue.

"Can you explain to me one more time what it's doing?"

Glenn's voice rose as he pointed at the computer screen. For the third time he explained, "I was adding receipts to that accounting program and the numbers kept disappearing every time I typed them in. Then I tried to add in the shipment we received yesterday and the perpetual inventory numbers started flashing and going crazy." Glenn stood up straight, remembering an additional detail. "When I hit that doohickey button…" He pointed an accusing finger at the screen. "It changed to the internet and stupid pictures of the new Star Wars movie started flashing on the screen. Some tall hairy thing and a robot made of balls."

"Uh-huh. That would be Chewbacca and BB-8."

"See," said Glenn excitedly. "I knew there were viruses! They always have such strange names."

Benton gave Glenn a sidelong glance from the computer screen to see if he was joking. Unsmiling, Glenn remained keyed up and tense.

"Um..." Benton returned his gaze to the screen. "Glenn, there's no problem I can find. No viruses. No worms. Nothing." Benton took a deep breath before finally letting the main thought on his mind escape his lips. "Have you and Glenda, um, talked about...well, limiting your time on this computer?" Sweat popped out on Benton's brow.

"What does that mean?" Glenn shot back. He moved closer to Benton's face. "And don't you dare say it's *user error*." (Even though Glenn wasn't supposed to hear Benton's diagnosis on some of his other visits, he had heard that phrase a couple of times in connection with his name.)

Benton's fingers flew over the keyboard as he ran some diagnostics. Then he opened the accounting program, took one of the receipts nearby and successfully added it to the last row.

"Well?" Glenn asked.

"User...competency."

Glenn had to restrain himself. A deep, guttural moan escaped followed by hand tremors. He wanted to pick up the computer and launch it through the roof. And for the encore—the amazing, albeit smug, Flying Benton!

Glenn closed his eyes and took five slow, cleansing breaths. When he opened his eyes he said calmly, "And what did you do to fix it?"

"I hit the magic button."

Glenn moved closer to the man and the computer, resisting an urge to wrap his hands around Benton's throat. "Show me—so I'll know the next time."

Benton closed down the program and clicked restart. He grabbed the bottle of water and took a big chug. Side by side the two watched as the computer screen turned from black to blue and finally to the Windows' home screen.

"Glenn?" the female voice called from the back door. It was Glenda returning from the salon/spa. "Glenn?" she called again from the bar.

"In here," Glenn said. "In the office."

"Thank you Jesus," Benton breathed. He took another long drink from the water bottle.

By the sound of her high heels clicking, they could track her as she entered the back door, moved across the barroom floor, dashed behind the bar to stash her purse and walked over to the window to adjust the blinds and change the sign from "Closed" to "Open". In a matter of seconds she would be in the office. Benton held his breath the whole time. Glenn glanced at the computer technician and wondered why he was sweating so much. *What the heck*, Glenn thought. *Is he scared of Glenda?* Glenn listened to the heel clicks as they headed toward the office. Well, he wasn't scared of his wife. He was going to tell her exactly what he thought about the computer and demand they get a more user-friendly machine.

Glenda walked in the doorway, stopping short when she saw Benton. Glenda immediately turned to Glenn. "What—did—you—do?" Her tone was even; her eyes flashing.

Glenn stood up straighter. "I called him. He just fixed the computer." As an afterthought he added, a tad quieter, "Your hair is really pretty."

"I had a massage," she responded icily.

"Oh…well, you look really relaxed," Glenn stammered, trying to recover. "But now you seem to have a twitch." He smiled weakly. "Perhaps you need a little more…kneading. If you want to go back, I'll…um, pay."

Benton stood with his water bottle clenched in a tight fist. Only his shaky hands told how he felt about being caught in the middle of marital melodrama. Glenda mouthed the words "user error" and Benton nodded his head slightly.

"Thank you, Benton," Glenda said as the man walked toward the front door. "Send us your bill. And tell Patti hello for us."

Glenda turned to her husband, hands on hips. "Well?"

Glenn gave her a sour look. "I was just adding in last night's late receipts and the shipment we received yesterday."

Glenda stood in front of him silently, her chin in the air. Slowly she lowered her head, her eyes drilling holes and an important message into him.

"Why can't I use the computer?" Glenn whined, somewhat like a teenage girl.

Glenda took a few steps closer to Glenn, her demeanor now sweet and innocent. "Do you notice anything?" she asked, fingers dancing as if she were playing a harp.

Glenn flinched, realizing this was a make-or-break moment. He had to admit he was a little afraid. He looked her up and down for a clue. Her nails! They were a bright, glossy pink.

"Your manicure is beautiful! I'm glad you treated yourself."

Glenda stepped closer. "Thank you, sweetheart. You are so attentive." She put her arms around her husband, giving him a long hug. While close, she whispered in his ear, "And if you ever touch my computer again, I'll cut your balls off."

The usual suspects started filtering into No Egrets around three thirty—early morning workers looking to wind down from their jobs; midnight shift workers dropping in for a cold one while running errands before work. Glenn surveyed the tables and realized if it wasn't for No Egrets some of the island residents would never have met. He had to smile. No Egrets—where half the people know your name.

A low mechanical buzz suddenly filled the bar. Immediately all conversation ceased. Most of the bar patrons knew the two second buzz was the only warning they would get. Cans, bottles and glassware slammed onto the bar and tabletops. Hands covered ears. And then it hit them— sound waves swept through No Egrets leaving no air molecules untouched. The ninety-five or so decibels of the Oak Island Fire and Rescue station siren showed no mercy on its next-door neighbors.

Matilda smirked, looking around. "Bunch of sissies," she said (or mouthed). No one actually heard anything over the deafening roar. Matilda sat through it all sipping her Tequila Sunrise (it was Thursday), her ancient ears uncovered.

When the third and final blast from the siren died down, Glenn uncovered his ears and moved down the bar to Matilda. His ears were ringing and his head was pounding. "How can you sit there like that with all the noise!" he said to Matilda, much too loudly.

Matilda blinked twice. "Why are you yelling at me? I can hear you fine. Fire alarms aren't loud...you want to know what's loud?" She stopped to take a long drink of her Tequila Sunrise. "The speakers at a Stones' concert, that's what. *That* was one hell of a tour! I remember one stadium show; backstage me and this Stones' roadie got naked and started banging to the beat. Bill Wyman's bass was my best friend that day!" Matilda cackled at the memory and combed her thin hair with her fingers. Glenda arrived just in time to hear, "Then there's the time Mick grabbed me, ripped my shirt off and dragged me...or was it Keith?"

"Enough!" Glenda shouted. "Enough! Enough! Enough!"

"Could you poke out my mind's eye?" Glenn pleaded, as his wife whisked by him.

Matilda sucked down the last of her drink. She sat for a minute, letting the drink hit her stomach before reaching for her helmet on the bar. "I think I'll ride out and see Bobby."

"NO!" Glenn and Glenda shouted together.

Glenn put his hand on top of Matilda's helmet and gently maneuvered it back to its place on the bar. "The hospital's not letting Bobby have any visitors right now." He didn't bother mentioning that security had been increased at the ICU and a Brunswick County Sherriff's deputy was stationed with Bobby. The guy who attacked him was a hospital employee for more than two years with a spotless work record. Rumors swirled but no one could quite figure out why he tried to kill a patient.

"Matilda dear, when Bobby is allowed visitors again, we will take you with us to see him," Glenda said, feeling an equal mix of responsibility and affection for the old lady.

Matilda sniffed a little. She picked up her empty glass and slammed it down on the bar, looking straight at Glenda. "Deal." Then the old woman laid her head back and croaked, "It's another Tequila Sunrise." When Glenn didn't respond, Matilda jammed her index finger on the bar. "Right here. Another Tequila Sunrise right here." Then she winked and added in a whisper, "Never got it on with Glenn Frey but I have Joe Walsh stories. Skinny little son of a bitch."

Glenn gave a slight shiver as he moved down the bar to mix Matilda's drink. Out of the corner of his eye he caught sight of just one of the Sonora sisters at a far table. Strange. He couldn't recall ever seeing the sisters apart. He was just about to walk over to her table when the front door jingled. In walked Hands and Sphinx in all their police seriousness. Apparently this wasn't a social call.

"Glenn," Hands said. "How's Bobby? We've been following up on the drowning victim and haven't had time to do much else. We heard you were at the hospital when it happened."

Glenn couldn't help glancing over at Bobby's empty barstool. "His condition is back to where it was when they first brought him in, back on the ventilator and heavily sedated. It was the damndest thing; he was just starting to wake up when that lunatic tried to kill him."

Hands gave Sphinx a look and they both nodded at the same time. "Don't repeat this to anybody," Sphinx said, lowering his voice. "One of the deputies told us he was there when they brought Mark Manganese in. That's the guy's full name. When they interviewed him, he just kept blubbering and repeating the same thing: 'He can't wake up, they'll kill her'."

"Her?" Glenn asked, frowning.

"Yeah," Sphinx continued. "When they finally got him calmed down, they got most of the story from him. He had been threatened by someone; he wouldn't tell who, although he did let it slip that he was a big guy."

Glenn scratched his head. "That doesn't make sense, does it?"

"Not until he told them about his daughter. He's divorced and his ex-wife and daughter live in Little River. He lives in Leland. It turns out this big guy was waiting for him on his dark front porch one night when he got off work. Manganese started to call 911 but the man told him he wouldn't do that if he wanted to see his daughter grow into a woman. He had pictures of Manganese's daughter on his phone and told him where she went to school, dance class, even the location of the birthmark on her leg."

"Wow!" Glenn exclaimed. "That's scary. But what does that have to do with Bobby?"

"The big guy told Manganese if Bobby woke up in that hospital bed, his daughter would disappear. Never to be seen again."

Juanita Sonora was obviously upset. First, she was sitting alone, no sister in sight. Second, she had been crying. Her eyes were red-rimmed and she was fighting back more tears. Glenda took the seat across from the sad woman.

"What's wrong? Where's Bonita?"

Juanita started to speak but a huge sob escaped. Her eyes grew wide and soon her body was quaking as she tried to hold it in. Glenda quickly moved to the chair beside Juanita, reaching an arm around her. Juanita broke down, crying uncontrollably. Glenda pulled her close, soothing her. After several minutes, Juanita sat up straight and wiped her eyes on her shirt sleeve.

"I'm sorry Glenda. I guess I needed that. I have to be strong for Boni."

"Is something wrong with Bonita?"

Juanita's voice was stronger when she spoke. "She's...got cancer. She's already received two chemotherapy treatments. I didn't want to leave her at home, but she's sleeping and I was hoping to talk with your husband. I need to talk with someone who knows medicine...healthcare. Doctors' offices."

Glenda looked to Glenn who was still talking with the police officers at the bar. "I'll get Glenn to come over in just a minute."

"It's just..." Juanita continued. "I've seen some things that bother me at her oncologist's office. Nothing big, just lots of little things. And it all happened so fast—it seemed like one minute she was diagnosed and the next she was getting chemotherapy there at the office."

Glenda's mind flashed to Karen. It seemed to have happened fast to her, too.

"And her doctor..." Juanita paused, not sure how to continue. "When we first met him, I thought he was the greatest doctor I had ever met, maybe even the greatest human being. He was calm, compassionate; all his attention was focused on Bonita.

"But after we signed the consent for chemotherapy, he changed. It's almost as if he were two people."

The images of Dr. Jekyll and Mr. Hyde floated through Glenda's mind.

"I don't know how to explain it to you, Glenda. Bonita has another round of chemo tomorrow..."

The sudden look of anguish on Juanita's face nearly broke Glenda's heart.

"And I don't want to take her back to Dr. Roshberg's."

A cold chill ran down Glenda's spine.

Glenn tried to think it through, but it still made no sense. "Somebody. Somebody out there. Somebody wants Bobby dead," he muttered. He tried to keep his voice to the level where his two cop buddies could hear him and the bar grapevine couldn't.

Hands nodded his head. Sphinx just shrugged.

"So, you're after the mysterious big guy now?"

Hands shook his head. "Can't do anything until Mark Manganese talks, gives us a name, a better description, something. Anything."

"Why wouldn't he help?" Glenn was baffled.

"The daughter. The deputy told me he's terrified. Must be one bad man. Has Manganese scared shitless."

Matilda banged her empty Tequila Sunrise glass on the bar. "Hey! Thirsty woman waiting," she sang out. "Gonna take my top off if I don't get some service!"

The crowd moaned and some began calling to Glenn.

"C'mon, Doc. She's not joking."

"Hurry please! I just ate."

Glenn held up an index finger to Hands and Sphinx and moved down to mix Matilda another. When he returned, the officers were preparing to leave.

"You mentioned the drowning victim. I haven't seen anything about him in the news lately," Glenn said. The man who drowned had been identified as Tommie Thomson from Bolton.

Hands and Sphinx stopped and looked at each other. A slight nod of the head from Hands and Sphinx spoke up. "Well, it's going to be on the news tomorrow, so I guess it won't hurt to tell you. The autopsy is back. He didn't drown. He was murdered."

"What?" Glenn said loudly.

Hands grimaced. "Shhh."

Sphinx looked around before continuing. "The Medical Examiner determined he was hit in the back of the head with a blunt object. Hard enough to cause a cerebral hemorrhage. In this case, from the massive brain bleed, the ME was pretty confident. He was dead before he ever hit the water."

Murder! Glenn swayed a little and grabbed the bar for balance. Bobby had ended up in the Intracoastal Waterway. Was there a connection? What had Bobby gotten himself mixed up in?

SIXTEEN

Glenn returned from the restroom and slid into the booth on the bench opposite his wife. He and Glenda had stopped at Duffer's Bar and Grill on Main Street in Shallotte for an early lunch. Glenda was devouring her fried green tomato BLT.

"Saw a great sign in the bathroom I think we ought to get for No Egrets," Glenn announced, casually picking up his glass of pink lemonade.

Glenda took a break from her sandwich and placed what was left of it back on her plate. "In the restroom? Let me get this straight—you were admiring the restroom decor." She took a drink of sweet tea and resisted rolling her eyes. "Well?"

"It said: 'I got a case of beer for my wife. Best trade I ever made'."

Glenda grunted and returned to her plate. She picked up a stray fried green tomato and popped it into her mouth.

"You don't like it?" Glenn asked, feigning hurt.

Glenda set her lips and raised her eyebrows. "That's fine. You can put the sign in the restroom of No Egrets."

"Really?"

"Yes. You and your second wife Teah Valentine can put the sign in the restroom. And then the two of you can just laugh and laugh."

Glenn started to laugh but caught himself. His little joke had turned awkward. "Who?"

"Don't give me that. You remember the little candy striper you were sniffing around before I showed up." Glenda fluttered her eyebrows and said in a high, giggly voice, "Oh *Glenny*, you're so strong. You're so smart."

Glenn grabbed his chicken gyro, spilling a little out of the pita and onto the table. "Huh. Very funny. You make it sound like she was underage; she wasn't a candy striper, she worked at the gift shop."

"Oh, so you do remember her."

"Of course. But once you walked into my life, I knew there was no other woman on earth for me."

Glenda laughed. "A little hokey, but I'll take it."

Glenn filled a spoon with pasta salad and shoveled it into his mouth. He had been married long enough to realize keeping his mouth full of food would be wise at this point. The pasta salad was a great choice and a small "yum" escaped his lips. Husband and wife settled into enjoying their food and both let their minds wander.

Their visit to Shallotte had been a last-minute thing. The day had started as usual, looking for Ernie the Egret through the kitchen window. ("No, I don't see him, but another goldfish has disappeared. It definitely has to be raccoons. Does Oak Island Hardware have a trap for coons?") Household chores and errands had been on their minds. Glenn wrestled with the idea of washing his truck and Glenda's car, but the weather forecast yesterday called for a fifty percent chance of thunderstorms. (Glenn was convinced the local meteorologists didn't even check anymore; just flipped a coin each day and changed the number under thunderstorms to somewhere between twenty and eighty percent.) Glenn looked out the window at the sky, searching for black clouds. Deciding to recheck the weather forecast, he turned on the morning news.

Glenda had just stepped out of the shower. Glenn was choosing his t-shirt for the day (he was really starting to love casual living). It was the top of the hour and the WECT news lineup was in its big news stories. Glenn referred to it as the "cops and mug shots" block. For now it was background noise as Glenn awaited the weather guy. Glenn turned to his wife holding up Steve Miller Band and Moody Blues' concert shirts.

"Pick," he told her.

"Both are black! Does it matter?" Glenda asked.

"Both are *classics!*" he insisted. "Moody Blues are *not* in the Rock and Roll Hall of Fame. Wearing it shows my support for a band that has been snubbed. Steve Miller Band was just inducted recently and wearing it shows my support for the choice. Each shirt represents *me*, sending a clear message to all I will meet today."

"Wearing a black t-shirt today will definitely send a message. It's going to be sunny and muggy out there, you looney bird," Glenda joked.

In the second before Glenn could react with silent indignation, the television changed the mood in the room.

"*...An autopsy is uncovering disturbing evidence in the death of a Columbus County man. Authorities earlier this week pulled the body of Tommie Thomson from the Intracoastal Waterway off of Oak Island. The state medical examiner says autopsy results could indicate foul play and that murder is a possibility...*"

The station then went into a heartbreaking sound cut from his grieving widow, Mabel. She wore what some called a "chemo wrap". It was a simple white turban that circled her entire hair line. She looked quite ill.

"*My Tommie was a good man. I loved him. He loved me. A good, good man. (crying) He always, always take care of me, 'specially while I been sick with the cancer. (crying) I don't know what I woulda done without my man; he always drove me to the doctor's office more'n an hour away. He didn't deserve to be kilt like an animal. (crying) The Good Lord will bring us justice!*"

The report ended. The station went into more cops and mug shots. Glenn and Glenda silently processed what they had heard: murder, cancer, doctor an hour away. Glenn performed a quick mental calculation—Bolton, doctor's office about an hour away. It could be Shallotte.

Thoughts of Dr. Roshberg had weighed on Glenn's mind since the previous night, when he had sat with Juanita Sonora for the better part of an hour in No Egrets. Juanita had a list of worries about her twin's oncologist's office and practice. He did the best he could to allay her fears, but he had nagging thoughts of his own. After she left, he had quickly googled the doctor to look for any red flags. The office webpage had been pretty cut and dry—very dry, with promises of great care and cutting-edge medical technology. The only curious thing Glenn had noticed was a link to a paper with Dr. Roshberg getting writing credit. The *only* writing credit. "Effect of Psychological Factors in Patients with Acute Myeloid Leukemia." Very strange. Not the topic but the fact Roshberg was the only author credited. Usually medical literature, especially major subjects like oncology, warrant more than one author—or at the very least some contributors. No references were listed at the end of the paper either.

So after the news report on the Thomsons that morning, there hadn't been much discussion as they jumped in the car and headed to Shallotte. It wasn't hard to find Dr. Roshberg's office—it was a new one-story building along US Route 17. It had impressive masonry with a huge decorative caduceus (which Glenda called a two-snake medical curlicue doohickey) above the door. Glenn noticed right away the lack of windows; usually physician offices were designed so the healing power of sunlight shone through. It looked more like a mausoleum.

They found the office easily, pulling into the parking lot without a plan. After ten minutes Glenn finally spoke, "I'm going in." Glenda usually tried to talk Glenn out of impulsive schemes, but in this case she simply nodded.

Glenn still had no particular plan in mind when he stepped through the door. The waiting room was three-fourths full and apart from two huge weird abstract watercolor pictures on the wall, it looked like any other waiting room in America. It wasn't hard to pick out the twosomes waiting together; one half looked ill and scared, the other healthy and nervous.

Glenn walked up to the front window. It was a sliding glass window, but it wasn't clear, frosted or tinted like many he had seen; this one reflected like a mirror. He stared into it, squinting. If he didn't know better, he would say it looked like a one-way mirror. Why would they need a one-way mirror? What were they trying to hide? After a couple of minutes, the window slid open—just about two inches.

"Can I help you?" asked a condescending, nasally voice.

Glenn felt like he was being asked a secret password. If a room full of sick people weren't listening, he probably would have said, "Swordfish". It was a password from an old Marx Brothers' movie.

Instead, Glenn's mind jumped into hyper-drive. "Directions," he replied. "I'm lost and I need some directions. I am hoping you could help me."

The window opened a few more inches. The tight-faced, purple-haired receptionist raised her purple drawn on eyebrows. "Directions to what?" she asked.

Directions to what? Glenn hadn't thought that far in advance. He was trying to think of something in Shallotte that would be believable. Suddenly the name of a dentist's office on the way into town popped into his head. "I'm trying to find Dr. Hagemann, dentist, here in Shallotte. Is he nearby?"

The receptionist turned to the inner office to ask if anyone had heard of Dr. Hagemann.

The workers all looked at each other like purple-hair had started speaking a foreign tongue. An older woman in the office asked if she meant Larry Hagman from "I Dream of Jeannie". Another told her she was wrong; Larry Hagman was that mean man on "Dallas".

As the troupe tried to figure out the identity and location of Hagemann, Glenn looked around the inner office. His eyes were drawn to a beast; a tall, burly, baldhead man in green scrubs standing in the inner hallway. He carried a menacing air about him. Glenn couldn't help wondering if the man was Dr. Roshberg but quickly discarded the notion. Surely not, hanging out in the hallway like he had nothing better to do. The man's demeanor and body language reminded him of a bouncer or maybe some kind of security that a rap star would have hanging around. He did not join in the conversation with the other workers. He just stood. And stared.

Finally, a gothic boy with a huge hole in his ear from a gauge pulled up maps on his phone. "The dentist is about two miles that way on 17." Glenn thanked him, not mentioning that he was pointing in the wrong direction. He wondered why Roshberg would hire a kid like that for a professional office. Any of them really. They made Groucho, Harpo and Chico look like ultimate professionals.

Glenn's mind snapped back to Duffers and his delicious pasta salad. He looked down and the bowl was almost empty. He wondered what Glenda would say if he ordered another helping.

"What you thinking about?" Glenda asked her husband. He looked like he was, as he liked to say, lost in the ozone again.

"Hmm? Oh, Roshberg's office." Glenn picked up his chicken gyro and resumed eating.

"Something bothering you about it?"

Glenn chewed and swallowed his mouthful of food before answering. "I don't know. I did get a weird vibe but it could've just been because I talked with Juanita last night."

Juanita had described Dr. Roshberg's ever-changing personality but that hadn't made too much of an impression on Glenn. He had known plenty of doctors with a god complex who put on quite a syrupy show at the patient's bedside, pretending they really cared. Worthy of an Oscar Nomination for Best Supporting Asshole. But there were three things she had mentioned that really bothered him. One was the unlabeled intravenous bag containing Bonita's chemotherapy; the second, a nurse not wearing gloves when taking blood; the last, the request for lab results. First Juanita had asked for a copy of her sister's lab results which had been rightfully denied. But when Bonita asked for the results, she was initially told she would get them; however there always seemed to be an excuse for the request being delayed and she had never received a copy. Withholding personal medical information from the patient was blatantly illegal and made Glenn mad as hell. Also very suspicious.

"Glenda, what's that website you can look up a doctor's credentials and find reviews from patients?"

"Healthgrades." Glenda started giggling. "Remember what that one patient said about you?"

"Ha-ha yes," Glenn said in monotone. "Very flattering. Can you be serious for a minute?"

Glenda sat up straight, raising one eyebrow.

"Well?" Glenn asked finally.

"Well what?"

"Can you access the website?"

Glenda frowned. "You can do it on *your* phone. You have the very same smartphone as I do."

Glenn glanced down at his phone on the tabletop. Strangely enough he thought of the Old Smithville Burying Ground. "I still say mine's not much of a smartphone if it can't kill zombies."

"Now who's not being serious?"

"I'm sorry," Glenn said. "Will you please look it up on your phone? I don't know how."

Glenda wanted to say *bullshoot* but she bit her tongue. She picked up her phone and started typing.

"Dr. Julius Roshberg, MD. Male, age 49," she read. She scrolled down to Dr. Roshberg's experience. "Specialties—oncology, medical oncology, hematology/oncology." Scrolling down she saw procedures performed by Dr. Roshberg. "Plasmapheresis, thoracentesis, bone marrow biopsy, chemotherapy."

Glenda scrolled down again. "Oh. There are too many conditions Dr. Roshberg treats." She handed her phone to her husband. "You'll have to read them yourself."

Glenn looked at the screen. "Acute leukemia, anemia, chronic myeloid leukemia, coagulation disorders (including hemophilia), Hodgkin's lymphoma, leukocytosis…" He stopped before pressing the "more" button on the screen. Most were related to the blood and Glenn found it a little strange that an oncologist didn't have the usual culprits listed in the conditions treated—rectal, skin, breast, cervical, lung.

A young waitress approached their table. "Would you like more tea?"

"Yes dear. Thank you," Glenda said, offering her glass. "Glenn, do you want a lemonade refill?"

"Huh? No." Glenn did not look up from the phone. He had just found "Background Check" for Dr. Roshberg. He grunted as he read: Malpractice claims not available—Healthgrades does not collect malpractice information for North Carolina. But instead of "none" under the next category, there was something listed. Glenn leaned forward.

·Sanctions:
·Disciplinary action in another state
·Action taken: Voluntary Surrender
·Summary: Dr. Julius Roshberg, License # 2A390; Nature of Complaint: The physician was disciplined by another state and failed to report this disciplinary action within sixty days after its occurrence to the Georgia Board of Medicine. Action Taken: The physician voluntarily surrendered his license to practice in the State of Georgia
·State: Georgia

Glenn scrolled down quickly.

·Sanctions:
·Unethical Business Practice, Unprofessional Conduct
·Action taken: Suspension
·Summary: Dr. Julius Roshberg, License #3698Z21; Nature of Complaint: The physician engaged in Unethical Business Practice and Unprofessional Conduct. Action Taken: The Florida Department of Licensing and Regulatory Affairs, Bureau of Health Professionals has placed the physician's Florida license on Suspension until a hearing is scheduled.
·State: Florida

Glenda noticed Glenn frowning and rubbing the side of his face repeatedly. "Are there reviews from his patients?" she asked.

"I'll look in a minute," Glenn answered absentmindedly. Unethical business practice and unprofessional conduct? That could be anything on the spectrum, from bad bookkeeping to outright fraud. The surrender of his license in Georgia was because he did not report the sanction in Florida. But one thing was clear, Dr. Roshberg was constantly on the move and he was moving north. What had he reported to the North Carolina Board of

Medicine and what had he kept secret?

The phone in Glenn's hand buzzed. Glenda reached and took it before Glenn realized what was happening.

"What are you doing?"

"I got a text. Something could be wrong with the kids. One of them may need us," Glenda said matter-of-factly, taking the stance of mothers everywhere.

"Or it could be Verizon telling you you've used all the data in your plan for the month. I wasn't finished reading."

Glenda didn't respond. She was looking at her texts. "Wow. It's from Karen. She heard about Bobby and wants me to call her or come to her house."

"That's good," Glenn said. "When you do, ask her about Roshberg."

"What did you find?" Glenda had heard most of Glenn's conversation with Juanita last night and she had her own suspicions.

"He got into some kind of trouble in Florida, moved to Georgia and then to North Carolina. He recently surrendered his license in Georgia because he failed to report his suspension in Florida."

"How could he keep his license in North Carolina then?"

Glenn shrugged. "Medical boards don't necessarily communicate with each other and each state's board is managed differently. It's difficult to explain."

Glenda gave one of her rare angry looks, usually reserved for Matilda. "What's difficult about it? This isn't the 1800s."

Glenn took her hand and kissed it. "You're absolutely right. You have a way of cutting through the BS and getting to the heart of the matter. I love you."

Glenda's face lightened and she smiled. She switched away from her texts and back to the Healthgrade website. She started to hand the phone back to Glenn, but he held up his palm.

"You read them," Glenn said. "You know how much I enjoy reading the average person's comments on the internet."

This Glenda could not deny; just the other night Glenn had thrown a mini tantrum while reading people's insensitive comments on local news stories on-line. She scanned down through the comments. "He's a great doctor...Dr. Roshberg is a saint...He saved my life."

Glenda stopped. "Oh!"

"What?"

Glenda read the next one verbatim. "Dr. Roshberg is a psycho, an insensitive SOB. He's only in it for the money and must be stopped!"

SEVENTEEN

Griselda, "Zelly", had been an ICU nurse for twelve years. She was known for being an exemplary nurse and professional in every way. She had cared for young, old, rich, poor, famous…well, almost famous. Initially she was convinced he was a NASCAR driver but later found out he did some driving on the K&N Pro Series East, an East Coast division of the Home Track series which is like level four of NASCAR. He was cute and she gave him her full attention. But she had never felt so attached to a patient as she did Bobby (of course she had never had to thwart a murder attempt on one of her patients either). The story of her "whipping the bad guy's ass" had spread through the hospital grapevine faster than a speeding Silver Bullet (also known as a bisacodyl laxative suppository in the hospital) and Zelly was basking in the limelight. Today she had on a touch more makeup than usual, so she looked less like John Goodman.

She checked all Bobby's vitals and was in the process of changing the propofol bottle when she saw a twitch. She put down the intravenous bottle without spiking it and moved to the bedside. She watched his eyes. There was slight movement!

In Bobby's head he could feel himself rising and sinking, rising and sinking. He wanted to scream. He had to wake up—he had to tell someone, *I am alive! Karen is in danger!*

Zelly moved closer to her patient. First she patted and stroked Bobby's hand; on sudden impulse she took his hand in hers.

Bobby felt the touch on his hand. Someone was there! *I'm here! I'm here!* He tried to focus all his energy. *Must…wake…up.*

Zelly closed her eyes tight, calling on a higher power, urging her patient to fight. "Come on Bobby. You can do it. Come back to us," she whispered.

A sudden twitch of a finger within her grasp caused Zelly to open her eyes. His eyes were fluttering! She wanted to shout, to leap and dance about, but instead she continued to hold his hand and look into his eyes. With two quick flickers, his eyes opened wide! Now his lips were twitching. He was trying to speak! She leaned closer with her ear to his lips.

Bobby spoke two words through the mask and collapsed into semi-consciousness again.

Zelly released Bobby's hand and quickly checked his vitals. He seemed to be stable. She finished spiking the propofol bottle and exchanged it with the empty one on the IV pole. Then she ran to the computer. In spite of the ventilator mask, she was pretty sure she heard him clearly but it didn't make a lot of sense.

Opening the Nurse's Note section in the computer, she documented the entire sequence, including the two words Bobby had spoken. Zelly wasn't sure if there really were any of the cute little mammals in the Intracoastal Waterway, let alone large ones, but she was almost positive Bobby had said, "Big otter".

"Unusual? Unusual. Hmm," said Karen. "I'm not even sure what *usual* is in cancer treatment. I haven't seen anything I would consider out of the ordinary." She paused as she seemed to be reviewing all her visits to Dr. Roshberg in her mind. Her eyes were half closed, her chin raised, her mouth tightly shut. Finally she said, "Nope, can't think of anything. Dr. Roshberg is hardly around for my treatments anyway. It's usually a couple of old bitches hooking me up."

Karen rearranged the scarf around her scalp, making sure her bare head remained hidden. She readjusted the thin blanket bundled around her. She was stretched out on a new recliner in the living room. It was positioned to face the television plus have a view of the kitchen and front door. An old TV table served as a desk to hold her cell phone, paper, pencil and crossword book.

"Dr. Roshberg is a…'seal the deal' kind of doctor. He diagnosed my disease, explained it, how he was going to treat it, then…POOF! He disappeared. He was nice enough, at least at first," Karen said, concluding her Roshberg assessment.

Glenda was perched on an old couch with huge orange flowers—very, very 1970s. She leaned forward, interested in everything Karen had to say but also having trouble hearing her words. Karen's once strong voice, which could be heard across the bar, was now strained and weak. Glenda's emotions were tumbling as if they were in a dryer. She was horrified to see Karen looking more pallid and emaciated than before. She was suspicious and strangely angry over anything Roshberg related. Yet she was happy to just be sitting with her friend.

Karen closed her eyes and Glenda thought she had drifted off. Karen raised her index finger and spoke. "You know, there *is* one thing, now that I think about it." Karen opened her eyes. "Bobby was royally pissed. Dr. Roshberg has this man. A goon really. A really big goon. His name is…"

This time Karen did appear to drift off. Suddenly she said, "Automobile. Big as an automobile. That's how I remember his name. Otto."

Karen took a deep breath. Glenda waited for her to continue.

"Bobby didn't like Otto from the start. He couldn't understand why Dr.

Roshberg would have someone like that around, let alone on his payroll. Well, you know how headstrong Bobby can be. The two clashed when Otto wouldn't let him come into the room during my treatments." She paused. "If I'd had the strength, I would have gone upside Otto's head myself."

She breathed a deep sigh. "I didn't think much about it at the time, but Bobby's right. What the hell is a muscle-head doing around a doctor's office? That's just bullshit.

"Me and Bobby," Karen said, choking back a sniffle. "What a pair. I'm...I'm...I am really...sick." Her throat tried to hold back the words but the tough woman in Karen forced them out. "And Big Bob." Karen managed a slight smile. "Well, something bad has happened to him—he's lying in a hospital bed." She closed her eyes and a quick shudder ran down her upper torso. "What a shit-heel I've been. I thought he was dumping on me because I've got...I'm sick. Bobby cares for me and I jumped right in there and thought the worst of him. *If* he didn't think of leaving before, he'll probably do it now. Or maybe he already has. I don't know if we're a couple or—"

"I think," Glenda interrupted. "Bobby still cares for you—a lot."

Glenda could almost see Karen's dull eyes light up. It even brought a tinge of color back to her face.

"Well, wouldn't that be something! From your lips to God's ear. Amen! And hell yes!" Karen said as loud as she could manage. "Hey, you and Doc visit Bobby in the hospital as often as you can and make sure they are taking good care of him. I want to be there, but this recliner doesn't have wheels."

"Sure, Karen."

"And keep an eye on those nurses—*and* their top buttons!" Karen insisted. "Bobby has always been a boob man."

Glenda laughed as she said, "All men are boobs as well as boob men at some point."

The one-way mirror window slid shut. Initially bewildered, Juanita stared at the glass until she felt the heat creep up her neck, ending at the top of her scalp. With a flushed face and narrow eyes, she banged on the glass so hard it wobbled in its tracks. The loud noise scared the purple-haired office worker on the other side and she jumped up quickly from her chair.

A very unprofessional, "What the fuck? You crazy bitch!" was the muffled response from the inner office.

Purple-hair's remarks gave away her position and without seeing her, Juanita knew she was looking right at her. Juanita scowled through the mirror, pointing at the woman, turning her hand over and crooking her finger three times slowly. The woman approached and opened the window as if in a trance, convinced Juanita had some kind of special vision to see her through the mirror.

Juanita gathered herself. "I'm not through with you. Don't you ever close this in my face again. Or you won't have any hair left to dye purple."

"I…I'm sorry,' the purple-haired, mousy woman squeaked.

Juanita took a deep breath. "Now—" she started, speaking slowly and forcefully. Her eyes remained narrow. Her left hand, its brightly painted nails shining, held the glass mirror, blocking the track to keep it from closing again. "My sister has asked for her lab results for several days. Where are they? Legally you have to give them to her."

Juanita leaned through the window, glaring at the woman until she answered.

"Y…yes."

Juanita nodded, congratulating the woman on the correct answer. "Now, you have a release form around here somewhere for a patient to get their entire medical record."

Purple-hair's eyes grew wide and she looked around nervously.

"Well, get one!" Juanita demanded, forcing her head farther into the office space. "When my sister finishes her treatment, she would like a form."

Sweat had broken out on the younger woman's forehead. "I don't know where we keep those forms. I'll have to ask. But the copies aren't free. You gotta pay." Then she remembered the spiel Dr. Roshberg made her memorize. "And…and I have…the office has three business days to provide the copies to the patient." She smiled somewhat smugly, thinking she had Juanita on the ropes. She was wrong.

Juanita slammed her fist down on the countertop and grabbed for purple-hair. The girl barely jumped out of Juanita's reach. Juanita's professional manicure brushed the young woman's blouse, snagging her name tag. The name tag went flying. No one looked to see where it landed but by the sound it ricocheted off a couple of file cabinets and a metal trashcan. "Come closer and tell me that!" Juanita roared. "We've been asking for the lab results for a week! And we're leaving with them today! If not the lab results, then we will be leaving with a *purple scalp*!"

The outer door opened and Otto's large frame emerged to stand by Juanita. Someone in the waiting room screamed. A nervous couple jumped to their feet and flew out the front door. Others appeared paralyzed with fear. Juanita stood her ground. She shot Otto a look. "What? You gonna throw me out, you big thug?" Juanita growled, leaning toward him. "I'm not scared of you!"

The whole waiting room cringed, sure they were going to witness a thumping.

Otto just stood there with his hands crossed. He didn't blink. He didn't speak.

Someone whispered a little too loudly. "I think this is where the villagers show up with torches and pitchforks."

Juanita broke her stare from Otto to look at purple-hair. The smug smile had returned to the woman's face. Juanita's eyes turned wild and she pointed a long, pink-tipped finger at the woman. The smugness quickly disappeared.

"Find—that—form," Juanita demanded. With a sideways glance at Otto and a loud, "Humph!" she pirouetted and returned to her seat. The office window slid shut.

Later that day, Bobby's eyes fluttered open again. Zelly was there by his side, ministering to his needs. Her shift was almost over but she couldn't leave him—not until he showed some sign of improvement. Zelly smiled widely. Bobby thought it was a beautiful smile although he couldn't remember if he had ever met her before.

"Hello Bobby. My name is Griselda. I am your nurse and you are in the hospital."

Bobby remembered hearing other voices, in his dreams, but this voice seemed to be the one he had heard the most.

Zelly checked Bobby's vitals; satisfied she removed the mask from his mouth and nose. Carefully she placed oxygen tubing around his head and inserted the cannula into his nose.

Bobby's eyes never left Zelly's face. "Do you have any pain?" she asked softly.

Bobby coughed. It felt like the inside of his mouth and trachea had been sandblasted. He tried to speak but nothing would come out.

"Just a minute." Griselda left the room and returned with ice chips. She gently placed tiny spoonfuls into Bobby's mouth and onto his tongue.

As the ice melted and coated his mouth and throat, Bobby felt relief. He thought it was the most wonderful drink he had ever tasted, possibly even better than Bud Light.

"Been long time—since woke up to a strange woman," Bobby managed to finally croak.

Zelly laughed out loud and actually blushed.

"Fred Flintstone and ancient Annie," Bobby stated in a raspy voice. "In my head."

Zelly gave him a funny look and shrugged. Long term intravenous drips of sedatives can cause a long list of side effects, hallucinations right there at the top and Zelly had seen most of them. She had one patient awaken who swore for the week he was under he had been Donald Trump's hairdresser and confidant. Oh the dirty little secrets he had told her of The Donald.

Zelly guided another spoonful of ice into Bobby's mouth. "What day? How long here?" he asked.

"A few days. Your doctor will be making her evening rounds soon and I will let her answer all your questions."

Zelly smiled and smoothed a strand of Bobby's hair away from his eyes. She had a feeling she would like this man, even when he was unconscious and lying there hovering between life and death.

Bobby looked at her name badge attached to her right breast. "Riseldia," he managed to say. "Thank you." Bobby's next thought, which was meant to stay in his head, actually made it through his lips. "Big boobs—I like."

A girlish giggle escaped Zelly and she blushed again. Highly inappropriate but flattering, nonetheless.

"You save me. Beat shit—out of him?" Bobby asked.

Zelly gently placed more ice chips in his mouth. This bought her a little time to consider how to answer him. He had surprised her; she didn't think he would have any memory of the episode. She wondered how much she should tell him. Professionally she knew the less he knew at this point the better. But, he had admired her...full figure so.

"His name is Mark. He was a nursing assistant here," she said slowly.

Bobby closed his eyes and she thought he had fallen asleep midthought, which was not uncommon at this stage of recovery. But then he opened his eyes and turned his head toward her. "Favor?"

Zelly nodded. "Sure. Anything." (She secretly hoped it didn't involve her boobs.)

"Who knows—awake?"

Zelly blinked. It was not a question she was expecting. "Uh, just me so far. Your doctor is in the hospital somewhere. You woke up for a short time earlier today and I documented it. But I guess I haven't really told anyone yet."

Bobby smiled. "Good. Tell—no one."

Zelly's smile faded into a look of shock and surprise.

"Please," Bobby begged. "Need talk to a friend first."

When Griselda left the room, she was shaking her head. *I must be crazy*, she thought. *I could lose my job. Worse, I could be reported to the nursing board and possibly lose my license.* But there was a little cloak and dagger excitement in the request. She walked to the nursing station phone and dialed the cell number Bobby had given her.

For a brief minute, Glenn felt like a real jerk. The woman was ill and grieving. Glenn tried to shake off the feeling he was like a sleazy personal injury lawyer swooping in on an easy target. He had found her husband's name and phone number in an old printed phone book that contained Brunswick and surrounding counties. Her dead husband. Mabel Thomson answered the phone.

"Hel—lo?" a tentative voice on the other end asked.

"Mrs. Thomson? Mrs. Thomson, my name is Glenn. I, uh, saw your story on the news." He paused for a deep breath. "First, I am very sorry for your loss."

"Thank you," Mabel responded guardedly. "You a cop?"

"No, I'm—"

"Newspaper?" A tinge of excitement in her voice.

"No ma'am. I'm a...a physician and I heard you say you had cancer. That you relied on your husband to take you to your doctor appointments."

Glenn's cell phone vibrated in his hand indicating an incoming call.

"Ma'am, if you could just wait a moment. I have another call coming in," he explained.

He held the phone out and looked at it. *Boil Grove Comm Hosp* was abbreviated on the screen. Boiling Grove Community Hospital? Bobby! Had something happened with Bobby? Glenn almost panicked and answered the call but stopped at the last second. He put the phone to his ear; Mabel Thomson had just finished speaking and he had missed it.

Glenn tried to recover. "Mrs. Thomson, I know how important it is to continue with your cancer treatments. I was concerned you wouldn't have a ride to get to them. I have two friends who are taking chemotherapy right now; perhaps they go to the same oncologist as you. There may be a way to find you a ride. Also there are free community service organizations that provide—"

Mabel Thomson's voice rose. "Hey!" she interrupted. Suddenly she didn't sound like a grieving, fragile widow but more like a feisty senior citizen. "I 'preciate your concern, doctor whoever. But I think you are after a old woman's money, 'cause nobody calls a stranger to offer a ride for free. Also, I think you need checked by one of 'em Ear, Nose and Neck doctors."

"I'm sorry," Glenn said, followed by a deep breath. "I'm not after your money. I am a surgeon. And why do you think I need to see a specialist?"

"Well," Mabel Thomson responded in an impatient tone. "I done told ya once! But you must not hear so good." Mabel began shouting into the phone so the hearing-impaired surgeon could make out her words. "I'll tell ya again. I'm all set. My nephew, little Ed is gonna drive me to Dr. Roshberg's!"

Dr. Julius Roshberg drummed his fingers on his mahogany desk. Otto sat opposite the doctor, filling a solid chair that had legs like tree stumps. A lot of the room's furniture had fallen victim to Otto's size so Roshberg had found the throne-looking monstrosity on eBay. Roshberg hated it. Otto hated it. But the chair would save on furniture repairs in the long run. The combination of the giant office furniture and the huge henchman made the room, and Roshberg, look as if they were not drawn to the same scale.

Roshberg drummed his fingers for a good ten minutes. Otto sat straight the whole time with his hands on his thighs, ready to pounce. Otto had locked the doctor's office door when he answered the boss' page. Now they both sat in silence, except for the finger drumming.

"We have two active problems." Roshberg stopped the drumming and tried to spell out what Otto already knew. "The second issue is Ms. Sonora's sister and this business over reports and the chart. That I can handle personally." The smile of a con man crossed his face. "If Ms. Sonora follows through, then she'll get a 'copy'." He made air quotes as he said "copy" and chuckled. "I will have to do a little touch-up work on it after office hours before it's ready, but so be it. It is a sacrifice I'm willing to make."

Otto nodded his understanding.

Roshberg's hand returned to the desktop. The tempo of his drumming fingers had increased. "Which leads us to our number one problem. Bobby Portis." Otto's eyes narrowed at the mention of the name. "A problem that just—won't—die."

"Do you have another contact at the hospital?" the doctor asked.

"Yes," Otto growled. Bobby Portis had become an embarrassment to Otto and he wanted nothing more than to take care of him—personally. But Dr. Roshberg wouldn't hear of it, wanting to avoid front page news for him and his employee.

"Good. So we will know immediately if he becomes conscious again." Roshberg hadn't posed this as a question but still Otto nodded. The security guard he had paid off was skittish after the initial attempt on Bobby's life and Otto wasn't sure if he could fully trust him now. A personal visit and an incentive may be in order; one involving the guard's family.

Dr. Roshberg stood up on his secret riser behind the desk, placed both hands on the shiny surface and leaned as far forward as he could without standing on tippy toe. He leveled a stare directly at Otto. "This will be our last chance to get Portis. Hopefully they don't have police stationed outside his room yet, but you can bet they will if there is another failed attempt. That would be most unfortunate for me. And sadly, a disaster for you.

"I'll take care of my 'problem'," Roshberg said in a singsong voice, again using air quotes. Then the tone changed to menacing. "You take care of *your* problem!"

If anyone else had been in the room, they would have laughed to see the little man threaten a beast who could squish him like a grape. But there were no witnesses and Otto did not laugh.

EIGHTEEN

Glenn had felt a little like a superspy since leaving the hospital last night. He snatched a cocktail glass by the stem from the overhead rack, placed it on the bar with great flare and said, "Vesper Martini. Gin, vodka and Lillet Blanc. And here's the important part…" Glenn paused for dramatic effect. In his best Sean Connery he said, "Shaken, not stirred." He then went through the motions of making a pretend Vesper Martini. Completing the reenactment, he danced around the room with an empty cocktail shaker whistling his favorite James Bond theme song: "Nobody Does it Better" from *The Spy Who Loved Me*. Glenda rolled her eyes. Last night he kept referring to her as "Moneypenny".

Glenn had hatched his plan late last night while in bed. Glenda wasn't thrilled, to say the least. In fact the only way she would agree to the plan was if she could be there by his side. (Initially Glenn had told her "absolutely not" but she convinced him by threatening to call the police chief and "roll over" on all involved.) They had opened No Egrets together and polished, prepared and stocked it so they could be gone most of the afternoon. Glenda called Joshua McCarthy (still refusing to call him "Ism") asking if he would be in charge of the bar while they were gone. Not surprisingly he was on the beach. The last part of his response had surprised her though. "Nice and steasy, Mrs. G. From the sandbar to the birdbar faster than you can turn and burn. Yo wait…" After a long pause he added in a deeper voice, "Our sandy shores have just been infiltrated." She figured the kooks, co-kooks, Barneys and spongers had invaded again.

Being Friday, Glenn mixed a large batch of Long Island Iced Tea for Matilda, hoping to take some of the burden off Ism for the afternoon. All Ism had to do was keep filling her glass and count how many times he did it. *With his flip flops, the kid can go to his toes to count if Tilly surpasses ten*, Glenn mused. Strangely, everything seemed a little funny and upbeat this morning.

Glenn had to admit his covert plan both excited and scared him, giving him the same feeling he used to experience when walking in the operating room before a challenging case. The first part of the plan involved the Oak Island Police Department. He had talked with Hands early this morning and Hands promised to be at No Egrets at ten-thirty. It was ten o'clock now.

While placing the Long Island Iced Tea batch in the refrigerator Glenn's gaze fell on Bobby's empty barstool. The memories of last night's hospital visit were still fresh and Glenn's heart swelled—his friend was awake! Bobby's nurse Griselda had filled Glenn in on the details before allowing him to visit. Somehow Bobby had convinced his nurse to keep his awakening a secret and Griselda had warned Glenn to be nonchalant about the visit and look very, very sad. As he walked toward Bobby's room, Glenn tried to think about something sad, but he had to lower his head and stroke his face to hide a huge grin. Griselda saw and shot him a disapproving look but said nothing. Remembering how Griselda had whipped Mark Manganese's ass, Glenn's grin immediately disappeared.

Griselda left her seat at the nurses' station to lead Glenn into Bobby's room. Without saying a word, she closed the curtain across the glass walls of the room and swiftly walked out the door. Glenn was left alone with her patient as he snored softly. Excited friend Glenn wanted to poke Bobby and wake him up. but clinician Glenn won out and he turned to head toward the bedside chair.

"Hey, Doc."

One corner of Bobby's mouth curled into a smile. Trembling with relief, Glenn smiled back, tears blurring his vision.

"Bobby, your big ole head, with eyes open, is simply the most beautiful sight I've seen in many moons."

"Aw shucks."

"And you sound a little like Rod Stewart, too," Glenn said, joking about the raspy nature of Bobby's voice.

"But can't—move like—Jagger yet," was the one-liner tossed back at Glenn.

Griselda popped her head into the doorway. "Everything okay in here?" she whispered. Bobby's right hand slowly rose with thumb up. The nurse slid out of sight.

"Zelly—wonderful," Bobby said, pointing to the door.

A worried look crossed Bobby's face. "Karen?"

"Her sister is with her. Glenda has been over a couple of times. She's still sick but doing okay."

Bobby closed his eyes and gave a huge sigh.

When he opened his eyes Bobby still looked concerned. "The Five plus One?"

Glenn nodded. "Feeding the critters on the same schedule I did when you were out of town."

Another sigh. Bobby put his hand to his chest and mouthed, *thank you.* "Turts hardy. Janet—petite and delicate."

Petite and delicate were not words Glenn would have used to describe the Chilean rose haired tarantula that had chased him around Bobby's house. He hadn't done much to take care of the spider now that it was back in its habitat. (Just in case he had Glenda google it on her phone and sometimes tarantulas don't eat for several months, especially when they are preparing to molt.)

"Trust me. Jermaine, Tito, Randy, Marlon and Michael are as wild as ever, splashing water all over the walls and floor. Janet, she doesn't shake her booty much, just sits there like a pet rock most of the time."

"Real friend." Bobby glanced nervously toward the open door and then motioned Glenn to come closer. Glenn bent his ear toward Bobby's mouth. "You and nurse—Zelly. Know I'm awake. Nobody. Nobody else." Bobby paused, regaining enough strength that the last words came out a lot louder. "Will—try to kill—me again."

Glenn let the words linger in the air. How in the world could Bobby know something like that? He started to dismiss his friend's paranoia but stopped. Two attempts had been made on Bobby's life and the saying "third time's the charm" popped into his head.

Who would want to kill Bobby? Then Glenn thought about the two words Griselda had mentioned. "Who? Big otter?" he asked Bobby.

Bobby gave him a funny look.

"That's what Griselda told me you said when you woke up briefly last time."

Bobby moved his head side to side ever so slightly with a look of understanding. "Not ot-ter. Otto. OT-TO. Big guy."

"Who's Otto?"

Bobby tried to move in the bed and grimaced. "All in good time. Going to have to—pace myself. Bring notebook? Zelly tell you?"

Glenn pulled a small stenographer's notebook out of his back pocket and a pen out of his front pocket. Bobby started talking and Glenn wrote down every word, pausing only occasionally to look up at Bobby incredulously. The story was a whopper, more Hollywood than Oak Island, and the only time Glenn interjected a comment was to tell Bobby about the body pulled out of the Intracoastal Waterway. When Bobby finished, he collapsed back on the bed and fell immediately asleep. He wouldn't have trouble convincing anybody he was still comatose, at least for a few hours.

On his way to the hospital, Otto had veered off for his first trip to Oak Island. He had parked two blocks from Bobby's house and walked back to it. It looked like there was nobody home from the front; Otto approached the back from a wooded lot two houses down. He peered in the back door and windows. When he was convinced there was nobody home, he retraced his steps back to his car.

Otto was thinking, stroking the scar on his face, as he drove. He saw a sign for beach access and turned. When he walked across the path through the dune in his black shirt and black pants even the shorebirds turned to look. Otto ignored the stares. Gazing out over the Atlantic he began absentmindedly tracing the scar down his cheek. He had hoped to find someone close to Bobby Portis at his house, someone to use as leverage. There was nothing like the threat of a missing loved one to make someone clam up. Now he would have to focus all his attention on the hospital security guard.

The vast ocean and the horizon brought on memories of his grandparents in the Russian Empire. They had been survivors. He thought of his friend and mentor Waldo Salt, blacklisted for his association with the Communist party. Also a survivor. His mind returned to the present and his boss. Otto knew the only chance for Dr. Roshberg's survival rested on his shoulders. Reflexively his hand found his pocket and his fingers slid through the holes in the kactet. As he pulled the brass knuckles out of his pocket, Otto's Communist Party USA card fell to the sand. Otto stared at the hammer and sickle symbol engraved at the base of the kactet and realized there was only one thing left for him to do.

As Otto turned to leave, he noticed two things: he had dropped his Communist Party USA card in the sand and a surfer punk on his cell phone was staring at him wide-eyed, mouth agape.

Glenn looked down the bar at Matilda. She still had half a drink, so she was good for fifteen minutes, maybe. Pinhead Paul, in the other direction, was sprawled out on the floor behind the Wurlitzer wielding his fish filleting knife. He was determined to fix the jukebox even though it hadn't played in days. Glenn shuddered; Bobby was the one with the magic Wurlitzer touch and he prayed Pinhead Paul did not do any permanent damage.

The front door opened and Glenn turned quickly, expecting Hands. Instead Richard strode in with an entrance on the lower end of his "attention-seeking, limelight-stealing" spectrum. The door didn't come close to banging the opposite wall. His outfit today was red, blue and reflective and looked otherworldly. Glenn found that a little amusing as he often wondered if Richard came from another planet.

"Did you get the part in the Welcome Back Kotter remake?" Glenn asked.

Richard plopped down on a barstool and huffed. "No, I auditioned for the Vinnie Barbarino character, but they said I wasn't right for the part. And for future reference it's reboot. *Reboot.* Not a remake."

Glenn didn't say anything. Richard was short and stout and looked nothing like John Travolta, not even remotely.

"They said I could audition for the part of the old, school vice-principal, Mr. Woodman," Richard continued. "I just turned and walked away. One has to have principles." He thought about what he said. "Not school principals, you know what I mean, scruples."

Glenn pulled a Pabst Blue Ribbon and placed it on the bar. "I'm sorry Richard."

Richard was distracted, gazing into the bar mirror. "What? Nothing to be sorry about. Richard Crabtree's motto is never, ever give up." He looked into the mirror again, holding up his arms to see his outfit. "That and never, ever wear a boring ensemble."

Glenn smiled and gave Richard a wink. "Well my friend, you succeed on both accounts."

Richard took a drink of his PBR. "Thank you, good physician and barkeep."

"Anything on the horizon at Screen Gems?" Glenn asked.

Richard ran his hands slowly down his outfit like a model. "Why yes. Next week—auditions for a science fiction film. Rumor has it it's a Tim Burton."

"Wow! That's pretty big for Wilmington. What's the movie?"

"*Mars Needs Beer.*"

Glenn had just enough time to think the rumor about the director was indeed a rumor and then to think maybe, just maybe, it was a crazy enough movie title for Tim Burton to be involved with, when the front door opened again.

Hands walked in, dressed in full uniform. Glenn looked to Glenda and nodded. She made her way behind the bar while Glenn walked Hands to a far table.

"What's this about?" Hands asked, sitting down.

Glenn pulled the folded, typed sheets of paper from his pocket. "Bobby." Last night Glenda had deciphered his handwriting (he had helped a little) and typed it into a Word file.

"Bobby!" Hands exclaimed too loudly.

Glenn put a finger to his lips.

"I'm sorry," Hands said. "Is he awake?"

"Yes."

"And why are we being quiet about it?"

Glenn looked around the bar. Matilda, Richard and the prostrate Pinhead Paul did not seem to be threats. "Bobby's life is still in danger."

Hands started reading the printed pages, stopping every once in a while for questions or exclamations.

"Dr. Julius Roshberg?"

"He's an oncologist in Shallotte."

"And this guy Otto?"

"He works for Dr. Roshberg. He's very large, kind of a bodyguard."

"Why in the hell would a doctor need a bodyguard?"

That was a question Glenn could not answer, but he had his suspicions.

When Hands got to the part about Bobby being assaulted by Otto, locked in a trunk and then bludgeoned with something metal in the back of the head on the banks of the Intracoastal Waterway, he looked up quickly. "Shit!"

Glenn nodded.

"Just like our drowning vic we pulled out of the water that day!"

Glenn nodded again. "Bobby knew him. They had talked about Dr. Roshberg."

Hands eyes were huge. He began reading the rest of the pages. When he finished, he looked a little dazed.

Glenn leaned forward. "Bobby wants to keep the fact he's awake a secret. He's still in danger."

"Who knows?" Hands asked.

"His nurse and me. Maybe some security guards at this point, I don't know."

Hands made a clucking noise with his tongue and teeth while thinking. The pieces were beginning to fall together and it wasn't going to take much investigation to link this fellow Otto to all of it.

"In your professional opinion Doc, can Bobby be moved out of the ICU?"

"It would be up to his physician, but he's off the vent so I'd say he could be moved soon."

"We'll have to work with the County guys, but maybe we can get him in a private room and provide protection, at least between us and the security guards."

Glenn had been holding his breath and let it out slowly. "That would be great, Hands. I would feel a lot better about the situation."

Hands started to rise. He had a lot to go over with the chief and then they would have to have the same conversation with Brunswick County. "Before I go, let me ask you Glenn. This guy Otto's not going to be hard to tie to the crimes, but what about the doctor? What was his name, Roshman?"

"Roshberg." Glenn thought about the question for a minute. "Apart from some highly unethical practices I've heard about from Bobby and others, I just don't know."

Hands stood up, placed the typed sheets into his pocket, shook Glenn's hand, and left.

Glenn's mind was still on Dr. Roshberg. "I just don't know," he repeated softly. "But I plan to find out."

Glenn joined Glenda behind the bar. "How'd it go?" Glenda asked.

"Good. He's going to talk with his chief and then they'll talk with the

Brunswick County office. I think Otto's in for a heap of trouble."

They had forgotten about Richard. He leaned forward on the bar. "Who's Otto?"

Glenn and Glenda looked at each other, not sure how to respond. Finally Glenn said, "Police business."

"Uh-huh," Richard nodded. "It has to do with Bobby, doesn't it? Was it Otto who threw him in the Intracoastal Waterway?" He looked from Glenn to Glenda and back again. No response. Richard decided to try a little psychology to get them to talk.

"Never trust a man named Otto," he continued. "I was once in a play and the bad guy was named Otto. He took this big syringe of…some kind of poison, I don't remember what…and injected it into the necks of his victims." Richard stopped to gauge the reaction—until he thought about it himself. A shocked look of pain crossed his face. "*Oh my God!* Is that what happened to *Bobby*?" Richard nearly shrieked.

Glenda leaned toward Richard. "We're not sure," she whispered. "But for right now we have to keep it quiet. Bobby's life may depend on it."

Richard nodded solemnly. "Promise me this, though. If there is anything I can do for my friend, please let me know. I will do anything to help Bobby."

Glenda placed her hands on both of Richards. 'I promise."

The back door creaked. Glenn rubbed his hands together. That would be Ism arriving early to relieve them so the second part of the plan could be put in motion. It had taken some convincing but Glenda had agreed to both of them going to Dr. Roshberg's office. Glenn was going to pretend to be a patient worried about his recent blood work and the possibility of cancer. An elaborate patient history with family members on both sides who suffered from cancer (he wouldn't have to make that part up) should help him become a patient of Dr. Roshberg's. At least that was the plan.

Joshua McCarthy (aka Ism) stepped out in front of the bar. He wore a gray suit jacket with extra wide lapels and a rolled newspaper sticking out of one deep pocket. His matching trousers were a bit baggy (in an old-fashioned way) but cinched tight with a large black dress belt. His black dress shoes looked out of date, but they matched the skinny black tie that hung over his white dress shirt. The usual stringy surfer hair was slicked back with grease over the top of his head.

"Oh shit," Glenn said.

NINETEEN

Glenn couldn't take his eyes off Ism's dress shoes. His whole ensemble was disturbing but the shoes most of all. Glenn hadn't seen anything but sandals, boat shoes or those godawful, ripped-up Converse high tops on Ism's feet since the day he met him. And that included the only other "episode" Glenn had witnessed.

Glenda walked right up to him. "Joshua, you look very nice!"

Glenda either couldn't see her husband making frantic slashing motions across his throat or she ignored him. "Is that your father's suit?" she asked.

Joshua McCarthy looked at her solemnly, eyes blinking slowly like a turtle.

Matilda and Richard moved from the bar and took tables nearby, their eyes never leaving the strange sight of the surfer dude/live history mutation standing before them. Matilda even left her Long Island Iced Tea at the bar. Pinhead Paul backed away from the bar and kept backing up until his hands, searching behind him, found the front door. He turned and ran out.

Glenn squinted, studying Ism's face intently. His eyebrows looked darker and bushier. How was that possible? He now had distinct jowls, something a twenty-something should never develop. It even seemed his ears had elongated (or maybe Glenn had never noticed Ism's ears under the long, stringy hair). A serious five o'clock shadow darkened Ism's face where Glenn had never noticed whiskers before. The color of the rest of his face was pasty, like he hadn't seen the sun in years.

Glenda put her hand under Ism's elbow and led him to the bar. Glenn collapsed into a chair at Richard's table.

"She ought not do that," Richard said, solemn as a Sunday school teacher.

Glenn turned to Richard with the look of a dazed deer who narrowly escaped Highway 211 unscathed. He tried to speak but it was as if his mouth and brain had stopped communicating. Throwing his arms in the air in the general direction of Glenda and Ism, all Glenn could manage to say was, "Urh…urh. Urh!"

"Now Joshua," Glenda said, guiding him behind the bar. "We have already cleaned the bar, stocked all the shelves and coolers, and—"

Ism cut her off by grabbing a shot glass and whiskey bottle. He slopped a little on the bar pouring the shot. Glenda let go of his elbow and stepped back, her eyes wide. Ism downed the whiskey with a slight tilt of the head, slammed the glass down and poured another.

"Joshua Ian McCarthy!" Glenda screamed.

It was like the room became an audience track for an old sitcom ("Happy Days" perhaps). The crowd collectively expressed shock with a long, "Ooooh!"

"Urh...urh. Urh!" Glenn gesticulated wildly with both hands. And then he covered his eyes.

Ism emptied and immediately slammed down the shot glass a second time. He locked eyes with Glenda. His eyes held defiance; her eyes shot beams of rage.

Richard reached over and shook Glenn into action. "You better go get your wife." Richard's voice was low but urgent. "The show will begin soon and *he* doesn't share the stage with anyone."

"Urh," Glenn said, getting up from the table. Richard pushed him toward the action.

The front door flew open, slammed the opposite wall and actually gave the building a little shake. Royce and Big John led a procession of firefighters into the bar. They all grabbed seats at tables like the clock had just struck the beginning of happy hour.

Glenn looked back at Richard, finally finding some real words. "Oh my God!" He was still throwing his arms around wildly, this time in the direction of the firefighters. "How did *they* know?"

The tips of Richard's mouth curled into a small smile. "Pinhead Paul Revere. He went to spread the word." The next part he said in a high-pitched mocking of Pinhead Paul's voice, "The Red Scare is here! The Red Scare is here!"

When Glenn still hadn't moved toward the action, Richard hoisted his beer in his direction. "Sir, I salute your cowardice. This will be a show to tell your grandchildren about."

Ism lifted the bottle to pour a third shot. Glenda swept her arm across the bar, launching the tiny glass not only out of his reach but nearly out of the bar. Firemen sitting at third row tables ducked. (Fade in "Happy Days" audience track to a few screams, a few cheers, a few claps and one old woman shouting, "Hell yes! Fight! Fight!")

The old woman's voice was all it took to snap Glenn back to reality. As he headed toward the bar the "Happy Days" crowd turned on their host and began to "boo" loudly. Glenn turned to face the crowd in disbelief. Then he heard, "You candy-ass, mama's boy!" It was the old woman's voice. "Let 'em settle it on their own—in front of us!"

"Tilly!" Glenn bellowed. "Sit down! And shut up!"

"Happy Days" crowd: "Ooooh!"

Glenn walked up and gently put his arms around his wife. She was trembling and turned to him immediately. "Did you see what Joshua did? We can't let him drink while he's on duty."

"Yeah, apparently whiskey is the senator's drink of choice," Glenn explained, leading her back to Richard's table. Glenda walked slowly, glancing back over her shoulder at Joshua as he took another shot.

Something outside the window caught Glenn's eye. A school bus? The front door slammed open again, plaster dust flying. A handful of people rushed into the room, most wearing some type of uniform. Richard leaned over, identifying the new arrivals. "School bus driver. The kid that pushes the Italian Ice cart on the beach. That's the golf pro at the Oak Island course." He stopped when the last three came through the door. "Holy cow, Glenn! How very allegorical. There's Preston and Abigail who work at the grocery store and Lila, the hippie bees wax artist. Do you know what this means? You actually have the butcher, the baker and the candlestick maker in your bar!"

Big John leaned over toward the owner's table and patted his gut. "Hey Doc, can we get some pitchers over here before the show starts. Don't matter what kind. And some beer nuts if you don't mind."

When Big John turned back to the guys, Glenn covered his face with his hands, plopped his elbows on the table and groaned. There was no way he was going to carry out the second part of his plan now. It was all ruined.

Glenda turned her attention to her husband. "Glenn? Glenn, are you okay?" She was a bit calmer now, but her voice wasn't as tender as usual when her husband was upset.

He removed one hand from his face but not the other. "We can't leave the bar now to go to Dr. Roshberg's."

Glenda reached over and gave his shoulder a squeeze. "Why? Oh, you mean because our bar has now been *transported into the Twilight Zone!*" She took a deep breath, realizing she was the one who was going to have to hold it together. "It's okay honey. Look on the bright side—today's receipts will be off the charts. Wow, you're tense!"

A cheer went up from the "Happy Days" crowd. Ism had downed another shot.

Glenn lowered his other hand, looking Glenda in the eye. "I think…no, I *know*, it's very important to Bobby that we go to Roshberg's today."

Richard leaned over the table until he was inches away. Glenn had forgotten he was there. "I want to help Bobby," Richard said with a look of determination. "Let me go to Dr. Roshberg's office."

Glenn shook his head. "No. I'm not sure what's going on there. It may be dangerous. I can put myself in that situation, but I cannot do it to you."

Richard's eyes narrowed and he forcefully restated his position. "I—want—to—help—Bobby." There was a pause while Richard looked from Glenn to Glenda and then back to Glenn. "What were you going to do?"

Before Glenn could answer, firefighters at another table were yelling for beer. Glenda surveyed the rowdy bunch. "Are they allowed to drink when they're on duty? I don't think so." She looked beyond the firemen at the rest of the crowd. "Hey, a lot of these people are in the middle of their workday. I am *not* giving alcohol to a school bus driver!"

Glenn sighed, turning to Richard. "Glenda and I were going to Roshberg's with a made-up story to see how he would react. To see if he would do a blood test and start a long protocol of cancer tests." Glenn moved in closer to talk with Richard. Glenda was getting squeezed in the middle of the two. "Something fishy is going on there and I wanted to get in the office and see for myself how he handles things."

The words came spilling out of Richard's mouth. "Let me do it."

Glenn was silent, studying Richard's face. He'd never seen that look from the actor before.

"Let me do it, please," Richard repeated earnestly.

At the bar Ism slammed down his glass and poured another shot of whiskey. He was killing the whiskey bottle an ounce at a time.

"No," Glenn said decisively.

Glenda spoke up. "I'll go with him."

Richard smiled at Glenda who was still squeezed between the two men. He gave a little nudge to her shoulder which in turn about knocked Glenn from his chair.

"Richard needs someone to explain it to him," Glenda said. "I can do it on the way."

"What?" Glenn exploded. "No! That's crazy!"

"Why is it crazier than us going and you pretending to be a patient?" Glenda asked.

"You forget, dear sir, that I am an *actor*," Richard said, his voice returning to normal.

That's exactly what worries me, thought Glenn.

Before Glenn could respond with an emphatic "No!" the front door opened and Pinhead Paul led in the standing room only crowd. There were additional grumblings for beer.

"Okay, okay," Glenn said, groaning. "But I was going to stop at Dosher clinic first and get lab work so I would have a baseline."

"Not a problem," Richard said, smiling. "Just had my annual physical for the actor's union. Includes lab work."

"And...and you have a copy?" Glenn asked.

"Of course. In my file cabinet." Richard shrugged. "I am an informed medical consumer."

Glenn shook his head in disbelief. The grumblings from behind turned into shouts for beer. A heavy sigh escaped Glenn's body and his entire form sagged to the table. "Okay, okay. I give. But keep your wits about you. You must be careful. And you—" Glenn turned to his wife. "Are you sure you can do this? Sure you will be safe?"

"Hey!" Richard shouted. His voice then fell to a near whisper. "She'll be with me. Of course she'll be safe. Besides, I just saw her stand up to Senator Joe McCarthy and slap a shot glass across the room. Girl's got power."

"Dear husband," Glenda said, stroking Glenn's face. "I will be fine."

"Very well. But before you go, help me take care of this throng!"

In his gray suit with wide lapels, black tie and black dress shoes, Ism looked more out of place than a reality show star in a presidential election. He paced back and forth in front of the bar, pausing occasionally to glare at the audience, as if waiting for a cue to begin.

Glenn, Glenda and Richard had a beer brigade going: Glenn filled the pitchers, Glenda handed Glenn empty pitchers and delivered full ones to the bar where Richard delivered them to the tables. Finally, after delivering bottles of beer to the patrons standing along the back wall, it appeared everyone was satisfied.

Glenda started to lead Richard toward the back door but stopped to give Glenn a long kiss. Richard looked forlornly at Ism, still pacing back and forth.

"I do hate to miss a good performance," Richard said.

Glenn pointed to a front table. "See Royce. He's holding up his cell phone already. It will be recorded and probably on YouTube tomorrow."

His wife's last words before walking toward the back door: "You better take care of Joshua!"

Glenn watched them leave and turned back to the bar. Joshua? He looked close at the man pacing. He wasn't even sure Joshua was still in there.

The packed bar became deathly quiet. Glenn thought it eerie. Pinhead Paul broke the silence. "Hey Joe! I thought I saw a commie at Walmart yesterday!"

Ism (Joe?) stopped pacing, slammed his shot glass down on the bar and turned to face his constituents. He somehow looked hairier than a half hour earlier and he was sweating profusely.

Glenn quickly returned to his seat at the table. He was joined by Pinhead Paul.

"My friends," Ism boomed in a voice which made Glenn flinch. Ism normally spoke in a sort of high-pitched whine, but this voice was deep and authoritative.

"Communists have infiltrated the state department, the United States army," Ism continued. "Why is it so surprising that Communists have infiltrated the local grocery and retail store?"

Someone in the crowd started to answer but Ism cut them off. "But wait! Let's look at this a different way. What is Walmart? Is it really a local store employing local people?"

"No!" an eager firefighter shouted, wanting to get into the act.

"Correct!" Ism exclaimed, a creepy half-smile on his face. "They are a multinational conglomerate; in fact, the largest retailer in the world. What better place to harbor…" Ism paused and put a hand to his ear.

"Communists!" the crowd roared.

Ism nodded, the creepy smile increasing, causing his eye on that side to twitch. Glenn heard someone on the back wall say, "Oh my God. My niece works at the Southport Walmart."

Glenn tried to remember what he had learned in school about Senator Joe McCarthy. At first all that came to mind was Republican from Wisconsin. Then he recalled something his professor had said, calling McCarthy's investigations an American version of the 16th century Spanish Inquisition.

"Friends and neighbors, I have seen it with my own eyes on this very day," Ism said, pulling out the rolled newspaper from a deep pocket in his baggy pants. "Communists have landed on the shores of Oak Island!" He whapped the rolled newspaper on the bar for added emphasis.

The crowd gasped and shifted uncomfortably in their seats. They looked around at each other, questioning looks on their faces. *Communists on our shore? On Oak Island?*

"You won't find it reported here," Ism said, unfolding the newspaper. "Because *your* government doesn't want *you to know*."

A smattering of boos followed this revelation.

"I have been accused by my colleagues," Ism continued. "Of smear tactics, distortion and misrepresentation. And there is nothing I despise more than…" Ism put a hand to his ear again.

"Communists!" half the crowd shouted again.

"Well, yes. Of course Communists," Ism muttered. "And," he said louder. "Self-doubting liberals! I truly despise self-doubting liberals."

The crowd roared. Ism strode toward them quickly, stopping in front of Matilda. "Are you a self-doubting liberal, ma'am?" He pointed at her with a large finger (Glenn was sure he saw hair on the large knuckle).

"No!" Matilda shouted. "I'm not a self-doubting liberal. I'm usually that Rosenberg bitch."

Ism's eyes grew wide. "Wherever there is a large group of people assembled, you can be sure there are Communists. Look around you; look at the person next to you." Glenn was shocked to see members of the crowd giving sidelong glances to the person on either side of them. Royce and Big John were actually eyeing each other suspiciously.

Ism put both hands on the table and leaned over Matilda. "So you admit to being the notorious Communist spy Ethel Rosenberg. Well, Mrs. Rosenberg, where is your husband?" Several hands shot up in the air behind them. "Is he passing secrets about the atomic bomb to the Soviets?"

Ism smashed his hand down on Matilda's table with a thud. "Where is your husband?" More hands in the crowd shot up; some of them made "ooh-ooh" sounds.

Pinhead Paul leaned over to Glenn. "Last time I was Julius Rosenberg."

"There you are!" Ism screamed, pointing to a firefighter at Royce and Big John's table. The man pumped his fist and said, "Yes!" The others at the table clinked their glasses and took celebratory drinks.

"Got to keep this moving," Pinhead Paul whispered to Glenn. "Hey Joe!" he yelled. "Isn't that Dwight D. Eisenhower over there in the corner? Didn't he say that Joe McCarthy was a pimple on the face of progress?"

Ism's countenance darkened. Glenn noticed Ism's hands shaking as he closed his eyes, trying to regain his composure. When he opened his eyes, he smiled that creepy half-smile again. "Ike is my president and I will not say anything bad about my president (at least not in a crowd). Besides..." Ism looked to the man sitting beside Matilda. "Are you a Republican, good sir?" The man nodded. "Good!" Ism continued. "And Ike is a Republican and...Republicans rock!"

The crowd went wild as Ism gave the man a fist bump.

Glenn looked at Pinhead Paul, shaking his head slightly. "I don't think Senator Joe McCarthy ever said 'Republicans rock' or gave anyone a fist bump on the senate floor."

Pinhead Paul shrugged. "Sometimes the real Ism struggles to the surface. But the next part involves Richard Nixon. He was in the Senate with McCarthy and they were friends at first. Then, when he became Eisenhower's Vice President, he set out to destroy McCarthy."

Glenn looked at Pinhead Paul with amazement. "How do you know so much?"

"I catch all the shows. You can't help but learn a little history along the way."

Ism was pacing again. He stopped in front of Matilda's table and eyed the man sitting beside Dwight D. Eisenhower (aka a normal Oak Island citizen). "You!" Ism screamed, spittle flying. "You are that prick, Nixon!"

Glenn leaned over to Pinhead Paul. "I guess McCarthy wasn't all bad."

The man designated as Nixon stood and took a bow to the cheering of the crowd. There was something familiar about him; Glenn leaned forward, trying to get a better look. All of a sudden, he recognized him.

Glenn turned to Pinhead Paul. "Oh my gosh! That's Kenny. He shaved his beard!"

"You dare to censure me!" Ism screamed, pointing a big hairy knuckle at "that prick Nixon". "And yet Communist subversion in *your* government is at an all-time high!"

The crowd cheered and drank. The one-man anti-Communist crusader continued his tirade.

TWENTY

"Hey wait," Richard called to Glenda, who was quick on her feet after exiting the car. She was already standing in the middle of the overflow parking lot behind Dr. Roshberg's office. Richard was struggling with his seat belt as well as some of the finer details of his role. As he pulled himself free of the car and stepped out, he could smell the new asphalt, but it was too late. He looked down.

"Dear God, woman! What have you done to me?" Richard gestured toward his feet and his rather plain looking, light suede shoes. "These are Tod's!" he exclaimed in his measured actor voice.

Glenda's face was blank until Richard's statement registered. "You are wearing Tod's!" she cried, moving in close to him. "I brought you on an undercover, blend-in-like-normal-people operation, where I had to stand up to my husband for you...and you are wearing *Tod's*!"

Richard was perplexed. "No, you dumped me off in the middle of a newly asphalted, backwater parking lot wearing *my new Tod's*!"

Standing nose to nose, the tense situation passed after a few beats as each decided the other was being ridiculous and it was time to move on.

Glenda looked at the shoes again. They look unscathed. "Glenn will pay for any damage. Let's go!" she said, giving the marching orders as she turned toward the office.

"You stop right there, missy!" Richard demanded.

Had she heard him right? Glenda stopped and turned to face Richard. He hadn't moved.

"I need some details. Details I cannot fudge. I have listened intently to all the reasons you and Glenn are suspicious of this Dr. Roshberg." Richard motioned toward the medical building. "I understand my character's motivation in this clandestine performance. But what is the backstory? Who am I? What is our relationship? Are we lovers? Am I your big, strapping husband?"

"Well..." Glenda said. She had calmed down and saw Richard had a point. They couldn't debate any background issues when they were inside the office.

"What?"

Glenda was watching Richard sashay toward her. "Don't take this the wrong way but Glenn doesn't walk like that."

"Oh, I see. You don't think I can play the macho part. Other directors have made the same mistake. Feast your eyes on this!"

Richard hitched up his pants, swiftly gave his crotch an adjustment and lumbered off. He turned back to her. "How's that?" he asked in a deep voice.

Glenda laughed. "Pretty good there, pardner. But Glenn walks more like this." She pulled in her butt cheeks and walked erect, trying to take long strides without shaking her hips.

"Hmm..." Richard commented. "Looks like the good surgeon needs a stick-ectomy."

"Sometimes." Glenda chuckled. "I tell you what, you are my brother."

"Oooh!" Richard exclaimed. "I've never had a sister. Can we tell juicy secrets to each other?"

"My crazy, creative brother."

He offered his arm to escort her through the parking lot. "Don't forget insanely talented."

"With great taste in shoes," she added, glancing down at his feet.

"Don't you know it!"

Richard tapped on the mirrored window. After a couple of minutes, the window slid open—about two inches.

"Can I help you?" asked a condescending, nasally voice.

"I'm sorry Miss—" Richard glanced first at her purple hair then at her nametag. "Fish...nutt. Fishnutt? Of the Charleston Fishnutt's I presume." The window opened fully.

Glenda, standing by his side, was shocked by Richard's voice. Not only did he not sound like himself, he didn't sound like any voice she had ever heard him use at No Egrets. She recited a prayer in her head, swallowed hard and refocused on the "scene".

"Of the whan?" the receptionist answered as she chomped down on a gob of gum in her mouth.

"Never mind, never mind. Miss Fishnutt, I..." Richard suddenly turned with a pleading look to Glenda. He leaned toward his "sister" and whispered in her ear, "Name? What name do I use?"

Glenda pushed to the window. "My brother, Richard, does not have an appointment."

"I don't have an appointment, but I was hoping you could help me." Richard smiled as he finished his line.

"Sorry," Miss Fishnutt said. "We are full today." She gave a slight point with a long pink fingernail toward the packed waiting room.

Richard kept his gaze focused on the receptionist. "My you keep it warm in here," he said with a slight chuckle. He started to remove his linen jacket. "I realize you are busy. Is it acceptable if I sit down for a few minutes? I...I seem to be feeling a bit overheated."

"No, it is not acceptable! So put your coat back on and head out the door," Fishnutt responded. "We are a doctor's office filled with patients. We don't need you in here spreading your beriberi or whatever you got."

"Just...for...a moment," Richard struggled to say. He clutched at his chest. He was wide-eyed and taking short, rapid breaths. He started to quiver and wobble in place.

"Richard? Richard!" Glenda screamed. She had to admit, he was really good.

Glenda threw her arms around Richard and he let his knees buckle for effect. Sensing another waiting room scene was about to unfold, Miss Fishnutt went for the window handle. Glenda was prepared and with one arm still around Richard, she jammed her purse in the opening, blocking the window. The receptionist immediately noticed the markings of Dooney and Burke and stopped trying to slam the window into it.

"My brother needs help!" Glenda cried. "He's having a panic attack!"

"He's not one of ours. Not our patient," said Fishnutt, fumbling for words, on the verge of her own panic attack. "We can't help him."

"You're kidding me!" Glenda yelled. Richard's breathing became rapid-fire. His face was deathly white. "Nurse!" Glenda screamed through the blocked window.

A short, stocky woman in cranberry scrubs ran down the hallway and out the door into the waiting room. Richard, with perfect timing, rolled his eyes up in his head and collapsed into the nurse's strong arms.

"Bring me a wheelchair!" the nurse yelled at Fishnutt. Fishnutt had no choice but to obey.

The husky woman wheeled Richard through the door and into the inner hallway with little or no special care. Glenda hurried through the door before she could be stopped, staying close behind. The sprint down the hallway reminded Glenda of a bull busting through a chute at the rodeo. Richard's wheelchair was just inches from scraping both walls of the hallway. Richard's head bobbled. His feet were not on the footrests and he was not keeping his arms and head inside the chair area at all times. The wheelchair nearly toppled when the nurse cut the tight corner into Exam Room 2.

The nurse locked the wheels and single-handedly lifted Richard to his feet. She took him to the only chair in the small exam room, placed him on the seat and without a second thought roughly pushed his head down between his knees.

"Keep your head down and take deep breaths," she instructed in a husky voice.

"Oh thank you, Nurse—" Glenda took a page out of Richard's playbook, glancing at the nametag. "Carole. I don't know what we would've done without your help. My brother had a panic attack. He always hyperventilates whenever it happens."

Miss Fishnutt stuck her head in the door. "He's not our patient," she proclaimed, disappearing quickly and shutting the door.

Glenda put on a sad face and dropped her head. "Now you know why he had a panic attack," she said, adding a couple sniffs at the end.

Richard started to raise his head, but Nurse Carole gently pushed it back. "Keep your head down, deep breaths."

Richard started to protest but then noticed his shoes (his head being only inches from them). *That bitch caused me to scuff my Tod's!*

Nurse Carole moved around Richard and took Glenda's hand. "Tell me what the problem is, maybe I can help."

Richard grunted and raised his head. Glenda stepped to him, took his head in her hands and whispered in his ear, "I got this, dear brother." She pushed his head back down and said loudly, "Now Richard. You need to do like Nurse Carole says. After all, she is a trained professional.

"Well nurse—" Glenda started.

"Please, call me Carole."

"Carole, I talked Richard into coming to Dr. Roshberg's office because I've heard such good things about him in the community. And Richard is starting to have some of the same symptoms as Chadwick, our older brother. God rest his soul."

Nurse Carole, with her back to Richard, was staring at Glenda so intently she did not notice Richard start to raise his head again or Glenda reach one hand behind her back and shove it down roughly.

"We didn't have an appointment." Glenda squeezed her eyes shut as tears began rolling down her cheeks. "But I'm just so worried about my brother. We just hoped...I just hoped...he could at least get lab work. He hasn't been to a doctor in so long. He's as stubborn as a mule and it took all the persuasion I had to talk him into coming here today. He just gets so upset. He's a mess, really."

Richard raised his head a little and glared at Glenda behind the nurse's back.

Glenda put her hands to her face, sobbing and shaking. Nurse Carole took her by the arm and led her to the small exam table.

"Sit here," she said softly to Glenda. She gestured sharply toward Richard. "*He* needs to keep his head down. I'll see what I can do. You wait right here." Nurse Carole gave Glenda's arm one last squeeze and left the room.

Richard's head shot up. "Scene stealer!" he hissed.

"Shhh," Glenda whispered. "It was your theatrics that got us back this far. I took over because I think the nurse likes me."

"You think? From my vantage point I saw her stealing at least a dozen looks at your derriere."

Glenda looked back over her left shoulder. Her butt did look good in her Gucci jeans.

"Besides," Glenda said. "The next big scene will be yours if we get to meet Dr. Roshberg."

Ism had the crowd at No Egrets worked into an anti-Communist frenzy; they were cheering and drinking to every accusation, obfuscation and untruth.

Pinhead Paul stood, deciding it was time to be part of the show. Before standing, he explained to Glenn he was going to be Ralph Flanders, a Republican Senator from Vermont who turned on McCarthy and gave a nasty speech against him in the Senate Chamber.

"Senator McCarthy," Pinhead Paul called. "Will you yield the floor to Senator Flanders?"

Ism glared at Pinhead Paul and gave a slight nod.

Pinhead Paul launched into an ugly, full-scale attack on Joe McCarthy and McCarthyism, causing the crowd to gasp and shift in their seats uncomfortably. The climax came when Senator Flanders/Pinhead Paul compared McCarthy to Hitler and Dennis the Menace and accused him of homosexuality and, perhaps worst of all, sowing dissension across the country.

Ism appeared calm as he walked over to Pinhead Paul and immediately bitch-slapped him. The crowd roared. If only Senator Joseph McCarthy had had the pleasure of bitch-slapping Senator Ralph Flanders back in the day.

With the crowd back on his side, Ism promised each and every one (with the exception of Matilda Rosenberg, Pinhead Flanders, Ike and Tricky Kenny Dick) a certificate designating them a card-carrying anti-Communist.

The last thing Ism roared, before collapsing into a heap on the floor was, "Remember, there are evil, evil men among you!"

Dr. Julius Roshberg entered Exam Room 2 without knocking, without fanfare, without a smile. He wore an air of arrogance like others wear cologne. His behavior made it very clear he was more than just a little dismayed to be in this room with these people. A glitch somewhere, somehow had allowed Richard and Glenda to clear all the barriers designed to keep just anyone from seeing the Great and Powerful Roshberg.

Glenda and Richard thought simultaneously, *He's shorter than I thought he would be.* The doctor stood over Richard, looking down on him.

"Why do you think you have cancer?" Dr. Roshberg barked at Richard.

No hello, how are you, or introduction, Glenda noted. And the doctor didn't even acknowledge her presence in the room.

Richard hesitated. Still bent over in the chair, he slowly straightened to an upright sitting position. The look on his face was difficult to decode; he was either about to laugh, cry, sneeze or pass out from having his head between his knees too long. He did not speak. He seemed to be mesmerized by Roshberg.

"I am a *very* busy doctor." Roshberg seemed to be holding back rage, but just barely. "People from around the world are calling me on my telephones…all numbers, work and private. They seek my counsel. I do not have time to stand here and pull words from your mouth. I cannot coddle or baby you." Roshberg took a deep breath and let it out slowly; unfortunately, it did not empty his body of hatefulness. "So again, why do you think you have cancer?"

"My brother—" Glenda started.

"Shut up!" Roshberg shouted without looking at Glenda. "You are not the patient! You have no right to speak! You have no right to be in this room!"

Roshberg had thrown down the gauntlet! A response started to form down deep within Glenda to his full-blown, head-on verbal assault. From the corner of his eye, Richard could see her nostrils flaring and the seething anger building in her eyes; there was a disturbance in the atmosphere as Hurricane Glenda began to form.

Sensing the need to distract Glenda, Richard found his voice. "You are my only hope for life, Dr. Roshberg!" He followed with a huge sob. "People say you are a pure and true man of medicine. You must save me!" He reached for Roshberg's hand.

Roshberg started to brush Richard's hand away but paused to look down again at the man in the chair. A transformation seemed to occur and Glenda watched it unfold with wide eyes. Roshberg extended his right arm. Richard grabbed the sleeve of the doctor's white coat, pulled the doctor to him and kissed his hand. Roshberg's mouth bloomed into a wide, approving smile.

Glenda couldn't be quite sure when her jaw dropped or how long her mouth remained open. Her mouth did dry out and she began to scrounge in her purse for her emergency bottle of water.

The actor immediately segued into the rest of his "big scene" with the soliloquy about fictitious older brother Chadwick, Hodgkin's lymphoma and fatigue, flaccidity and all the other symptoms that had supposedly been plaguing him. Glenda watched Richard's performance in awe. He had memorized it in the car and was regurgitating it in such a way that even she believed his story. He paused, his voice quivering, as he looked at the doctor with tears in his eyes.

The doctor had only stopped him once with a question. "Yes, doctor.

The best. I have full coverage," Richard answered truthfully.

Nurse Carole entered the room and the doctor gestured to her. "Nurse, please get this patient into the computer system and take his blood." Before Richard could spit out the effusive thanks that followed, Dr. Roshberg was out the door.

Glenda thought it strange they weren't led back to the waiting room to fill out the four-page form. Nurse Carole brought it directly to them in the exam room.

"Fill it out quickly and I'll be back to take your blood," the nurse instructed.

Richard glanced at the first page of the form after the nurse left. "We didn't think about this part," he said. "If I have to give my insurance card, I'm going to have to use my full name and address."

Glenda grimaced. They sure hadn't thought it through. "I'm sorry Richard. If you want to leave now, I'll support you."

"No way! If I can help Bobby even a little, then it's worth it. Besides, I pay for the insurance and hardly ever use it. My family has always been healthy as horses."

Glenda cocked her head, pursed her lips and waggled her finger at Richard. Richard looked down at the "Family History" section of the form. "Oh yeah, except for poor brother Chadwick."

Richard filled out the form truthfully, except he put down his fake symptoms and riddled the family history with cancer.

Ten minutes later Nurse Carole reentered the room. She had lab tubes, a butterfly needle and a tourniquet.

"All done?" the nurse asked, grabbing the clipboard from his hands and not waiting for an answer.

Nurse Carole quickly applied the tourniquet and began tapping Richard's forearm. When she found a good vein, she slipped the needle in and filled up four tubes.

"That's it," the nurse said. "We'll be in touch. Is that a good number to reach you during the day?"

Richard nodded. Nurse Carole gave Glenda a quick smile and a wink. "I've got to run. We've got chemo patients stacked four deep today. If you could get out of here quick it would be great."

Richard and Glenda just looked at each other as the nurse slammed the door.

"I don't know much about healthcare," Richard said. "But this whole episode has left me with a weird vibe."

Glenda just shook her head. There were so many things wrong she didn't know if she could list them all. Her only comment: "She didn't even wear gloves to take your blood."

TWENTY-ONE

Glenn had to admit he was a little jazzed. Not only did he own a majestic piece of medical history, he had made a shrewd deal to get it. As soon as he could find an electrical outlet...

"Hold on," Glenda called to him as he navigated through cardboard boxes of old clothes beneath an old kitchen table. "I'm going to pass you the nozzle of the sweeper. You can clean while you're down there."

Was she serious? "Are you serious? It's tighter than a coal mine down here!" He felt the crevice attachment to the sweeper make an indecent proposal to his rear end (crevice attachment indeed). "Very funny!" He pulled it under the table with him and adjusted his position to sweep. And then it occurred to him. "Where do you have the sweeper plugged in? You said the outlet was—" The last part was drowned out as the old Kirby fired up. Glenn had no choice but to suck up the old spider webs and lint.

He backed out from the chaos that was laundry room storage, where old socks and his band t-shirts from college got sucked into a black hole. Glenda greeted him like he was home on leave. She threw her arms around his neck and planted a big, wet kiss on his lips. She moved in closer, knocking him back against the boxes.

"You think this is going to make up for that?" Glenn asked, pulling a cobweb out of his hair.

"Yes." And she started to shimmy against him. She was right—it was making up for it. But first he wanted to plug in the old X-ray Film Viewer.

"Outlet?" he asked with a bit of mock indignation. Glenda pointed to a collection of wall outlets about waist high near the ironing board. He moved across the room and plugged in the viewer. This was a big moment for Glenn, although no one else would understand. It was an X-ray Film Viewer; a big light box on the wall. But he thought owning it was so cool. He flipped the switch and the electrical buzzing of circuits that hadn't been zapped in years started filling the room. Glenn backed up to admire the splendid illuminated sight.

Where Glenn saw beauty, Glenda saw junk (on her laundry room wall of all places). When questioned by her husband, she admitted it was a quaint piece of medical history now that x-rays had gone digital and there was no need for x-ray film or X-ray Film Viewers anymore. But did it have to be in her house? And if it did have to be in her house, couldn't it be in the attic with Glenn's high school track trophies and ribbons, comic books, and vinyl classic rock albums piled on top of it?

Glenda noticed another addition to the laundry room wall. A picture had been placed near the viewer. Honestly, she had never considered hanging pictures in her laundry room and wondered what print Glenn had chosen—portrait, abstract, landscape? As she got closer, she recognized it. The same one hung beneath Swordy at No Egrets. Where did he find another framed Hippocratic Oath print on Oak Island?

It was late; Glenn had spent most of the day in the No Egrets' office. Glenda was glad to give him his space since the bar had not been crowded and he seemed preoccupied. There were just a few regulars there throughout the day and evening as there seemed to be quite a letdown after Ism's performance the day before. Pinhead Paul had explained to Glenda that the ones who missed it were depressed for obvious reasons and the ones that were there had the "post anti-Communist blues" (plus hellacious hangovers).

In the office, Glenn looked like some kind of miser, hunched over the desk with only the cheap desk lamp for light. He had closed the blind on the one small window. Occasionally she heard sounds coming from the room which warranted investigation: sighs, groans, gasps. The few times Glenda had walked into the office she had noticed her husband with his x-ray film. He had painstakingly labeled each film sleeve with a Sharpie and used a special pen to write on the x-ray film.

Thank goodness the maintenance guy at the hospital in West Virginia had thrown in cases of used x-ray film when he had unloaded the X-ray Film Viewer on Glenn. Whatever would they do with an X-ray Film Viewer if they didn't have x-ray film to go with it?

Glenn noticed his wife looking at the X-ray Film Viewer on her laundry room wall and shaking her head disgustedly.

"I told you I think better when it's all displayed and illuminated at eye level. Like back in the good ole days when all we had were x-rays. We had to study several different angles until we finally found the problem and knew where to operate."

"Yes dear. Show me what you've been working on all day," she added quickly, hoping to cut off the second part of the "good ole days" speech before it started. She knew it word for word.

The first sleeve on top of the pile was labeled "Karen" in black Sharpie. Glenda was surprised when Glenn pulled the black x-ray film out of the sleeve—a picture of a healthy Karen, smiling broadly, was taped in the right-hand corner.

"Where did you…" And then she remembered him asking her to log on to her Facebook page when she was in the office early that morning.

"You creeper," she said without much conviction. As Glenn placed the black x-ray film on the X-ray Film Viewer the words he had written with the special pen came to life in bold letters. Glenda made note that Glenn had printed carefully, without a hint of chicken scratch.

Beside Karen's picture Glenn had printed her full name, including middle initial, and her birthdate. Below, in smaller letters, he had written, "Patient of Dr. Roshberg's for approximately three months. Diagnosis: non-Hodgkin's lymphoma."

Glenda thought back to the times she had visited; Karen had never told her the name of the cancer and she had never posted anything about her illness on Facebook. "How did you find out her diagnosis?"

Glenn cleared his throat. "I investigated, or as you would say *creeped* on her sister's Facebook page. Her sister had posted it there for the world to see."

Glenda thought about Karen and her sister. She was sure Karen would be furious with her sister if she knew it was posted.

"Now, did Karen tell you how long she has been getting chemotherapy?" Glenn asked.

"I don't think so. I'm not sure."

"Okay," Glenn said, writing *Chemotherapy Regimen, Frequency and Length of Therapy* and drawing a line under it. "We need this information. Do you think you can get it from Karen or her sister?"

Glenda nodded. Karen may tell her, but her sister wouldn't give her the time of day. "I'll do the best I can."

"Good, good," Glenn said, reaching for the next sleeve labeled "Sonora". Glenn placed the black x-ray film on the viewer and this time the picture taped to the corner had both Bonita and Juanita's smiling faces on it.

"Their Facebook name is BonitaJuanita and every picture is of the two of them," Glenn explained. "And Juanita has been very, very helpful." Juanita had been one of the visitors to the No Egrets' office and had supplied Glenn with her sister's lab printout and other information. "Patient of Dr. Roshberg's for three weeks; Diagnosis: Acute myeloid leukemia; Lab findings—low platelets, high leukocytes; No bone marrow biopsy; Chemotherapy Regimen: bortezomib combined with daunorubicin and cytarabine on selected days of the month."

The next sleeve had Richard's name on it. "Don't have much on Richard yet," Glenn said, placing the film on the viewer. "Hopefully he will get a call from Dr. Roshberg's office soon."

"Where did you get that picture?" Glenda asked. The Richard in the photo was thin, had curly hair and was standing next to a woman that looked a lot like the actress Katie Holmes.

"He has an actor Facebook page. This picture was labeled *Richard Dawson's Creek* which is weird because neither Richard Dawson nor a small body of water is in the picture. But it was the first picture I came across."

It only briefly occurred to Glenda to explain to her husband the television series "Dawson's Creek", starring a young Katie Holmes was filmed in Wilmington starting in the late 90s and Richard must have had a small part. Realizing the futility of that line of thought, instead she said, "Next."

The next sleeve had a name Glenda did not recognize until Glenn put the x-ray film on the viewer and she saw the printed WECT on-line story and a picture of Mabel Thomson during her interview about her husband's death. Under the name Glenn had written "Patient of Dr. Roshberg's for ?; Diagnosis: ?; Chemotherapy Regimen: ?"

"We'll probably never know Mrs. Thomson's cancer diagnosis or treatment, but I think that's beside the point for the Thomsons," Glenn said. "Bobby said the last time he saw Mabel Thomson was in Dr. Roshberg's waiting room. Her husband was at the window to the inner office and things were not going well. According to Bobby, not by a long shot. It seems Mabel's husband was demanding a copy of her chart and an itemized bill of all the charges."

Glenda could tell her husband was becoming agitated as he talked; his voice continued to rise until it echoed off the laundry room walls. He stopped talking and paced back and forth in front of the X-ray Film Viewer, stopping to review each piece of film.

"Something not right here," he muttered. He looked from Karen's picture to the Sonora's to Mabel Thomson's. "Is there a connection? Malignancy comes in all shapes and forms, attacking all tissues and organs but both Karen and Bonita have cancers of the blood."

"Perhaps this is a different kind of malignancy," Glenda said softly but with a touch of venom.

Glenn stopped pacing and looked to her. "What do you mean?"

Glenda picked up the special pen from the top of the washer and handed it to her husband. She tapped the x-ray film with Richard's picture.

"These are my observations." Glenda began her list, counting off her concerns on her fingers as she called them out. "Dr. Roshberg seems more concerned about insurance coverage, money, than patient well-being. The patient, Richard, was not admitted into Roshberg's computer system before his blood was drawn." She paused and waited for Glenn's writing to catch up.

"Remember I told you about the sloppiness of the nurse. She didn't wear gloves to draw blood, didn't have labels to put on Richard's blood tubes. She didn't even have any way to write his name on the tubes. They could easily be misidentified or thrown away. Sheesh!

"She even left the clipboard and Richard's paperwork in the room when she walked out with the blood samples. The nurse never asked for his name—he wasn't in the system. What happened to the blood tubes? At the very least it means the office charts are most likely a mess. And if the other rooms were anything like the one we were in, the floor was filthy. Good grief! There were bloody gauze pads and syringes with needles on them in the regular trash can!"

Glenda stopped, realizing she was the one shouting now. She had to laugh a little. "It's easy to get angry and carried away with Roshberg," she said, smiling sheepishly. "But you know…" Her thoughts and voice trailed off.

Glenn looked up as he finished writing the abbreviated version of Glenda's report. She was standing with her arms crossed, her eyes burning angry. She appeared in deep thought. What had she said during that last part that he didn't hear? Something about carried away?

"Glenda. Glenda? Hey!" She snapped out of her trance. "You okay? You seem to be off somewhere."

She shook her head. "Nothing I can put into words; not as facts. Just…a feeling I had when I was there. A bad, sleazy…wrong feeling." Glenda narrowed her eyes as she thought back on the visit to Roshberg's office. "Something is up with this guy. He's up to no good. I think we should call our friends and tell them to stay away from him until we can get answers."

Glenn wrapped his arms around her and held her close. Glenda buried her head into his chest and took a few deep breaths.

"We can certainly register a complaint with OSHA about workplace conditions and practices," Glenn said in a positive tone, his way of assuring his wife that Roshberg would have to answer to somebody.

"No, no." Glenda sighed. "If OSHA shows up and gets involved, he might get spooked and take off in the middle of the night. I *want* him to leave town, but in the back of a police cruiser," Glenda said with brutal honesty.

Glenn slowly looked up at the film viewer. As he held Glenda, he studied the faces of the patients. "I can't shake the feeling something's wrong with the actual treatments."

Glenda raised her head and noticed three remaining x-ray film sleeves on the washer. "Are there more patients?" she asked. She released her husband's waist and reached for the envelopes.

"Not patients," Glenn said, taking the sleeves as she offered them. He slid out the x-ray film from the first one and Glenda saw the same WECT on-line story printed out and attached to the film. But this time there was a grainy picture of a man. Glenn had written "Tommie Thomson" by it. Under the name he had written "Befriended by Bobby at Dr. Roshberg's office—very vocal about the way his wife was being treated by staff and excess charges to his insurance."

Glenda was chilled by the next line and took an involuntary step back.

"Murdered. Clubbed in back of head; drowned in Intracoastal Waterway."

Glenda glanced at the next sleeve and saw Bobby's name written on it. It made her heart hurt. Bobby and Karen. She wanted nothing more than to rewind several weeks and make the world right for her two friends.

Glenn noticed his wife's gaze and pulled Bobby's x-ray film out of the sleeve and placed it on the viewer. Bobby's smiling face greeted her and Glenda couldn't help smiling. Her thoughts returned to the first time they had met Bobby outside No Egrets, to the many happy days Bobby had spent on his barstool. His general good nature and occasional goofiness made her smile broaden.

"Where did you get that picture?" Glenda asked as she scoured the background for any clue to what Bobby was doing when it was snapped.

"Had it at the bar." Glenn pointed to the edge of the picture where you could just make out the edge of the old Wurlitzer. "Damn thing still isn't working," he muttered.

"Glenda," Glenn said hesitantly. He took her face in his hands and turned it away from the viewer. By his actions Glenda knew he was about to drop some news on her. The anticipation caused her whole body to tense.

"Bobby told me a lot of things when he called me to the hospital— some of it I didn't put in the report you typed for the police. He didn't know the name of Karen's drugs, but he knew how often she was getting them. It started out he was worried about the awful side effects she was experiencing. And like everybody these days he went to the internet."

Glenda pulled away and her husband released his grip. "I need to sit," she explained. "You go on." She found the old kitchen chair, moved the stacks of old clothing from it and sat down.

"Now I'm certainly not an oncology expert myself," Glenn said, picking up the rhythm from where he left off. "And I told this to Bobby because there are many different chemotherapy regimens for a single cancer type."

"And?" Glenda asked.

"Well, Bobby was not only convinced Karen was receiving chemotherapy more often than recommended but that she had exceeded all of the treatment regimen time periods listed on the internet."

Glenda pulled her eyes away from Glenn and looked at Bobby's x-ray film. Glenn had written "Bobby vocally questioning and agitated in Dr. Roshberg's office over Karen's treatment."

The next lines chilled her again. "Clubbed in back of head, thrown in Intracoastal Waterway."

"Oh Glenn. I don't get it. Roshberg is a little man. He's not strong enough to overpower Bobby."

Glenn picked up the last sleeve, slid the x-ray film out and displayed it on the viewer. The picture showed a large, brown mammal swimming in the water. Under the picture Glenn had written "Big otter".

Glenda didn't look close at the picture and didn't read the words before she cried, "Oh my gosh! There's a beast in the water? Some kind of animal did this to Bobby and Mr. Thomson?"

"An animal, yes, but not the kind from the animal kingdom."

"Glenn, what is that?"

"I couldn't find a picture of the man Bobby accused of attacking him." Glenn shrugged. "When Bobby briefly woke up the first time the only words he spoke to his nurse were 'Big otter', or at least that's what she thought he said. He actually said, 'Big Otto'.

"A very large man named Otto is employed by Dr. Roshberg. Bobby's testimony can convict him of attempted murder and most likely murder in the case of Tommie Thomson."

"Oh my!" Glenda exclaimed, her hand going to her mouth. She looked at Bobby's smiling face and then at Tommie Thomson. She lowered her hand, suddenly mad. "So let's just go get the bastard!" She actually scared Glenn a little. "What are your cop buddies doing about this maniac?"

Glenda had noticed Hands and Sphinx visiting the No Egrets office earlier in the day on official police business. They wanted to know if Glenn had seen the man named Otto when he had visited Dr. Roshberg's office. Glenn could only give them a partial description of the tall man he had seen through the office window standing in the hallway.

"They are looking for him but haven't been able to find a last name or place of residence. So far, as big and odd as this guy looks, they can't find him. Hands and Sphinx told me the Brunswick County deputies went to the office to question Otto and he wasn't there. They also told me the office staff and particularly Dr. Roshberg weren't very cooperative."

Glenn and Glenda clasped hands as they stood staring at the seven pieces of x-ray film on the viewer. They reread the words under each picture. When Glenda came to Bobby's, she picked up the special pen. Under the words "Clubbed in back of head, thrown in Intracoastal Waterway" Glenda wrote one word in big, block letters: SURVIVED.

TWENTY-TWO

Bobby had just started to drift off when the piercing alarm sounded. He was immediately awake and on high alert. Looking to the left of the hospital bed he saw nothing; to the right there was no movement. He was eyeing the bathroom door when the room door slowly opened. Bobby quickly scanned the bedside table for a weapon—only a Styrofoam cup, a bendy straw and a half-size ginger ale can. The only other thing within reach was the small, bedside pulse oximetry machine with one end of a gray wire plugged into the monitor and the other end clipped on his index finger.

The security guard's head appeared in the doorway. "You okay? I heard an alarm."

Bobby let out his breath in a long, slow exhalation. "Yeah, thanks Matt." He looked over to the pulse-ox machine as it continued to alarm. "It's the darned machine. Respiratory Therapist told me it measures the amount of oxygen in my blood, but she said the lead to this one was acting wacky. She even tried to unplug this," Bobby said while holding up the gray wire. "And take it with her but she said it was stuck. She was supposed to bring me another one, but I haven't seen her." Bobby reached over and pressed the button on the front of the pulse-ox machine and the alarm stopped. "She showed me how to silence the alarm. I guess since I'm awake and talking to you that I've got enough oxygen in my blood."

The security guard chuckled. Since being moved to a private room on the Telemetry unit Bobby had become friends with all the security guards and policemen who were stationed outside his room. But Matt had taken the longest to come around. He was aloof at first and seemed nervous to talk with Bobby.

"Stay awhile, Matt. We'll play some cards." Bobby was just happy to be around human beings again.

"Can't, Bobby. Gotta stay on the job. They catch me in here and there goes my retirement," Matt said.

"How's the family? Your kids?" Bobby asked, playing the family card to try and get him to stay.

A pained look spread over Matt's face. "Fine. Everybody's fine," Matt said hurriedly. He checked his watch. "I gotta go, Bobby."

The security guard walked through the door and returned to his post. Bobby looked forlornly at the closed door. Supposed to still be in a coma. What a stupid plan—*his* plan. "Shit-for-brains," Bobby said to himself.

He shifted to his left side on the bed. Not comfortable. He made the head of the bed go up. And he made the head of the bed go down. Up. Down. Up and then a quick shift to down. He was bored and restless. His Mawmaw would say he had his days and nights mixed up. He refused to turn on the television, having read it was bad to fall asleep to the TV. Besides late-night television was even worse than mid-morning television. Bobby looked at the clock on the wall at the foot of his bed: 1:24 a.m. *Well,* Bobby thought. *A whole ten minutes have passed.* Up. Down. Feet up. Head down.

Bobby missed Zelly. When he had been moved from MICU to a different unit he had lost the best nurse in the hospital, in his opinion. Bobby looked at the machines around him, studying the numbers and screens. The numbers meant nothing to him. He touched a button, the screen changed. He touched another, the screen changed again. The next one caused a piercing alarm to sound.

Bobby fumbled with the buttons. Where was the dang mute button? He suddenly remembered which nurse had just started her shift and nearly panicked. She made Nurse Ratched look like Little Bo Peep. He started pushing all the buttons, trying to silence the alarm.

The door to the room opened and the "no-nonsense" nurse flew into the room. She gave Bobby a sideways glare as she went to the IV pump and pushed two buttons. The screeching stopped. She rolled the pump as far away from Bobby as the tubing and cords would allow.

"I could have done that if somebody had given me a manual on all these machines like I asked," Bobby explained. "I'm good with machines. I fixed this old Wurlitzer for the bar—"

No-nonsense ignored him and checked readings on the other machines. She reached over to the table beside Bobby's bed, snatched the remote from its resting place and turned on the television.

"I've read it's bad to fall asleep to the TV," Bobby told her weakly.

No reaction.

"It's the exposure to the flickering light."

No response.

"My days and nights are switched around," Bobby called to her as she headed toward the door. "I hope you're happy!" he yelled at her disappearing backside.

Bobby glanced at the television screen and noticed the time on the station guide on the screen—1:29 a.m. It was impossible to sleep in a hospital and Bobby was looking forward to his own bed (and his own bathroom and kitchen). Some of his strength was returning and his doctors didn't think it would be much longer before he could go home. He was eager to get home. And just as eager to get away from Nurse No-nonsense. He stuck out his tongue and blew a raspberry in the direction of the hallway.

His hand slid across the sheets until he found the remote. The one built into the bed frame didn't seem to work but Bobby couldn't tell for sure—no one had brought him the user's manual for it.

Bobby flipped through the channels stopping on a black and white movie. It seemed to be a vampire movie complete with fog and an eerie castle. The vampire suddenly appeared. Bobby wracked his brain to remember the old actor's name but came up empty. He flipped through more channels: Shopping Channel—high-end purses—not interested; infomercial for country music CD collection—interested in music—not interested in sales pitch; infomercial on acne treatment—would've been interested twenty years ago. He stopped suddenly on the local PBS station. Bobby couldn't help letting out a little squeal. It was "Monty Python's Flying Circus"! Growing up, he used to watch it in his room when he could only get four channels on his tiny black and white television. He settled back to watch, picking up the Styrofoam cup and sipping some tepid ginger ale through his bendy straw.

Terry Jones and his new bride Carol Cleveland ran into a department store and were desperate to buy a bed. Bobby giggled. He remembered the sketch. It was (of course) rather silly. They had to divide the number salesman Eric Idle said by ten and multiply the numbers of salesman Graham Chapman by three. Oh, and the best part they couldn't say *mattress* to Graham Chapman or he would put a bag over his head; instead they had to refer to it as *dog kennel*. Whoops! There went the bag as the newly married couple let the "m" word slip.

Bobby was laughing loudly at the absurdity when the door to the room began to inch open. The door was halfway open before he even noticed it. Bobby expected to see No-Nonsense stick her head in the door and yell at him to be quiet.

"*You* turned the TV on," Bobby said in an accusatory tone. Let the blame of his insomnia fall on her hateful shoulders.

But the dark figure in the doorway was not his nurse. The figure was backlit by the bright lights of the hospital corridor and yet Bobby had no doubt it was the creature from his nightmares. The one who viciously attacked him, stuffed him in the trunk of a car and rolled his body down the bank and into the water. And, there was no reasonable doubt in Bobby's mind, the one who had engineered the attack on his life in the ICU.

Where was Matt? Bobby could just see the edge of the chair outside the room and the security guard wasn't in his usual spot. That was a bad sign.

Otto closed the door and stepped toward Bobby. He had on dark glasses and a Myrtle Beach Pelican's baseball cap in a weak attempt to camouflage his massive frame. He didn't try to hide the snarl or the obvious contempt he felt for Bobby; a low growl steadily grew in volume.

"You have caused—many problems—for the doctor," Otto said between growls and breaths.

Bobby slowly reached his hand out to the bedrail until he found the nurse call button. Frantically he began pushing it. Otto lunged, grabbing the button and ripping the wire from the wall.

Otto's giant hand shot forward, attaching to Bobby's throat; Bobby struggled to draw in air through the crushing, vice-like grip. Wrapping his fingers around his attacker's wrist, Bobby lamely tried to pull it away. In spite of the hopelessness of the situation, Bobby felt surprisingly calm. He repeated, *No panic, no panic. Look for a weakness,* over and over in his mind.

Otto reached into his pocket and pulled out the kactet, inserting the fingers of his right hand through the holes. Slowly Otto brought the brass knuckles toward Bobby's face, teasing him. Otto smiled, admiring the weapon that had never let him down.

With his attention focused on the kactet, Otto loosened his grip on Bobby's throat slightly. Realizing it might be his only chance, Bobby located Otto's ring finger and in one quick motion pulled the finger away from the pack, bending it backward at an unnatural angle. Bobby didn't hear a snap, but Otto cried out in pain.

Bobby looked around quickly and continued the attack with the only things within reach. He grabbed the Styrofoam cup and flung the tepid ginger ale into Otto's eyes. When that didn't seem to have any effect, he smashed the cup and bendy straw into Otto's face. In a last-ditch attempt, he bonked the half-size ginger ale can off Otto's forehead. Otto had snapped his finger back in place; he just laughed and moved forward, cocking his right hand with the kactet behind him.

Time seemed to slow for Bobby. His mind was threatening to shut down. He looked over Otto's shoulder and saw Monty Python on the television. It was the beginning of the Dead Parrot sketch; John Cleese was returning a dead parrot sold to him by pet store owner Michael Palin. He loved that one and it seemed an appropriate farewell to Bobby Portis.

Bobby managed to roll his head just enough to avoid the blow as the brass knuckles whistled by his ear and punched the pillow. Otto laughed and grabbed the thick gray call light wire and wrapped it around Bobby's throat. He pressed it down hard at first, then released the tension, playing with Bobby. It was as if Otto was enjoying watching the redness creep into Bobby's face, the eyes that seemed to want to pop from their sockets, the protruding tongue. Bobby gurgled, coughed, wheezed.

Otto moved his face down; Bobby had a close-up view of Otto's nose hairs. When Otto spoke, Bobby could smell his sour breath.

"Time to die." Otto cocked his right arm back slowly.

As Bobby put his hands on Otto to try and push him off, he felt the wire of the pulse-ox machine. Miraculously the monitor was still clipped on his finger. Without much thought his right hand followed the wire to the machine on the bedside table. Just as Otto turned his head to see what Bobby was doing, Bobby picked up the machine and smashed it into Otto's nose with all the force he could muster. Otto backed away from the bed, holding his nose, emitting animal grunts.

Bobby jumped up from the bed, pulse-ox machine still in his hand. Otto screamed in rage and charged. Bobby swung the pulse-ox machine once over his head by the wire and in a moment of perfect timing, used the momentum from the swing to crash the machine into the side of Otto's head just above his ear. The Myrtle Beach Pelican ball cap and dark glasses flew off; Otto fell to his knees. Bobby stood above him whirling the pulse-ox machine over his head like a demented cowboy.

"C'mon you sum-bitch!" Bobby taunted. "I'm mad as hell. I'm not going to take it anymore. You don't have the element of surprise this time; I'm not comatose in a bed. It's finally a fair fight."

Otto shook his head and suddenly lunged at Bobby's knees. Bobby snapped the pulse-ox machine down with great force between Otto's shoulder blades. Otto hit the floor with a whump. He started to rise and Bobby whirled the machine twice around his head with such a velocity that it made a whirring noise like a radio-controlled model airplane. When it smashed into the side of Otto's head, blood and spittle flew and he bounced off the side of the bed and crashed into the wall head first.

The only sound came from "Monty Python's Flying Circus". Bobby looked up and was surprised to see the Dead Parrot sketch still running on the television. He looked down at Otto's inert body just as John Cleese's character proclaimed, "This parrot is no more. It has ceased to be. It's expired and gone to meet its maker. This is a late parrot. It's a stiff. Bereft of life, it rests in peace. If you hadn't nailed it to the perch, it would be pushing up the daisies. It's rung down the curtain and joined the choir invisible. This…is an ex-parrot."

In another five minutes, Matt, two other security guards and a policeman would barge into the room. (Matt had experienced a change of heart after allowing Otto to access the hospital through a back stairwell—he would lose his job but in the end, Bobby would refuse to prosecute).

Within those five minutes the Respiratory Therapist returned, opening the door nonchalantly. She had a new pulse-ox monitor wire in one hand and her cellphone in the other. Staring at her phone screen she didn't even notice the large man on the floor leaking blood.

"I've got a new monitor wire for you," she said.

"No thanks," Bobby replied, dangling the bloody, busted pulse-ox machine by the wire which was still attached tightly. "This one worked just fine for me. I think I'll keep it."

In the darkened bar area of No Egrets the first sound was a "zzzzt" accompanied by the sudden flashing of multi-colored lights. The old Wurlitzer kicked back to life, changed records and the sounds of Gloria Gaynor singing "I Will Survive" filled the empty bar.

"First," Dr. Roshberg said. "I recommend you get IVIG for your low antibody levels."

Richard stared at Glenda stupidly, not sure what to say. Dr. Roshberg's office had called Richard at 8 a.m. and told him the doctor wanted to meet with him at 10:30.

"I'm sorry," Glenda spoke up. "What is IVIG?"

"Intravenous immunoglobulin," Dr. Roshberg answered flatly. He thumbed through some papers on a clipboard and returned his attention to Richard. "And we need to take care of your low iron levels with intravenous iron."

Richard looked stunned. Glenda wasn't sure if he was acting now or not. The doctor sat behind his desk examining Richard's lab work.

Finally Richard spoke. "I understand doctor and I trust you implicitly. I kind of understand the iron but not the immunoglob...whatever it is you called it. Why do I need it?"

"If you don't get the immunoglobulin you will be susceptible to recurrent infections when you get your chemotherapy." Roshberg yawned, showing no empathy or regard for his patient's mental state.

"Chemotherapy!" The word rocketed from Richard and Glenda's lips at almost the same time. Richard started shaking and crying. Glenda moved to comfort him, again not sure if he was acting.

"How long...what kind of chemo will my brother need?" Glenda asked, her arms around Richard. She was trying to remember the list of questions Glenn had tried to drill into her that morning, expecting such a moment. But she hadn't anticipated it would be so dramatic, so emotional.

"Three months, maybe six," the doctor said matter-of-factly.

Richard buried his face into Glenda's shoulder and let out a piercing wail. The sound nearly broke Glenda's heart.

Roshberg was unscathed. Taking a golf club leaning against his desk, he used it to push a box of tissues across the massive desktop to Glenda. "There are several chemotherapy regimens and I will have to evaluate them for the best course," the doctor continued.

Richard sobbed uncontrollably on Glenda's shoulder. Glenda had to speak loud to be heard. "What kind of cancer is it and...um...how long...what are his chances?"

Richard wailed and began shaking in her arms. Tears streamed down his stricken face. She wanted to comfort him, to tell him it was going to be okay—that it was all just a cruel con.

Dr. Roshberg sat back and clasped his hands with index fingers touching. He bent his head slightly forward and bounced his index fingers off his chin. "Perhaps we better wait until the next appointment to discuss the disease and prognosis."

Richard was still blubbering but he looked up at Glenda and pointed to the desk.

"Oh yes," Glenda said. "Richard hasn't been to a doctor in a very long time. But he got into trouble with his insurance company one time because the office did not bill correctly. So he keeps copies of all receipts, everything. And any paperwork. He's type A personality and very fragile now—" Glenda pointed to the printed lab work. "Please?"

A dark, dangerous look flashed across Roshberg's face, startling Glenda. It was gone in an instant and he smiled at her. "Absolutely." He walked over to his office copier.

Glenda held on tightly to Richard and stroked his back. His sobs lessened but every once in a while, one would hit that caused his body to jerk with the spasm.

A copy of the lab work tucked into her purse, Glenda had to use both hands to help Richard to his feet. She had to support his whole weight to get him moving. His legs wobbled and she had to struggle just to get him through the doctor's door. Glenda noticed Roshberg did not move to help his new patient.

In the outer office a nurse did try to help but Richard screamed, "Don't touch me!" As they entered the waiting room, all the occupants couldn't help but stare at the man who had apparently received devastating news from the doctor. He gave a high-pitched, wild wail in the middle of the packed waiting room. A child began to match Richard sob for sob. Unexpectedly the domino effect came into play: an older woman dabbed her eyes; a husband and wife clutched each other as they recommitted their love. The whole room was crying.

Richard did not calm down when the two reached the outside walkway. He was still crying and dragging his feet. It took all of Glenda's strength to keep him moving. *He really believes it*, Glenda thought.

"Richard. Richard!" she cried. "I either have to leave you here on the sidewalk and come pick you up...or you'll need to walk across the asphalt again. Do you want to keep moving?"

He answered only in sobs but started moving. Turning the back corner of the office, Glenda wondered if she should try to take Richard home or call Glenn for help. In a flash Richard broke free of her grasp, stood up straight and smacked the wall of the office with an open palm. In an angry voice he said, "That man is the quack of quacks. In fact, he's the sleazeball of quacks. Let's get him!"

TWENTY-THREE

Glenda did not look happy; Glenn was trying not to notice. Daniel smiled ear to ear. And there they stood—the three of them (two of them holding beers)—in the laundry room, looking at an X-ray Film Viewer mounted above the washer and dryer.

"Is that an X-ray Film Viewer?" Daniel asked, barely suppressing a silly laugh.

"Yes," Glenn and Glenda responded in unison, one sounding a little prouder of the wonder of illumination than the other.

"You, um, using it for something other than viewing x-rays?" Daniel asked. He and his two hosts continued to just stare at the medical monstrosity. "You know, what's the word? *Upcycle?*" Daniel was proud he could remember the trendy term. "Upcycle. Are you upcycling it?"

"No," Glenda answered flatly.

Daniel fired off his next question. "Spin cycle not make it wobble?"

"Not that we've noticed," Glenn answered.

Ding! A timer with a rather bland tone drew the attention of the room.

The two men looked at each other. Glenda turned around, grabbed a laundry basket and opened the dryer. She began pulling warm and tangled sheets and towels out of the machine and dumping them into a wicker basket.

"I put on a load before I realized we would be entertaining…in the laundry room," Glenda explained.

Daniel inhaled deeply. "Wow! How do you get your laundry to smell so fresh? Mine always has this musty scent."

"I got married," Glenn answered quickly. "Can we please get back to the viewer and the matter at hand?"

"Okay," Daniel said, returning his attention to the light box. "So what do you use it for—vacation slides?"

"Not even close," Glenda answered. "Oak Island was our last vacation anyway. I think you've already seen the many wonders of nature the island has to offer."

Daniel continued to stare at the viewer, taking a long drink of beer. He asked the next obvious question. "Where did you get it?"

"It was Glenn's parting gift from the hospital."

"How…unusual. Did they give you an enema bag and a bedpan, too? They must have really liked you," Daniel said.

149

"Very funny," Glenn said, switching on the viewer. "Like many things in the ever-changing world of healthcare, the X-ray Film Viewer has been replaced by computers and new technology. But it will always have a special place in my heart."

"And in my laundry room," Glenda responded dryly.

Daniel began studying the x-ray film on the viewer. Glenn had called the pharmacist earlier in the day with questions about chemotherapy medications and intravenous immune globulin.

"Truth be told," Daniel said. "I've been out of hospital pharmacy for a while, so I called a buddy to double-check me; especially on the reimbursement side. That stuff changes every freaking year."

They were looking at Richard's picture and x-ray film. Glenn took the special pen and wrote "intravenous immune globulin, iron and chemotherapy yet to be determined; diagnosis—mystery cancer".

"I am so sorry to hear that about Richard," Daniel said, putting a hand on Glenda's shoulder.

"Don't be," Glenda said, handing two sets of papers to her husband. Glenn took the pages and taped them below Richard's x-ray film. Daniel was eyeing Glenda, wondering when she had turned so hard-hearted.

"Take a look at Richard's lab work, paying special attention to the dates on the top of each set." Glenn instructed.

Daniel scanned the first set, which was dated just a few days ago. "Wow! There are more high and low levels than normal levels. Richard's body must be a royal mess."

Glenn tapped his finger on the next set. This lab work was dated only a couple of months before. Daniel briefly studied the numbers and then looked up at the two of them with a puzzled expression.

"I don't understand," Daniel said. "The only level out of normal range was bilirubin and that was only one point higher."

"Exactly," Glenn stated. "Which means?"

Daniel thought a minute. "Either Richard's health has gone down the crapper at super warp speed or one of these two laboratories can't be trusted."

Glenda tapped her finger on her nose. "Bingo!"

"Wait…what are you saying?" Daniel scanned the second printout. "The one a few months ago was done at Boiling Grove. I would trust the hospital's laboratory to be accurate. Where was the other—"

"Roshberg's office," Glenn interrupted.

"I don't understand." Daniel frowned, thinking. "The intravenous immune globulin, IV iron, chemotherapy…*are you freaking kidding me?*"

Glenn put his hand on Daniel's shoulder. "I've run the scenario through my head hundreds of times and it always comes back to the same thing, appalling as it is."

"Heartless, disgusting and evil—that's what it is," Glenda added.

Daniel placed his beer on the dryer and used the washer to brace himself. "Damn! The meds he is pumping into people are really, really expensive," he said, looking back to the list written on Richard's x-ray.

"Immune globulin, IV iron, chemotherapy—all can be given several times to cancer patients!" Daniel's voice became louder as the enormity of what Glenn suspected began to sink in. "Hospitals are reimbursed at a fairly high percentage for outpatient treatments. It would be the same for doctors' offices."

Silence fell over the laundry room. The three people stood facing each other, each lost in their own thoughts. Daniel grabbed his beer from the top of the dryer and chugged it down. Glenn held his bottle out and looked at it, as if surprised it was in his hand; Glenda grabbed it and took a long drink.

It was Glenn who spoke first, searching for a possible motive. "So, a doctor could charge private insurance and Medicare patients for the drugs administered at his office and make money?"

"Yes," Daniel answered, spitting out the word. "Honestly, a doctor wouldn't bring in as much with Medicare patients, but private insurance patients would make up for it nicely. And don't forget office visit charges, supplies, administration fees."

"Volume," Glenda interjected.

"What?"

"Roshberg's parking lot and waiting room are always packed," Glenda said. "He must have hundreds and hundreds of patients and apparently no cutoff number. He gladly took on Richard—*after* making sure he had insurance. The more patients he treats for cancer, the more drugs he can give, the more he will be reimbursed. Volume."

Daniel and Glenn were staring at her. Daniel glanced at the framed Hippocratic Oath print on the wall near the viewer. "This asshole has no respect for people, medicine or the Hippocratic Oath! What happened to first do no harm and all that?"

"If what we are suggesting turns out to be true," Glenn answered. "I'd like to read the oath again to Roshberg. Preferably right before his rights are read to him. And as he is found guilty. And as he walks through the prison gate."

"I'll make a special cake for him," Glenda said thoughtfully. "And lace it with chemo drugs!" she finished vehemently.

Daniel balled his fist tightly and shook it. "It makes me want to hit something." Glenda looked at him, surprised. She deftly positioned herself between Daniel and her front-loading washer and dryer. Daniel laughed in spite of himself. "Don't worry. I've learned never to take on large machines."

Glenn started pacing like a caged tiger, mumbling the names of drugs and diagnoses. At one point he threw up his arms in frustration, scraping his knuckles on the low laundry room ceiling. Smiling sheepishly, he crossed his arms, putting his reddened fingers in his armpits.

Daniel laughed. "Now that we've all gotten that out of our system…" He scanned the other pictures on the top row of the X-ray Film Viewer. "I recognize the Sonora sisters but not the other two."

"That's Karen," Glenn said pointing to her picture.

"Karen!" Glenda exclaimed. "I almost forgot. I talked to her today. When she found out Glenn was concerned about her treatments, she talked more about them. She remembered part of the name of her chemotherapy drug because the word *tux* was in it. She thought it was retux-something."

"Probably rituximab," Daniel said.

"That helps," Glenn said. "She's been going to Roshberg for three months or so."

"And," Glenda added. "She's had nineteen treatments. She noted each one in her datebook."

Glenn was writing the drug name and number of treatments on Karen's x-ray film; he stopped and turned back to them. "Nineteen?"

Glenda nodded. "That sounds like a lot," Glenn said, looking at Daniel. "Her diagnosis is non-Hodgkin's lymphoma."

"I'm on it boss. Can I borrow your cell phone?" Daniel asked, pulling a piece of paper out of his wallet.

"Isn't it about time you got a cell phone of your own?" Glenn asked, holding out his phone.

"Why do I need one when I can borrow yours?" Daniel took Glenn's phone and walked into the kitchen to call his colleague.

Glenn reviewed all the information on Bonita Sonora's x-ray film, realizing he hadn't talked to Juanita recently. He'd have to call her if she didn't show up at No Egrets tonight or tomorrow.

Daniel returned in about ten minutes. "Hey, I saw an egret in your back yard."

"That's Ernie," Glenn said absently, still staring at the film on the viewer.

"He visits our goldfish pond," Glenda added.

Daniel started to tell them their goldfish were on the endangered list as he had witnessed Ernie gulping down a big one, when Glenn asked, "What did you find out?"

"Oh, I waited while my buddy consulted with the main oncologist there, but he said a non-Hodgkin's patient would normally get twelve treatments—"

"Twelve!" Glenn exclaimed. "We may be on to something."

"You didn't let me finish," Daniel said. "Twelve rituximab treatments—

over the course of *two years*."

Juanita was acutely aware Bonita was the last patient in Dr. Roshberg's office building. They were waiting in his office for him to "pop" in. He had specifically asked Bonita to remain after her treatment ended and Juanita couldn't think of any reason to refuse, try as she might.

The short man charged into the office, bypassed them without a word and sat behind his large desk. It was getting so Juanita couldn't stand the sight of him.

"Well, Ms. Sonora, I have the results of your latest lab tests and PET scan." He shuffled papers and pulled some notes from Bonita's chart. "Your levels are better but still not where I would like them; the PET scan however is about the same."

Bonita immediately began crying and Juanita hugged her tight. Juanita looked the doctor squarely in the eye (once she found out the "look" made him squirm, she used it all the time). "What do you recommend, *doctor*?" Juanita asked, unable to keep the irritation out of her voice.

"First, she's going to need a blood transfusion."

"What?" Juanita frowned. "Blood transfusion? Boni hasn't had to have blood yet. I thought you said she was improving?"

The doctor leaned back, smiling. "She is! Getting there but it's a long road. She'll probably need some IV iron as well before we can continue the chemotherapy."

Bonita sobbed hysterically; Juanita could not comfort her. Caught in her sister's death grip, Juanita wanted nothing more than to stand and confront the doctor. She tried to lift, maneuver and suck in, like she did to escape Boni when they were kids, but she wasn't as limber as she used to be. Finally she pulled Bonita to her feet along with her.

Juanita looked down on Roshberg and she thought he actually cowered a little. "My God, doctor! How many more treatments is my sister going to have to endure?"

Dr. Roshberg steepled his fingers and studied the women. Finally he spoke, "Once we get the cancer under control your sister will still need maintenance doses of chemotherapy."

"What do you mean?" Juanita demanded. "I've never heard of that."

"Well, I'm afraid once a patient has chemotherapy, they need it for the rest of their lives."

"What kind of animal is that?" Daniel asked, pointing to the picture on the lower level of the X-ray Film Viewer.

"Big otter," Glenn answered.

"I see," said Daniel. "As opposed to a petite otter."

"It represents Otto, Roshberg's goon," Glenn explained as he tapped the photo with his index finger. "The one who attacked Bobby and killed Tommie Thomson. Actually he attacked Bobby more than once."

"Any chance the police can tie him back to the activities at Dr. Roshberg's office?" Daniel asked.

"Not now," Glenn said. "I guess you haven't heard."

Glenda stepped forward and held out her hand. "May I?"

Glenn deposited the special pen in her hand and she walked up to the viewer. She pressed hard and made a large X over the animal picture. "May you rot in Hell, Big otter!"

She then moved the pen under Bobby's picture and circled the word "Survived".

There was a slight knock at the door followed by a soft voice. "Mr. Portis?" A woman had pushed Bobby's hospital room door open just enough to stick in her head.

Visitors had been quite common for Bobby of late. People he didn't know would stop by just to see how he was doing, ask if he needed anything. Most of the time they just wanted to say hello and meet him. So far, the news had only spread through the grapevine (and Twitter, Facebook, Tumblr and several blogs) and not the actual news media, but Bobby's pulse-ox pummeling of Otto had already become legendary.

"Please, call me Bobby."

The woman eased her way into Bobby's hospital room. She was middle-aged, dressed in green scrubs and a white lab coat.

Bobby was in his bedside chair with his dinner and had just taken a big bite. He tried to chew it quickly. His strength had returned and the only machine present was an IV pump where a bag of saline slowly dripped into him. (He no longer needed the fabled pulse-ox machine which had been removed by the police and bagged as evidence.)

"My name is Stacey Sparks. I'm a Nurse Practitioner in the hospital's clinic down the road." She pointed in the general direction of "down the road". "I'm really sorry to bother you."

"No bother," Bobby said. "What can I do for you, Stacey?"

She moved closer to Bobby's chair. "I think you've already done it. I heard...well, that you killed a man named Otto who attacked you."

"Yes," Bobby said slowly. "It was self-defense."

Stacey smiled in relief. She quickly moved toward Bobby, grabbing for his hand. Bobby was caught off guard but didn't stop her.

"I just wanted to shake your hand. And to say, thank you from the Sparks' family. All of us! We are so grateful."

She let go of Bobby's hand and lowered her head. "Otto threatened my life," she said in a whisper. "And my husband's and son's." Suddenly she raised her head with a flash of anger. "The son of a bitch even threatened my daughter-in-law and grandchild!"

Bobby moved his dinner tray away from his chair. He was no longer hungry. "I don't think it has sunk in yet. That I've taken a human life."

"Not human. Otto was Satan's disciple!" Stacey yelled. "He was not human!"

Bobby said nothing and watched as Stacey gathered herself. She seemed to be trembling.

"Please," Bobby said, pointing to the bed. "You can sit on the bed."

Stacey collapsed on to the bed and put her hands to her face. "I've tried to forget those four months, but I just can't. They were horrible."

"I think I can relate," Bobby said. "Otto not only threatened me, he came at me twice...and tried to get someone else to kill me."

She removed her hands from her face and looked him square in the eye. "No, no, no. You don't understand. Not the time I was living in fear of Otto. I mean the four months I worked in Dr. Roshberg's office!"

Bobby couldn't hide his surprise; he had assumed Stacey or one of her family was a patient of Dr. Roshberg's. "You worked there?"

"Yes. I should've walked out the first day when I saw the bone marrow biopsy performed by a nurse without gloves." Stacey paused, gazing out the window. "It was stupid on my part, but I needed the job."

Bobby tried to speak but felt like he had swallowed his tongue. The color had drained from his face.

"I've never seen anything like that place. The way chemo is administered there..." She shuddered.

"It wasn't uncommon for patients to get the wrong medication—bags were rarely labeled. Documentation was an afterthought, if it was done at all. Personally, I think the doctor wanted it that way. And the way Dr. Roshberg pushed chemotherapy...just plug in the drugs and charge."

She turned back to Bobby. "Naturally every patient was billed at the highest possible code, even if the doctor only saw them for two minutes."

Bobby was fidgeting with his IV tubing, rolling it back and forth between his fingers. He blinked slowly, holding his eyes closed for a minute. Opening his eyes, he said in a scared voice, "My girlfriend is getting chemotherapy at Dr. Roshberg's."

Stacey jumped off the bed and grabbed Bobby's arm. "For God's sake, get her out of there!"

TWENTY-FOUR

Karen snarled, "Are you out of your mind?" Throwing off the blanket covering her, she gestured toward her body. "Look at me! Do I look healthy to you? I have cancer!" She was so loud a dog out on the street starting barking. "The doctor says I have cancer! The tests prove I have cancer! Doctors do not do the kind of things you are talking about!" Karen crossed her arms and huffed.

Glenda was stunned. She hadn't expected this kind of reaction from Karen. Denial maybe, but not a full-blown hissy fit. *It's almost like she's defending Roshberg,* Glenda thought. *Stockholm syndrome?* She made a mental note to discuss it with Glenn.

Karen adjusted the bill of her new ball cap. It proudly proclaimed: *Redneck, Ass-Kicking, Crazy Bitch.* Apparently she had found it in the back of the closet—Bobby had won it for her on The Claw at the Oak Island Jungle Golf arcade several months ago. Glenda read the front of the hat and deemed it apropos.

Brandi was standing in the kitchen doorway, watching her sister's theatrics in the recliner. Glenda looked to her, silently pleading for help to convince Karen to leave her doctor. Brandi smiled smugly, lifted a hand and began examining her cuticles. Glenda sighed, hoping Glenn was having a better time of it.

Glenn shifted from foot to foot on the Sonora sisters' front porch. He checked his watch—6:50 a.m. He was ten minutes early.

"Oh! Is that you, Doc?" asked a muffled voice from the other side of the door.

"Yes," Glenn answered. "Sorry. I'm a little early."

"No problem. No problem." The muffled voice appeared to be closer to the door.

"None at all. None at all," called out a weaker, softer voice. Glenn smiled, realizing the second voice was Bonita. The girls seemed to be in rare form this morning—almost like days of old.

Juanita: "We're nearly ready."

Bonita: "Almost dressed."

Juanita: "Don't make him think we're naked."

Bonita: "He's a doctor. He's seen plenty of naked women."

Juanita: "But he hasn't seen two pair of gazongas on twins like these babies here!"

After a short pause, loud, hearty laughter could be heard through the door.

Juanita: "We are *not* naked, Doc!"

Bonita: "So quit trying to picture it."

More hearty laughter.

Glenn heard the lock on the front door click.

"Doc?" Juanita called through the door. "Count to ten Mississippi and then come on in and have a seat. Starting...now!"

Glenn didn't hear movement on the other side of the door at first. Then the sisters squealed and laughed as they hurried back to their rooms.

Glenn shook his head and counted to thirty Mississippi before pulling open the storm door and pushing through the front door.

The sweet scent of flowers nearly overpowered Glenn as he walked into the house. He expected to see old style furniture covered in plastic, but the couch and chairs were bright, new and uncovered. As Glenn finished his quick survey of the room, he made note of the absence of weird home accessories like Buddha statues or black velvet Elvis paintings. Before entering, he would have bet money on it.

Glenda glanced hopelessly at the tote bags at her feet. She had arrived armed with medical books, studies and a testimonial from Glenn. A dry erase board she had prepared with a timeline poked out of one tote bag. In her pocket she even had a folded, printed outline of her presentation to Karen. (That morning she had practiced her opening line, just like she had learned in speech class. Glenn had smirked when he caught her practicing—in the laundry room.)

In the recliner, Karen still had her arms crossed and had turned away from Glenda. The prep work had been as much for Brandi as it had been for Karen. Glenda had told her husband about Brandi getting inside Karen's head, giving the specific example of convincing her that Bobby had dumped her. But now Glenda wasn't so sure.

All the evidence against Roshberg had been presented and yet Karen dug her heels in and refused to quit seeing him—even refused to see another doctor for a second opinion. Through it all Brandi stood silently nearby. Glenda felt annoyed and defeated.

Glenn grabbed a seat in the middle of the big, blue couch, wondering if he should have prepared better for his meeting with the twins. He hadn't brought anything with him, not even a copy of Richard's lab results. Down the hallway he heard laughter which soon started moving toward him.

Glenn stood as Bonita entered the room. Her head was bald and she had wrapped a big, pink bow around it. She smiled broadly.

"Sorry to make you wait, Doc," Bonita said, a little louder than necessary.

It seemed to be Juanita's cue to enter as she joined her sister and they both started singing, "A pretty girl is like a melody..."

"Juanita!" Glenn cried out. "What an incredible look for you! And very touching."

Juanita had shaved her head to show support for her sister. The two women hugged. And then they laughed some more. They were dressed in coordinated outfits of different colors—coral and yellow (with a touch of Be-Dazzle, of course).

"You two are beautiful! Next time you come to No Egrets, drinks are on me," Glenn announced as he clapped his hands.

The women squealed with delight.

In another Oak Island neighborhood, Glenda felt like crying. The drapes in the room were drawn and she wanted to walk over, rip them open and let in the gorgeous North Carolina sunshine. Maybe that would help the mood of the room. It was as if she had been kicked in the stomach. Who *was* this woman sitting across the living room in a new recliner? She looked a little like the Karen she knew and loved but the resemblance ended there.

Karen had just screamed an ear-splitting, "Get out!" directed at both Glenda and Brandi; other dogs in the neighborhood joined in the barking.

Glenda took a step toward the door, stopping suddenly. She turned back, trying to contain her anger. "You know we are just trying to help you. We care about you! Bobby will be discharged from the hospital soon—have you talked to him about this?"

Karen's features softened slightly and Glenda thought she may have discovered a chink in the armor.

"He did call but..." And just as suddenly her features hardened, closing the chink. "Bobby has been in the hospital. He doesn't know *anything* about my treatments now!"

Out of the corner of her eye, Glenda saw Brandi sneering and nodding. Briefly she thought about grabbing the dry erase board and using it to erase that look off Brandi's face.

"Karen," Glenda said. "Please look at some of the things I've brought. I was *there* when Roshberg told Richard he had cancer. And Glenn—"

"I told you, doctors do not do the kind of things you are talking about!"

Brandi marched over to the tote bags. "Time to leave. Let me help you gather your things." She paused to give Glenda's outfit and accessories the once-over.

"Hey!" Brandi exclaimed, looking at the small, bright yellow, pyramidal leather handbag strapped to Glenda's wrist. "Is that a Jil Sander wristlet?"

Glenn patted the couch next to where he was sitting. The twins plopped down beside him. "I need to talk to you about—"

In an instant Juanita was back on her feet. "Oh, good grief! I forgot the refreshments." She took off toward the kitchen.

While they waited, Glenn felt like he should make small talk. "How are you feeling?"

Bonita offered a weak smile. "Oh…" Her voice trailed off for a moment. "Terrible, really. But I skipped my last treatment, so honestly, not as terrible as before."

Glenn's mouth opened to speak, but he wasn't sure what to say. "Uh, Bonita, that is—that's—it's great that—Glenda and I—we—that's actually why I wanted—"

He remembered his wife practicing her opening line that morning and wished he had joined her. As a surgeon he had many consultations with patients. But that was on a professional level and his friendship with the Sonoras made this highly personal.

Bonita giggled to see him tongue-tied. "Doc, I don't think you've had your morning coffee."

Juanita dashed into the room. "Coffee? No coffee here." She carried a pitcher of Bloody Marys while balancing three glasses in her other hand.

Juanita blushed. "We know it's early and all, but we are celebrating!"

Bonita began clapping her hands as Juanita danced around singing, "La cucaracha—la cucaracha."

In a bizarre version of a dream he had been having since his teenage years, Glenn sat on a couch, holding a Bloody Mary while twins sang and danced for him.

Brandi reached out to touch the pretty Jil Sander wristlet. "I saw that on eBay. You buy it from them?"

Glenda reached down and picked up a tote bag. With her other hand she roughly grabbed Brandi by the elbow and led her into the kitchen.

Glenda held up the wristlet while placing the tote bag on the kitchen table. "I will have you know this was purchased years ago. I saved every penny I came across to buy it. It is *not* a used purse from some crackpot on eBay."

Glenda unzipped the wristlet and pulled out credit cards, her license, lipstick, a box of Chiclets, pepper spray, a mini bottle of hot sauce and a wad of receipts and threw them all in the tote bag.

Glenda dangled the wristlet in front of Brandi's face, swinging it slowly back and forth like a pendulum. "It's yours. Take it."

Brandi's eyes, large and glassy, never left the wristlet as she slowly reached for it. Glenda yanked it out of her reach.

"Yours…" Glenda narrowed her eyes. "If you get Karen to leave Dr. Roshberg."

Brandi reached for the wristlet again. "All I have to do is get her to leave Dr. Doucheberg?"

Brandi had always known the value of finer things. For instance, she was aware that particular Jil Sander wristlet was going for around five hundred dollars. (Back at home friends had urged her to try out for "The Price is Right" but, truth be known, she had absolutely no idea what a jar of spaghetti sauce cost.)

Brandi shot out of the kitchen like a big cat after prey. Karen had the back of the recliner as far back as it would go and in an instant Brandi was on top of her with arms and legs on either side, hissing into her sister's face. "You! You! You bitch!"

The chair teetered on flipping but Brandi shifted her weight, distributing it evenly between the back and seat. Karen was at the mercy of her sister and her movements.

Glenda ran toward the chair holding out the wristlet. "Look, it could be a knockoff. I think I got it in Chinatown—on Canal Street. New York City." Glenda was waving the purse, trying unsuccessfully to distract the Brandi-monster she had created.

Brandi's eyes were locked on Karen's. "Do you know what you're putting me through? I have to wait on you—clean your vomit—wipe your ass. And *you* want to keep me in this prison. You won't even consider that Dr. Doucheberg is a lying dick! Do you know what this has been like for *me*? No dates—no clubbing. I haven't had sex in one hundred and fifteen days! I have to stay with your sorry ass night and day! Now, you are going to do what Rich Bitch says. You are going to leave Dr. Doucheberg!"

Brandi backed off a few inches from Karen's face to make sure her message had been received. Her eyes stayed locked on target, but Brandi addressed Glenda. "That ain't no knockoff. I watch the TV shopping channels and scan all the websites."

Hiking up her leg and twisting off the top of the chair, Brandi left her stunned sister and deftly grabbed the wristlet as she turned toward Glenda. She peeked at the lining—zipped the zipper—tugged on the handle. Then she looked at Glenda. "You have it registered?"

"We're off to Mexico!" Juanita announced. "Sun, sand, muchachos." She continued to dance and sing.

"No, no, no," Bonita managed to say as she nearly drowned in her own laughter. "Muchachos are *boys*. I don't want a boy. I want a *man*!" She continued to laugh until she was gasping for air at which point the party stopped to make sure she was okay.

"I'm a cougar," Juanita stated without shame, punctuating it with a feline growl. She pressed a button on her iPod and the sounds of Tito Puente playing a mamba filled the room. "Anyone twenty-one or older is fine with me." She started dancing again.

Glenn watched them dance and wondered how he was going to gain control of the situation and turn the conversation to Bonita's health. He decided he would have to wait until Bonita tired.

"Ask us, 'Why Mexico?' Doc," Bonita called to Glenn as loudly as she could.

"Why Mexico?" Glenn took a big gulp from his Bloody Mary and made a face. "Whoa! That's one strong drink."

"Alternative medicine!" Juanita shouted in order to be heard over the song "El Agitador".

Glenn was imagining the impact Mexico would have on the Sonoras and vice versa when he realized what Juanita had said.

"What? You're going to Mexico...for *what*?"

Juanita put Tito on pause as she and Bonita exchanged a look.

"You tell him," Bonita said.

"Doc, we know outside of the U.S. are some medical treatments that are not...respected here," Juanita said, searching for the right words.

"But I want to try them," Bonita continued. "I can't put up with Dr. Roshberg anymore; his rudeness, his secretive behavior. Juanita has done some research. We've chosen Mexico."

"We respect you, Doc," Juanita said, jumping back into the conversation. "But this is our decision. Together." And then she added, "Roshberg is crazy."

It was Glenn's turn to burst into laughter. He raised his glass for a toast. "To your health!" Everyone clinked glasses and took a long drink.

"Girls," Glenn said. "It's your decision whether you seek alternative medicine in Mexico, but if you'll hear me out first, there are some things I want to tell you about *crazy* Roshberg."

TWENTY-FIVE

Glenn glanced down the bar, dazed. *What day is it?* Focusing on Matilda's Rose Kennedy Cocktail, he realized it must be Sunday. The last week had alternated between crazy insane and a snail's pace.

Finally, with the help of several phone calls from Bobby, Karen had been convinced not to return to Dr. Roshberg. Bonita and Juanita had agreed to get a second opinion before flying off to Mexico. Daniel had called his nurse girlfriend, Jaclyn at Boiling Grove Community Hospital to get her recommendation for oncologists while Glenn had called a physician he had met from Whiteville. They both had a Wilmington oncologist at the top of their list. Karen and Bonita had appointments scheduled with their new oncologist for Thursday. Glenn planned to call the oncologist to personally discuss their situations and care (or lack thereof).

Daniel O'Dwyer walked into No Egrets and plopped down at the bar with the other regulars. He held up three fingers in a salute and said, in a decidedly British voice, "Fat Tire, my good man."

Richard, on Daniel's left, was wearing a pink Hawaiian shirt and fluorescent green shorts. Pinhead Paul, on his right, was adorned in dungaree, scales, and bits of fish intestines.

"How's it going, Daniel?" Glenn asked, sliding the Fat Tire pint glass over into his waiting hand.

Daniel took a slug of frothy beer. "Not so good. When I woke up this morning my plan was to go for a swim. Instead, I grabbed the keys, jumped in the Cube and drove to Shallotte."

Daniel took another drink. "Damn it, Glenn. Roshberg's parking lot is still full!"

Richard looked at Daniel in shock. "You must be kidding!"

"I wish," Daniel said sadly, shaking his head.

"Is there no way to stop this madman?" Richard wailed.

"I've talked to the Oak Island Police and Brunswick County Sheriff's office," Glenn said. "Glenda typed up all the information from my X-ray Viewer and I gave it to both of them. The Sherriff's office called me back after talking to the Federal Office of Inspector General. Apparently it takes a lot of time, resources and money to prosecute a physician for Medicare and Medicaid fraud. Richard's blood results aren't enough, but it did get the ball rolling. They said they would have to send in undercover agents as patients and it may take months."

"Meanwhile," Daniel said. "Unwitting patients are still flocking to this lunatic."

"I repeat," said Richard. "Is there no way to stop the madman?"

Pinhead Paul leaned forward. "I can take my knife and insert it here," he said, pressing his fingers into his pubic area. "And slit him up to here." He ripped his hand up to just below his neck. "Then I'll pull out his intestines, kidneys, heart and lungs." He made a scooping motion and threw the imaginary organs onto the bar floor.

The other three looked at him. They blinked and looked at each other. Glenn finally broke the uncomfortable silence. "We will keep filleting Roshberg as a last resort, but thank you for the image, Paul."

"Is there any way to tie Otto to the doctor and get him closed down that way?" asked Daniel.

"We just have Bobby's side of the story now. Otto has been removed from the equation and any hope of a confession died with him," said Glenn. "I was told Roshberg ordering Otto to commit any of those acts is all hearsay and can't be proven."

Daniel took a drink of Fat Tire and slammed his glass down. "At least Bobby took care of the thug! And—" Daniel chuckled. "He created a new verb along the way. Otto was *pulse-oxed*. I mean, farmers in olden days may have died from being trampled by their oxen, but they were never pulse-oxed."

They drank in silence. Richard turned his attention to Glenn. "How long will the federal investigation take?"

"Six months, maybe nine. That's what they told me."

Richard's eyes grew wide. "And it's business as usual at Dr. Roshberg's office in the meantime?"

Glenn nodded and they all lapsed into a morose silence. They didn't even notice when the front door opened and a customer entered. The man strode over to the old Wurlitzer, gave the jukebox a loving pat, walked to the bar and sat down.

"Why is everybody so sad?" the man asked.

All heads in the bar turned and watched Bobby nestle his large buttocks snugly into the indentions in his barstool.

"Bobby!" they all screamed at once.

Richard was pumping Bobby's hand; Pinhead Paul gave him a pungent hug. Daniel let out a "Whoop" and slapped Bobby on the back. Kenny came running from the other end of the bar.

Bobby held Kenny at arm's length, studying him. "Who do we have here?" Bobby asked, stroking Kenny's smooth face. Kenny just laughed. "What happened to the beard, Kenny my man?"

"I just had a hankering to shave it one morning and the next thing I know Ism is calling me Richard Nixon. I took that as a sign to keep shaving."

Bobby let out a deep laugh and it was infectious. They were all laughing when Bobby looked down and discovered Matilda leeched on to his side. The top of her head only came up to the bottom of his ribs. Matilda had her head buried in Bobby's shirt.

With a mechanical convulsion the Wurlitzer came to life, changed records and the beautiful voice of Patsy Cline emerged singing "She's Got You".

"Miss Matilda!" Bobby exclaimed. "I've sure missed you. What's wrong?"

Matilda shook her head and wouldn't remove it from Bobby's shirt.

When Daniel said, "You were right Tilly, the sun *will* come out tomorrow," Matilda let out a loud wail and burrowed her head deeper into Bobby's shirt.

Stunned, Bobby looked to Daniel. "You mean…" He glanced down at the top of Matilda's white head.

"Yep," Daniel said. "Bobby, meet ancient Annie who serenaded you when you were incapacitated in the hospital. I knew it was something that would sink in and you would never forget." ("I know I'll never forget it," he added softly with a shudder.)

Bobby lifted Matilda up until her face was level with his. Her eyes were red and she was sniffling. Bobby gave her a big smooch on the lips and hugged her frail body to his massive chest. "You tough old bird. I didn't know you cared."

"Okay, okay," Matilda rasped. "Put me down before you get too sexually aroused, you big behemoth. I need to get back to my Rose Kennedy Cocktail."

Glenda entered and moved beside Glenn behind the bar. "I thought you were taking Bobby home," Glenn said to his wife.

"Are you kidding?" Bobby interrupted. "*This* is my home. The last place I wanted to go after leaving the hospital was my house. I spent too much time alone in the hospital." He looked slowly around the bar. "Hello, No Egrets! Hello, friends!" he boomed.

Glenn placed a Bud Light bottle on the bar; Bobby beamed and began peeling off the label. "This is more like it," Bobby said. "Everyone happy. Why were you such sad sacks when I walked in?"

Glenn thought about glossing over the question but changed his mind. Bobby was an integral part and deserved to know everything. Glenn filled in the parts Bobby had missed.

Bobby listened intently, alternately peeling the label and drinking the Bud Light. He looked to Richard. "That was very brave of you, Richard." He placed his big hand on Richard's shoulder. "Thanks, man."

"My pleasure, Robert. Anything to help."

"And you, Glenda. I owe you and Doc more than I can ever repay." Glenda smiled and wiped a tear from her eye.

Glenn replaced Bobby's empty with a new Bud Light bottle and finished by telling Bobby what the police had told him about the Office of Inspector General timeline for investigation.

"Wow! Now I understand the long faces when I walked in. Is there no way to make it faster?" Bobby asked hopefully.

"Well," Daniel said. "I knew a physician investigated by OIG in West Virginia. They came in, shut his office down and removed computers and boxes of paperwork. But I think there was a whistleblower in that case."

"A...whistleblower," Bobby said thoughtfully.

"Yes. Someone who worked there turned him in."

Bobby leaped off his barstool and jumped in the air. He danced around in a circle; everyone in the bar thought he had lost his mind. He put two fingers to his mouth and a piercing whistle followed.

"Bobby, please," Glenda begged. "Don't overdo it. You don't want to end up back in the hospital."

Glenn looked at his large friend with amazement. "What in the world?"

"Doc!" Bobby screamed. "I got us a whistleblower!"

Bobby plopped his gluteus maximus back into the indentations and took a large gulp of beer. Everyone gathered around him in a circle, waiting for him to continue.

"She came to see me in the hospital; she was a Nurse Practitioner at Dr. Roshberg's office for a few months. She works at a clinic near the hospital now. I think she would have told somebody what was happening at the office a long time ago if Otto hadn't threatened her and her family."

The mood of the bar, which had been on an emotional pendulum, shifted back to jubilant. Drinks flowed faster and voices became louder. Bobby peeled the label off his second bottle of Bud Light, smiling ear to ear.

"Hey wait," Bobby said. "I just realized I missed No Egrets anniversary celebration." He turned to Glenn and Glenda. "I'm sorry guys. I really wanted to be here."

Glenn and Glenda exchanged a glance. Glenn motioned for his wife to speak. "You don't think we could have our one-year celebration without our first customer? We postponed it."

"I didn't miss it!" Bobby said excitedly.

The record changed on the Wurlitzer and four drumbeats signaled the start of "Celebration" by Kool & the Gang.

Glenn smiled. "Nope. You didn't miss it."

"Well, when is it?"

Glenn and Glenda looked at each other blankly. "I don't know. We haven't thought about it," said Glenn.

"How about next weekend?" Glenda asked excitedly. "We could change the date on all the signs and banners. I can check to see if the band is available."

Glenn grimaced. "I don't know. The back room and stage aren't finished yet."

"Not a problem," Bobby said. "Next week is my off week. I don't go back to work until a week from Monday. I'll be in early tomorrow with my tool belt on."

"I'll be there, too," said Richard. "The Tim Burton movie is on hold for the moment so no auditions for me."

Glenn shrugged. "Well alright. Sounds like a plan."

In the background, Kool & the Gang sang, "Yahoo! It's a celebration."

Bobby checked his watch, chugged the last of his second Bud Light and slapped the label back on the bottle. "If you don't mind Glenda, could you take me to Karen's now? She told me to come after three."

"It would be my pleasure."

Glenda was standing as far away from Karen and Bobby on the front porch as she could, but it was her job to guard the front door and run interference if Karen's sister, Brandi tried to come out. Brandi wasn't happy Bobby was back in the picture. Glenda tried her best not to eavesdrop, but she was just too close.

"I didn't want you to see me like this," Karen said to Bobby shyly. Glenda didn't think Karen looked any worse than the last time she saw her, but she certainly didn't look any better.

Bobby put his arms around her. "Karen, you are simply the most beautiful woman...ever. I didn't know if I'd ever see you again. That made me very sad."

Glenda tried to look away but couldn't help noticing Karen begin to cry.

"Oh Bobby, when I heard what happened to you."

Bobby hugged her tight. "Karen, I love you. I won't ever leave you again."

Karen cried and held tightly to Bobby.

"Is it okay if I go with you to your new doctor on Thursday?" Bobby asked.

"Yes." Her whole body shuddered in his arms.

Bobby held her at arm's length. "You're going to beat this. I promise."

Bobby pulled Karen close and kissed her. Glenda didn't bother looking away; she laughed and cried tears of joy.

Glenn was clearing the empty bottles from the bar when the label flew off the Bud Light bottle and fluttered to the floor. He tossed the empty bottles into the bin and turned to pick up the label. It was face down on the floor, but he stopped before picking it up. Bobby had written on the back: "I love you guys."

TWENTY-SIX

Glenn struggled to be quiet, casual, cool. When the day began, he had no idea he would be in Shallotte standing around a newly paved parking lot.

His morning schedule had been dedicated to an early island run with Daniel and just as they were stretching and groaning, Sphinx called. It was the policeman's day off, but the chief had phoned him at home; the Brunswick County Sheriff's deputies were moving in on Dr. Roshberg. Glenn had put him on speaker so Daniel could hear the conversation.

"They think he's going to destroy records and make a run for it," Sphinx said, using his authoritative cop voice. Glenn and Daniel immediately looked at each other, surprised. Glenn thought about Roshberg's previous stints in Florida and Georgia and it made sense. Time to run away.

Sphinx gave the highlights: the Feds about to seize the records; Brunswick County heading to the office to secure the building and everything inside including, with a little luck, Roshberg.

And then the words that were music to Glenn's ears. "Hey, how about you and Daniel join me for a nice, leisurely drive to Shallotte this morning?" Sphinx asked.

"Hell yes!" Glenn responded, punctuating it with a fist pump.

No one spoke much on the drive. Outside the windows they watched the beginning of a typical, small southern town workday. All quiet on the western front...for now. Sphinx had 80s rock tuned in with the volume low (in order to hear the police radio over Sting and The Police). Glenn, in the passenger seat, turned to check out the back seat of the cruiser. Daniel was looking around the back seat contentedly.

"Lots of leg room," he explained when Glenn caught his eye.

Sphinx slowed down about a quarter of a mile from Roshberg's building. He eased off US 17 and pulled into a parking lot behind the last deputy cruiser.

Plain clothes deputies were out of their cars and gathered behind a deserted Laundromat. As the three walked up to them, Glenn could see two other men and a woman, also wearing guns and badges on their belts, circled around with the deputies, explaining the operation. Glenn noticed Sphinx had his gun and badge, too.

Sphinx was welcomed by name, then all conversation ceased. Glenn and Daniel could sense the uncomfortable "cop stares" focused on them. (Glenn felt like he should confess to something and had the sudden urge to call his mother: "Mom—it wasn't the cat! I broke your Blenko vase!")

"These gentlemen are healthcare professionals instrumental in building this case," Sphinx said. "They are on a ride-along with me and are only here to observe."

The circle widened, allowing the extras to join. Details for the raid had already been spelled out and Sphinx was directed to watch the exits. Glenn and Daniel were given the important jobs of "observing only and staying the hell out of the way".

The professionals loaded into two cruisers; Sphinx shrugged as he took the last seat and looked up at his friends. "Well, you *are* dressed for jogging."

Glenn and Daniel took off running toward the distant building.

"Do you think we should have guns?" Daniel asked with a touch of concern in his voice. "Otto was the dangerous one. Roshberg—he's—well, you never know how an animal will act when it's cornered."

"Don't want a gun," Glenn responded, beginning to huff a little. "Makes my running shorts droop to one side. Ruins the whole athletic look I'm going for."

"What do you think spooked the fine and ethical Dr. Roshberg?" Daniel asked.

"I don't know. I doubt if he knows about Stacey Sparks and her whistleblower claim yet. She just entered it on Tuesday."

The two finished their short run and began walking toward the back parking lot, acting like they were cooling down from their run. They spotted Sphinx crouched behind a huge Rolls Royce in the front and he gave them a thumbs up.

"Maybe Otto's death spooked him," Daniel offered quietly. "The little weasel can't survive without hired muscle to protect him."

At that moment, the back door creaked open. A man in a white lab coat was backing out the door struggling to hold on to two desktop computer cases.

Neither man had ever had direct contact with Roshberg and curiosity got the better of them. Forgetting their nonparticipation promise, Glenn and Daniel moved forward.

"Dr. Roshberg?" Glenn asked.

The doctor turned, nearly dropping one of the computers.

"Oh here, let me help you," Daniel said. He grabbed both computers from the stunned doctor's grasp so quickly Roshberg didn't have time to resist. "I'm sure you are just taking these to be fixed. Hey, I know a great computer technician. Why, he can recover any kind of information from a hard drive, even if it's been wiped. He's a real wizard like that."

A panicked look crossed the doctor's face. He backed up like a cornered beast. When the doctor turned to run Glenn blocked him. "Where are you going Dr. Roshberg? I need your help. You see, I have a pain right here." Glenn thumped his chest with a fist above his heart. "My wife says it's because there are scumbag doctors in the world who are only in it for the money and don't give a shit about their patients. But it might just be acid reflux. What do you think?"

"Leave me alone!" Roshberg cried.

"That doesn't sound like a diagnosis to me. Does it you, Glenn?"

"Why no, Daniel. It does not. Perhaps we ought to escort this fine excuse for a physician back into his office so he can examine me proper like."

As Glenn pushed Dr. Roshberg backward through the door, he looked down on him and said, "You know. You are really, *really* short."

They entered directly into Dr. Roshberg's office, complete with antiquities, rare books and a bust of Napoleon. The parallel with the French leader was not lost on Glenn or Daniel.

"So, you have an escape hatch directly from your office. Interesting," said Glenn.

"And boy what an office. Look at that desk." Daniel stooped to examine the large mahogany desk.

Dr. Roshberg backpedaled until he made it to the wall behind the desk. His beady eyes examined the two men who were clad in t-shirts, shorts and running shoes. "Who are you? What do you want? I have money. I can pay you if you give me back my computers and let me leave."

Glenn and Daniel exchanged looks.

"Lots of money," the doctor promised. "Cash!"

Two sheriff deputies appeared in the doorway.

"I love it when they try to bribe their way out of trouble," said the taller of the two deputies. "Makes it easier for all the charges to stick. So, where is this cash? Or are you going to make us look for it?"

"Days like these make me love my job," said the other deputy.

Glenn was only half listening. His attention had been drawn to the wall above Dr. Roshberg's head.

"Oh—my—God!"

Daniel turned to his friend. "What?"

"He's got a Hippocratic Oath on his office wall. Framed!" Glenn stared at it and felt sick to his stomach. He remembered the reverence he had felt upon the oath being administered to his graduating class before they were all presented with a copy and sworn to uphold high ethical standards.

Daniel noticed his friend clenching and unclenching his fists and turning red. He approached the deputies. "Did you notice the boxes in the hallway? I think somebody was getting ready to move out. Or he may have stashed the cash there." Smoothly, he led the deputies into the hall.

A crash and the sound of breaking glass followed. Daniel tried unsuccessfully to get out of the deputies' way and ended up impeding their progress. When the deputies finally ran through the office door, Roshberg was kneeling on the floor, clutching the side of his head with a bloody hand. Glenn was standing in the same spot. The Hippocratic Oath frame was on the floor beside the doctor. Shards of broken glass were scattered around the floor.

"What happened?" demanded the shorter deputy.

Glenn pointed to the wall and made a circular descending motion with his hand. Daniel took up the story from there.

"I told you that frame was dangerous when we came in. It looked like it was going to fall off the wall. I think the frame was much too heavy for the nail. Gravity—physics. It was an accident waiting to happen."

Glenn looked at the deputies, a satisfied smile on his face.

"Happy Anniversary, No Egrets! One year and still growing!" yelled Whitney, the bearded leader of The Lost Cause Band into the microphone. The band had just finished "Tequila", always a bar crowd hit. But Whitney's dirty sax solo had taken it to a new frenzied level. When the crowd saw him lift his sax above his head at the end of the song, they began demanding more of the same. The cheering bounced back and forth off the walls.

Glenn gazed around the bar with pride. No Egrets was packed and the atmosphere festive. The new stage the band was jamming on looked spectacular. Bobby had helped Glenn finish the back room, but it was Bobby's stroke of genius to tear out the wall and open up the room and stage to the rest of the bar. Bobby had even designed and installed a special sliding door that locked so the room could be closed off when not needed (and, more importantly to Glenda, Jujitsu for Jesus wouldn't be left without an alternative place to practice).

Glenda stood beside her husband, a slight smile on her face. She was thinking about how No Egrets looked when they had first walked in with the real estate agent. A waitress moved past her swiftly. She was so glad Glenn had agreed to hire bartenders and waitresses from a contract company for the party. It gave them a chance to really enjoy the festivities, the band, and of course be good hosts. Ism didn't seem to mind either; he and his girlfriend Allie were front and center of the band twerking their tushies off.

Bobby walked out of the bathroom to a chorus of cheers. It had been a little over a week, but he was still being treated as a hero. Glenda had been overjoyed when Bobby had brought Karen to the party. Whitney and his singer wife, Vicki were her neighbors and Karen had wanted to hear the first couple songs of the set. She told Glenda she was feeling better since her appointment with her new doctor on Thursday (and it really helped having Bobby back by her side). She had actually made it through four songs before getting tired; Bobby was preparing to take her home.

"Play 'Bela Lugosi's Blues'!" yelled Daniel O'Dwyer.

"A request from a big tipper! 'Bela Lugosi's Blues' it is," replied Whitney from the stage. "Right after a short break."

Glenn had to weave his way through the crowd to get to Daniel who was seated at the bar. Beside him was his friend, Willie. Daniel had described Willie as "socially imbalanced" and explained he didn't come out of his houseboat much (the Silent Cow was "moored" on the back lot of Daniel's property amidst the trees, vines and shrubbery) but he was a big fan of The Lost Cause Band, having seen them once at the Oar House Lounge. Willie was sporting an old fashioned flat-top haircut, wearing a Jethro Tull 1979 tour t-shirt and seated on a stainless-steel barstool that Daniel had brought special for his friend. He only drank organic beer and in his hand was a bottle of Organic Wild Salmon Pale Ale which Daniel had delivered to the bar cooler the day before.

Willie had been waiting all evening for one of the bar owners to swing by his seat. Glenda turned out to be the lucky one. As she tried to find a foot of space in which to stand, Willie asked her, "What do you have against egrets?"

Glenda was momentarily taken aback. "Um…nothing. We have one that visits our goldfish pond. The name of the bar is more a play on words."

Willie's face lit up. Daniel groaned and dropped his chin to his chest. "Willie is the king of wordplay games," Daniel explained. "And he doesn't give in easily." Daniel considered being Willie's wordplay sparring partner one of his biggest crosses to bear in life. Willie was the reigning champ and if he issued a challenge now, Daniel's response would be flight rather than fight.

"I'll take you on, big *boy*," a crusty voice challenged from the other side of Willie. Daniel breathed a sigh of relief.

"Matilda! You beautiful, mature lady!" Daniel cried. Matilda responded by tossing back the last of her Sake Bomb (it was Saturday).

Daniel moved between them and made the introductions. "Willie, this is Tilly. She's the queen of No Egrets."

Matilda snorted. "I'm not the queen of anything, although I was crowned Miss Ring Girl at the 1981 Toughman Contest in Charlotte."

Glenn, Glenda and Daniel exchanged startled glances. ("Don't get an image," Daniel began repeating under his breath.)

Matilda and Willie eyed each other like Saturday night wrestlers on Wrestle Mania circling each other in the ring. Willie interlaced his fingers and inverted them, producing loud cracks.

"Another Sake Bomb, barmaid," Matilda demanded. "I need to get my mind right."

"Another Organic Wild Salmon Pale Ale," said Willie.

"Wussy drink. Bring it on!" Matilda taunted.

"This is your house. You go first," Willie said with a sweep of his arm.

Matilda looked around. Her gaze focused on the bottles behind the bar. Suddenly her frown dissolved. "It's my *Bicardi*—and I'll cry if I want to!"

Daniel "oohed"; Glenda "aahed". Willie smiled. The game was afoot.

Willie scanned the bottles. He put up his index finger and pointed. "Moves like *Jager*—meister!"

Daniel was amazed. He didn't know Willie knew any songs by any band other than Jethro Tull. Plus the song wasn't thirty or forty years old.

Whitney, his saxophone still hanging around his neck, walked to the bar and Daniel turned his attention away from Willie and Matilda's two out of three falls, winner-take-all match. "Hey! Remember me?" Daniel asked.

"Sure," Whitney said. "I never forget a good tipper."

"'Bela Lugosi's Blues' is my favorite Lost Cause song."

Whitney laughed just as his wife, a fabulous redhead appeared beside him. "This is Vicki."

"Hi Vicki. I've got someone I want you to meet. He's a really big fan of yours." Daniel moved her between Willie and Matilda, but the game had heated up.

"Wine section!" Matilda yelled.

Willie ignored Daniel pecking him on the shoulder. He leaned forward, trying to read the wine labels. He sat up straight, a smug look on his face. "Bad moon *Riesling*!"

Matilda slammed her mug on the bar, mixing more of the sunken shot glass of sake into the beer. She took a short drink followed by a long burp. She turned and glared at Willie. Willie laughed, clearly thinking he had won.

Slowly, Matilda sneered. "*Chardon—nay*, boy, is that the Chattanooga Choo-choo?"

All those around them cheered. Willie had no choice but to bow before Matilda and he did so with a grin on his face.

"Willie. Willie!" Finally Willie turned to Daniel. "This is Vicki."

Willie grinned even wider and bowed before Vicki. "Your voice is terrific. You killed Bobby McGhee."

Vicki squealed and gave Willie a big hug. Daniel was amazed his friend didn't try to pull away.

Whitney, laughing at his wife's antics, caught Glenn as he walked by. "I've got somebody I want *you* to meet." He motioned the frizzy haired guitar player from the band over. "Glenn, this is Len. You two might have a few things to talk about. When Len isn't belting out Crosby, Stills and Nash, he's a surgeon at Boiling Grove."

As the two surgeons converted to med-speak, Glenda followed a waitress to a table near the door. She waited while the waitress delivered two strawberry daiquiris. This was the first time the Sonora sisters had been back to No Egrets together since the start of their ordeal. Other than Bonita's short hair and pale complexion, she looked healthy, happy and sassy.

"You sure you're up for one, Boni?" Juanita asked. "I can drink them both."

"Give it to me," Bonita told her sister. "And keep your sticky fingers off it, Sis."

Juanita smiled at Glenda. "She's been feeling pretty good. We really owe you and Doc a lot."

"I really like my new doctor," Bonita said.

Juanita was beaming. "I think everything's going to be okay."

Bonita moved over and hugged her sister. "Yes, I think everything's going to be okay."

Glenda looked around the community she and Glenn had created. Everyone was smiling and laughing but Glenn's smile was the biggest of all. *Yes*, she thought, *everything's going to be okay*.

Glenda weaved her way through the cars in the packed parking lot, stopping when she made it to the sidewalk. She turned, admiring the outside of No Egrets. The band had just started their third set and she could hear the strange sounds of an electric "Bésame Mucho" wafting from the bar. The streetlight illuminated the No Egrets sign and Glenda noticed the first hints of corrosion on their original metal sign. Might just be time for a new, fancy, brightly colored illuminated sign.

Glenn poked his head out the front door and noticing his wife, walked over to join her.

"I wondered what happened to you. What are you doing?" he asked.

Glenda didn't answer, instead looping her arm around Glenn's waist and hugging him tight. She let out a contented sigh.

Glenn wrapped his arm around his wife. "Yes, it is good, isn't it?"

She looked up at his face, a little surprised. "Why darling, I think you may actually be ...happy."

"Hmm, perhaps." He bent down and gave her a long kiss.

Holding hands, they didn't speak for a long time, gazing at the bar.

"I'm not going to lie to you," Glenn said, breaking the silence. "It did feel good to help people again. I hope Karen and Bonita are going to be okay. But after seeing the seedy side of the medical profession, I think I'm happy here, at least for the time being."

Glenda pulled her husband tight, hugging him.

"I've got a good idea," she said. "After the tourist season ends, let's go on a long vacation. Where would you like to go?"

"An African safari," he replied immediately.

When Glenda didn't respond, he said, "I know. Camping is not your forte and I can go on the safari with my second wife, Teah Valentine."

Glenda laughed. "Actually, I wasn't going to say that. I was going to offer a compromise. How about Disney's Animal Kingdom Lodge?"

"What do you mean?"

"The animals are right outside your window. And I can have a bath, a nice bed, and excellent food."

"Hmm."

"I'll take that as a maybe."

For a long time they stood gazing at the business they had created. The band had just finished a song and all was quiet.

"You guys finally open for business?"

They both gasped and turned around. Déjà vu. There he stood, all six feet eleven inches, three hundred and fifty pounds just like he had a little over a year ago.

"Karen insisted I come back to the party."

Glenda wrapped her other arm around Bobby. Together they walked back into No Egrets.

EPILOGUE

Glenda used her "magic band" to unlock the room door. Glenn ran in like a little kid. It had been nine months since they had celebrated the anniversary of No Egrets and Glenda had finally convinced Glenn to take the vacation. He had started talking about an African safari again, so naturally they had just arrived at the Jambo House at Walt Disney's Animal Kingdom Lodge in Orlando.

Glenn grabbed the room's Wildlife Spotting Guide from the nightstand, fumbled with the sliding glass door and finally charged out onto the second-floor balcony. Glenda unpacked their carry-on bags on the bed.

Glenn's view to the right was partially obscured by the side of the hotel, but on the left the room was situated near the corner of the buildings with a watering hole and several large trees directly in front. He glanced through the Wildlife Spotting Guide quickly; they had roan antelope, kudu, scimitar-horned oryx, impala, red river hogs! This was going to be great! He scanned the watering hole for movement. Nothing. He searched between the trees for shapes. Nothing.

Glenda was surprised when the sliding glass door opened and Glenn came storming in.

"What's wrong?"

"There are no animals out there. I knew it was too good to be true."

Glenn slammed the bathroom door. Glenda sighed. Patience had never been one of her husband's strong points. She made her way out to the balcony and stopped to pick up the Wildlife Spotting Guide where it had been dropped. No sooner had she looked up when a beautiful giraffe loped around the side of the building, stopping at a tree where it extended its long neck and munched on leaves. It was so close she could see its tongue! A smaller giraffe appeared followed by a several exquisite zebras.

"Glenn! Glenn! Giraffes and zebras!" She ran to the bathroom door and knocked. "Giraffes and zebras," she said breathlessly.

"Yeah right," said the voice from the other side of the door. "And lions and tigers and bears. I wasn't born yesterday. You're not pulling that trick on me."

The trial of Julius Roshberg was a media circus. Federal prosecutors called him the "most egregious fraudster in the history of this country". His former patients called him "monster". One patient testified that due to excessive chemotherapy treatments, the shape of his jaw changed and all of his teeth but one fell out. He punctuated the testimony by standing, opening his mouth and pointing out his lone tooth to the jury. Another patient spoke out posthumously. His wife read a statement he had written four months earlier before he passed away claiming none of his tumors were helped, instead increasing in number and size and how he believed Dr. Roshberg knowingly and purposely treated him for the wrong cancer and gave him the wrong chemotherapy. Stacey Sparks, the Nurse Practitioner testified about the four months she was employed at the office and the issues she had witnessed with patients receiving wrong medicine or medicine out of sequence, poor record keeping, unsafe practices and questionable billing. The star witness, however, was Richard. His emotional testimony, along with three exhibits, was very damaging to the defense. The three exhibits were shown on a large screen and consisted of Richard's initial lab work at Boiling Grove, his abnormal lab results at the oncologist's office and a normal set drawn a week after Roshberg's labs. Dr. Roshberg, who had pleaded not guilty, was put on suicide watch soon after Richard's testimony.

Richard's testimony had been on a Friday and on Monday when the trial resumed, Dr. Roshberg changed his plea to guilty. It was widely speculated the defense hoped to work out a deal. Roshberg made an emotional apology in court claiming "the quest for power is self-destructive" and "the patients came to me seeking compassion and care" and how he had failed them. The judge threatened to clear the courtroom when a chorus of boos followed the speech.

Thankfully the jury bought none of the defense's tactics and the prosecution refused to even talk about making a deal. Julius Roshberg was convicted on thirteen counts of Medicare fraud, one count of conspiracy to pay or receive kickbacks and two counts of money laundering. He forfeited $15.9 million he collected from Medicare and private insurance companies. He lost his license to practice medicine. The list of patients who received medically unnecessary treatments continued to grow until it was well over four hundred. Roshberg was sentenced to forty-five years in prison and is expected to serve at least thirty-four years of his sentence at a low-security prison in North Carolina.

Richard became a local celebrity almost overnight. His televised testimony made him a sought after party guest at all the entertainment events in Wilmington. A fan base started to grow which boosted his career. A better agent pursued and signed him. The offers came pouring in and Richard won the part of the head alien, Zordick in Tim Burton's upcoming production of *Mars Needs Beer.*

Karen's new oncologist, after carefully consulting with two other physicians, declared Karen's cancer to be in remission. She had taken only a few chemotherapy treatments of a different drug and regimen and her doctor was quite pleased with the result. It was amazing to Karen how she had tolerated the new chemotherapy with absolutely no side effects. The chemotherapy given to her by Dr. Roshberg had been like torture, making her physically sick for days. She had overheard her new doctor telling his nurse that Dr. Roshberg should be forced to endure the same drug and number of treatments he had forced on Karen.

Bobby went back to work at the nuclear plant. One day in the middle of the usual suspects at No Egrets, he got down on his knees, took Karen's hand, slipped a ring box out of his pocket and proposed. Karen cried and accepted. Matilda began singing "Tomorrow" from Annie and soon they all joined in: "The sun will come out tomorrow…"

Bonita Sonora did not have cancer. She had some abnormalities in her blood work, but the new oncologist determined it was not cancer and with a few lifestyle changes, she was deemed healthy. It took her longer to recover from the toxic effects of the unnecessary chemotherapy than it did to get her lab results back in the normal range. Bonita and Juanita did take their trip to Mexico but the only alternative medicine they tried was strawberry margaritas instead of their usual strawberry daiquiris.

Mabel Thomson of Bolton did have cancer and it was in its advanced stages. After reviewing her scans and results, a new oncologist determined she had been in an advanced stage for almost a year and should never have been administered chemotherapy during that time. "She should be allowed to die in peace," he said. Mabel Thomson passed away in Hospice surrounded by her loving family. They buried her beside her husband Tommie.

Pinhead Paul became obsessed with Richard Nixon and collected books which included many of Nixon's public speeches. While cleaning fish, he could be heard reciting many of Nixon's lines. "I am not a crook!" he would often say to the lifeless yellowfin tuna, wahoo, or mahi-mahi (depending on the season).

After weeks of staring into the full-length mirror outside the kitchen door, Kenny decided to grow his man beard back (much to the delight of his mother who kept running in to him when she left the kitchen).

Daniel had been shocked to receive a call from human resources at Boiling Grove Community Hospital. The hospital pharmacy director was retiring after forty-four years and they wanted Daniel to interview for the position. It only took him ten seconds to say, "Hell no!" but it did produce the curious side effect of causing him to ponder his future. What exactly awaits Daniel O'Dwyer around the next corner?

Tropical Storm Ora arrived on the island during hurricane season causing Ism to froth and develop chicken skin. Down at shredquarters, the sphincter factor quickly approached a 10. Jazzing the glass that day, the crewbies experienced more Neptune cocktails, pearlitis, rag dolls, sand facials and premature eshackulations than all the months before. By the end of the day they were totally Burnt Reynolds. Redonculous.

The Lost Cause Band's YouTube performance of "Bela Lugosi's Blues" came to the attention of American Movie Classic executives who paid for the song to be included in their annual AMC FearFest commercials for Halloween. Sara Karloff, the daughter of the movie great objected to the lines "I was the King of Horror, 'til I met that damned Karloff" and "Still hatin' on Karloff—got the Bela Lugosi Blues" which brought more press, notoriety and YouTube views. The Lost Cause Band is currently working on a new album tentatively titled "Bela Rules".

Although she wouldn't admit it, Bobby's brush with death had shaken Matilda and she decided to make some changes. She interchanged the Tequila Sunrise she always drank on Thursdays with the Zombie she always drank on Tuesdays. Oh, and she got a rabbit's foot to hang from the handlebars of her Vespa.

Glenn had decided to take a shower since he was already in the bathroom. Glenda knocked on the door and stuck her head in halfway.

"Honey, I'm telling you, you need to get out here! Wildebeest! They are so cool looking. And I checked in the guide and the little antelope-looking thingies are Thomson's gazelles. I've seen about four of them. And three of these huge birds came to the watering hole. They are called griffon vultures and it says their wingspan is eight feet!"

"Yeah, yeah," Glenn said. "I told you I'm not falling for it."

Meanwhile, back in Glenn and Glenda's backyard on Oak Island, Ernie the egret swooped down and scooped up the last goldfish from their pond. But that's a mystery for another day.

ABOUT THE AUTHOR

Lance Carney is an award winning 30+ year hospital pharmacist (5 year award, 10 year award, 15 ...). He has been writing medical/pharmacy based fiction since the 1980s. He has written four novels, "Ripped Tide: A Daniel O'Dwyer Oak Island Adventure" , "No Egrets: A Glenn and Glenda Oak Island Mystery", "Mantis Preying: A Daniel O'Dwyer Oak Island Adventure" and "Of Vamps and Vampiros: A Finnian O'Dwyer Universal City Crime Cape(r).

Lance's short stories have been published in magazines, anthologies and trade paperbacks. He often collaborates with David Moss, a buddy since junior high school. David is mostly grown up now, working for state government and having every holiday off, including Peter Rabbit's birthday. "Truth is Stranger than Fishin'" with David was chosen for publication in The Year's Best Fantastic Fiction. One of Lance's own, "Snare of the Fowler", was published in the trade paperback "Monsters from Memphis" and recognized by a nomination from the Darrell Awards Jury for Best Midsouth Short Story.

Lance lives in West Virginia with his wife and the last cat standing-named #4. His daughter graduated college in 2017 in film studies and is currently in Los Angeles working for Walt Disney Animation. His son graduated from Mississippi State University College of Veterinary Medicine in 2018 and is currently practicing in Fairfax, Va. Somehow, at times, they still manage to throw the empty nest into turmoil. He escapes to Oak Island, North Carolina, whenever The Man isn't keeping him down

NOTE FROM THE AUTHOR

A huge thank you to my readers. If you are reading this, then you made it to the end (or maybe you are holding the book upside down and backwards and just ended up here). Either way I am grateful; I hope you enjoyed the story. If you decide to go the extra mile and take time from your busy schedule to leave an honest review on Amazon or Goodreads, it would be very helpful. Reviews are extremely important to Indie authors and I appreciate each review I receive. As a special incentive, all those who leave a review will be entered into a drawing to win "Tea with Tilly" (Long Island Iced Tea, of course.)

"MANTIS PREYING: A DANIEL O'DWYER OAK ISLAND ADVENTURE" OPENING CHAPTER

The following chapter is from Lance Carney's "Mantis Preying: A Daniel O'Dwyer Oak Island Adventure" (Oak Island Series Book 3) available on Amazon in paperback, e-book and audiobook.

1 - PIRATES AND WANKERS

"I don't know if I can spend eternity with this guy when he goes. I mean—just look at him."

"Aye mate. I know what you mean. He's only been on our vessel for what seems like a fortnight and yet his voice scrapes on me like barnacles. Witness the parley between these two; I'd rather dance the hempen jig than listen to more."

"In our day it would have been easy to get rid of a scurvy landlubber like him. Drop him on a deserted island, make him walk the plank, keelhaul, wait 'til the rum flows and bump him over the side."

"Sounds easy 'nough, except for two problems. No water, thanks to this fool. And the best we can do is move a glass or knock over an empty bottle of his grog."

"Yes…yes. Tis hopeless. We're doomed."

Fiddling with my ear, I stared at the wall. Something was missing. I had only glimpsed it through the cabin door before, but now the bare wall looked out of place. Something was definitely missing.

"What are you doing with that Q-Tip?" Willie shrieked. Then he gasped in that way that teeters between overacting and a teenage crisis.

I stopped mid-twirl, looking at him like I always did when he asked a stupid question—incredulously. "What's it look like?"

"Like you have no regard for your ear canal or otic health."

I removed the Q-Tip and purposely tossed it onto an end table that looked like an antique nesting table but appeared as sterile as an operating room. Willie responded to my callous action with another gasp and a fast exit into the galley, returning quickly with forceps and a small plastic bag emblazoned with the fluorescent orange biohazard symbol. With extreme caution, he used the forceps to extract the Q-Tip from the end table and place it in the plastic bag. You would have thought my ear canal contained radioactive wax.

Germophobes are a unique breed and Willie could be their king.

When he had disposed of the toxic waste and wiped up its remnants, he returned to his chair and looked at me sourly.

"What?" I asked, preparing for a lecture.

Instead I got a "tsk-tsk" and a head shake. I waited him out, my way of torturing him slowly.

Finally, he broke. "I don't care what you do in your own house, but this is my home and I will not have you throwing caution to the wind."

Willie's "home" was actually an old houseboat he had fixed up (with the help of handyman extraordinaire Moses and my money). He had dubbed it the Silent Cow and planted it in the middle of the wooded lot I owned behind my house. Living on it in the water had been out of the question—too many waterborne illnesses. (I had asked him to prove it and he brought up the CDC website and started ticking them off: Legionella, Vibrio cholera, Norovirus, typhoid…)

This was actually the first time I had been allowed inside the Silent Cow—and thanks to my dirty aural openings, perhaps the last. Could I help it if it was something passed down through generations of O'Dwyers? Back in Ireland, my great-great grandfather and namesake was often called Daniel Derdy Ears.

"Um…caution to the wind?"

"Yes," Willie answered indignantly. "Don't you ever read the cautions on product packaging?"

"Heck no! Those are only for—" I started to say "morons" but caught myself. "Uh, lawyers."

Willie walked into his bedroom and returned with a rectangular Tupperware container.

"What's in—"

Ignoring my question, he popped the lid and began reading from something within. "**Warning: Do not insert into ear canal.**" (Written in bold letters, he read it that way.) "**Entering the ear canal could cause injury,**" he finished.

"Oh, come on!" I started.

He silenced me with his hand and continued. "Keep out of reach of children."

Keep out of reach of morons, I thought. "You mean to tell me you've never used a Q-Tip to clean your ear? The whole world uses Q-Tips to clean their ears!"

He shook his head. "I value my ear drums and do not wish to puncture them with a stick."

"A stick!" Willie had done it again. I was visibly upset—over Q-Tips for God's sake. I leaned over and looked in the Tupperware container and read from the Q-tip box myself. "It's a cotton swab; has soft cotton on the end."

My eyes went back to the box. "It's the Ultimate Home and Beauty Tool."

"It's a dangerous lance," Willie said matter-of-factly.

Not wishing to give in, I offered one last jab. "And why do you keep the box sealed in a Tupperware container?"

"Cotton."

"Cotton?"

"Yes, cotton is a breeding ground for deadly bacteria."

My hands were raised in front of me; I let them drop, surrendering. But I had to ask: "Then why do you have Q-Tips in your—" I looked around the Silent Cow. "Home—house—houseboat?"

"I dip them in isopropyl alcohol and clean the keyboard of my laptop twice a day. More often if necessary. The Q-Tip was invented in the 1920s by Leo—"

"Stop," I interrupted. "I don't care. So why did you leave three Q-Tips out of the box, within my reach, if the cotton was absorbing all the nasty bacteria floating through the air?"

"Madame asked for three Q-Tips. Oh, that reminds me, she also asked for something else." Willie carefully placed a third Q-Tip on the remaining two and returned to the galley in a hurry.

Madame? He had told me he had a surprise in store. Had he invited Ginger, his lady-friend bartender from the Oar House Lounge? His mother?

I looked around the living room, er…lounge. Salon perhaps. Stateroom? (No wait, I think the stateroom would be Willie's bedroom.) Well, whatever it was called, the room was immaculate. Our ultimate handyman Moses had worked his magic on the Silent Cow, as well as my house (which I refused to call the Prescription Pad as christened by Willie and my friends). I looked closely at the flooring. It appeared to be planks off shipping pallets but they had been cut, planed and sanded to fit perfectly together. Some of the boards were stained and some not, creating a beautiful one-of-a-kind floor. I touched the surface, noting it had enough of a top coat sealer on it to give it an ice rink appearance. If there were any bugs or germs in the wood, they were trapped as tight as a wooly mammoth in the La Brea Tar Pits. Over in the corner was a marble-topped bar, complete with octagonal mirror behind. A small but intricate stone fireplace with logs filled out the far wall from where I sat on the plastic covered couch.

Willie returned with a Fat Tire bottle for me, an organic beer for him and a rose-colored drink in a tumbler glass.

"How in the world do you burn wood in that fireplace without burning down the Silent Cow?" I asked.

"Those are electric logs."

I didn't need to ask him where his electric came from; coming down the path I almost tripped over two of the heavy-duty extension cords snaking from the back of my house to the houseboat.

"Oh yay," I said weakly. "Do they produce heat?"

"Of course. Electric fireplaces have the highest heating efficiency of any type of fireplace. When I crank it up on cold nights, the whole underbelly of the Silent Cow stays warm. Without having any nasty, dirty wood laying around."

"Let me guess. Cut wood is a breeding ground for insects and disease."

He gave me a blank look, like I had just said a truth as simple as "The sky is blue".

When Willie looked away, I examined my "adopted" friend (a school mate from junior high in West Virginia, he had magically materialized on Oak Island in almost the same way his houseboat had appeared on my land). Willie—pale, squat and muscular, with a flat-top haircut he had kept longer than most of his coiffures—actually looked better than he had last week. He smelled better too, as he no longer walked around with a tallow poultice wrapped around his upper body in a flannel cloth. ("The fat from a cow," he had explained, "Applied in a poultice around the chest will keep a deep cough from becoming pneumonia." Picture a silent cow lying in the pasture with four stiff legs skyward for months—that's what Willie smelled like.)

I tilted my Fat Tire bottle toward him and he clinked the top with the neck of his Eel River Organic Amber Ale.

"Where'd you get the beer?"

"The Fat Tire is from your refrigerator—"

"Not the Fat Tire! The organic beer." I had long given up getting mad at Willie for rummaging through my refrigerator—and kitchen cabinets—and mail.

Willie glanced at the red and white label with a picture of a bridge in a black circle in the middle. "I finally convinced the Food Lion manager to stock organic beer. I can be very persuasive."

I nodded. Persuasion, in a Willie-type way, meant the manager hoped if he stocked organic beer he would never have to have another tiresome, exasperating, make-you-want-to-claw-out-your-eyes-and-feed-them-to-the-seagulls conversation with Willie ever again.

My eyes found the bare wall once more, and suddenly it dawned on me. "Ian Anderson!" I cried.

"Where? Where?" Willie jumped to his feet and ran to the porthole. "Where?"

"Yes, Willie. Ian Anderson is on Oak Island," I said sarcastically. "And I invited him to the Silent Cow." Ian Anderson, the face of the band Jethro Tull, as far as I knew, lived on a farm in England and maybe had a house in Switzerland. Chances he was on Oak Island ranged from remote to nil.

"Hey!" Willie shot back, picking up on my tone. "It could happen!"

Willie owned a picture of Ian Anderson, which, until recently apparently, had hung on that wall keeping watch over the Silent Cow from his 8 x 10 frame. Willie's eyes shot to the empty place on the wall, he looked away quickly, and he actually shuddered. I decided to ask about Ian's whereabouts later.

"So, what's this surprise?" I asked instead.

Willie's countenance darkened as his eyes darted around the cabin. He actually looked terrified. Like he had been lowered into the middle of a room full of strangers who all turned toward him and coughed at the same time.

I placed my hand on his arm and he didn't pull away from my touch. Another sign this was something serious. "What is it? Did your cold from last week turn into pneumonia, despite the tallow? A relative from home passed away? Did you discover that organic beer is only a marketing gimmick?"

His eyes were wide, flickering all about the cabin. In a hushed voice, his lips barely moving, he said, "The Silent Cow is haunted."

"I—wait—what?"

I stared at Willie, waiting for the punch line. He said nothing more, just continued to scan the cabin nervously. I followed suit—aft, stern, port, starboard, there was no movement, nothing out of place. If there were ghosts on board, we were going to need a bigger boat. My eyes fell upon the tumbler with the rose-colored drink. Something about it looked familiar.

Bam! The cabin door exploded inward, knocking over a chair before hitting the wall. Instinctively, I jumped up from the couch, banging my head on the low ceiling. I rubbed the spot furiously and despite the immediate pain, determined I would live. It was probably only a skull fracture.

The being in the doorway was a tiny figure, dressed head to toe in black. With the sunlight behind, the vision was surreal, eerie. I shivered (or perhaps it was a slight seizure from my head trauma).

"I always imagined ghosts to be much…taller," I whispered to Willie.

I leaned forward to get a better look. Based on the wardrobe, it appeared to be a woman. Black dress to the floor, black shoes, black lace veil pulled down over her face (which looked more like a black half-slip with the waist band tied in a knot). I noticed the top of a white, flat box sticking out of a huge, black bag hanging at her side. The top of a bottle was also visible. Gin? Did ghosts drink gin?

The lace rustled as her head turned back and forth, surveying the Silent Cow.

"Madame!" Willie cried, relieved. "Welcome."

Madame?

Willie turned to me. "I have asked the Madame here," he said. "To rid the Silent Cow of ethereal beings." He locked eyes and issued a warning. "Behave and believe, Daniel."

What? What did he mean by that? Why, my mind is as open as the next guys. I mean, I don't really think ghosts are real, but today should turn out to be—

She took one step into the Silent Cow and stopped, extending her arms out and up, pope like. (She was either trying to summon the spirits or bracing for a phantom rogue wave to hit the Silent Cow.) Her hands were obscured by an oversized black shawl; a thin, gnarled, trembling finger found an opening through the dark garb. Like the Grim Reaper, she pointed it at Willie.

"Where's my Rose Kennedy Cocktail, Germ Boy?"

I laughed and clapped my hands. As I was saying, today should turn out to be most entertaining.

Willie ran over, grabbed the drink and took it to the old woman. She threw back her veil, revealing the familiar weathered face with thin, stringy white hair falling all around it. She grabbed the glass with both hands.

"I really need a damn drink," she said.

"Miss Matilda!" I cried, running to hug her. "How come you're here? Won't Glenn and Glenda miss you at No Egrets?"

I should have recognized the rose-colored drink as soon as Willie brought it into the room. I had been at the local bar, No Egrets, on enough Sundays to see her down close to fifty. (She only drank Rose Kennedy Cocktails on Sundays, having a different drink for each day of the week.)

Matilda pushed me away. "Keep your distance, Pill Man," she said, referring to my previous life as a hospital pharmacist. "Get ahold of your carnal urges. I have a job to do." For the first time, I noticed she was wearing jewelry. Matilda never wore anything more than a grimace or sneer, so I was quite surprised. (I could only assume the extra bling would serve as some kind of conduit to "the other side".) She dripped with Mardi Gras beads, somebody's old prom ear rings (circa 1962) and finger rings that looked like they came from a gumball machine.

"Besides, it's been too uppity at No Egrets since the anniversary party," Matilda continued. "Too many people and it's 'Mind your manners, Tilly', 'Be nice, Tilly', 'That's not for polite company, Tilly'." She paused in her mocking of the owners long enough to growl (I had to admit she had Glenda's voice down pretty good). "Glenn and Glenda think they're hot shit now. If it weren't for the smoking hot firefighters next door, I'd be long gone."

I couldn't suppress a laugh. This was too much. I was in a landlocked houseboat with Matilda, the local barfly, known all over the island. Whether riding her Vespa through town or in her usual seat at the end of No Egrets' bar, her sarcasm and razor-sharp tongue would cut people to shreds. She was also quite blue for an elderly woman, and I don't mean the color of her hair. Vulgar may be a better description, so I wondered how much Glenn and Glenda were actually missing her today.

"Tilly, Tilly, Tilly," I said, smiling.

"It's Madame Matilda today," she snarled.

I started to laugh again but noticed Willie shooting me a nasty look. Instead, I bowed to her and swept my arm into the interior of the houseboat. "Madame."

Madame Matilda slowly walked into the living area (Lounge? Salon?) of the Silent Cow, slowly turning and surveying the hull of the vessel. She stopped suddenly, shivered and pulled her shawl tight around her thin body.

"I just felt a cold chill. Has anyone died aboard this boat?"

Willie took two steps back and seemed to pull into himself. He looked around, horrified. I imagine any type of blood spill, even imaginary, would be enough to send him into a full-blown panic attack. I could hear him now, ticking off the list of bloodborne pathogens.

"Well," I said. "Last week Willie wore a tallow poultice and it smelled like someone had died."

Willie shot me another dirty look, but at least the distraction seemed to ward off his panic attack. "Daniel, if you aren't going to take this seriously, I'm afraid you're going to have to leave."

"Oh, no!" Matilda cried, grabbing my arm and leading me to a chair at the small round table Willie used for a dinner table. "We must have the Power of Three."

The Power of Three? Are you kidding me? Wasn't that from some witches show on television? An episode of Dr. Who?

I started to make a snide comment, but Willie, sensing it, smacked me in the back of the head with the handle of a nearby Swiffer Wet Jet mop.

"Ouch! What's that for?"

Willie looked at the cleaning gadget in his hand. "It's a wonderful all-in-one mopping system. The best I've found because of the disposable cleaning pads. Traditional mops just spread the bacteria around and are breeding grounds—"

"Shut up, you wankers!" Matilda screamed. "Cut out the Abbott and Costello routine and make me another Rose Kennedy Cocktail." Her eyes seemed to roll back in her head, leaving only the white. "Time to get started," she added in an otherworldly voice.

I jumped back. Willie scurried into the galley to mix another drink. I looked closer at Matilda. Maybe I had misjudged her, maybe she really did have psychic ability. I really didn't know a whole lot about her past (except she had been crowned Miss Ring Girl at a Charlotte Toughman Contest sometime in the 80s and she had banged a Rolling Stones' roadie backstage to the rhythm of Bill Wyman's bass).

Matilda cackled, showing crooked teeth through a crooked smile. "You like that? Scared the little guy silly. I've been able to roll my eyes back in my head since I was a teenager. If I didn't like a feller, used to do that after I faked an orgasm. They'd think I died and would run from the house!" Her whole body was shaking with laughter at the memories. "God, those were good times!"

I grinned and took a slug of my Fat Tire. Yep, this was going to be entertaining.

Willie entered, placing a fresh Rose Kennedy Cocktail in front of Matilda and taking the third seat at the table. Matilda attacked the drink like a lizard with a long, sticky tongue ensnaring an insect. It was somewhat disgusting to watch (and very messy).

"Willie" I said, trying to keep the skepticism out of my voice. "What makes you think the Silent Cow is haunted?"

His eyes flicked about the cabin again. He shivered. "Drinking glasses move on their own—on this very table. And just yesterday, my empty bottle of Eel River Organic Amber Ale was knocked over four times! Every time I set it upright it was knocked over again." He ran his hand over a spot. "I had to scrub the tabletop five times."

"Maybe ghosts don't like organic—"

He silenced me with an upraised hand. "And...they knocked my autographed Ian Anderson photograph from the wall and broke the glass in the frame."

I gasped. So that's what happened to Ian. And the picture was signed? The way Willie worshiped Jethro Tull's music left no doubt that an autograph from its flutist front man would be his most prized possession.

I could see Willie's eyes were beginning to tear. "It crinkled the edges of the photo," he wailed. "It's ruined."

I placed my hand on his shoulder and again he did not pull away. He really was out of sorts.

"Maybe—" I scanned the floor of the houseboat. "Have you gotten out your...er, my level recently? Maybe the Silent Cow has shifted and she is no longer flush, um plumb. We did have some big winds from Hurricane Matthew."

"A skewed deck could not produce what I saw," he said simply. "And then there's the toothbrush."

We waited for him to continue but all he did was crinkle his nose and begin retching. Matilda looked to me for guidance; I shrugged my shoulders, letting him cough and sputter. When Willie was repulsed and nauseated by something he considered revolting, there was no reeling him back in. Best to let him flounder around until he bobbed back to the surface.

Willie carefully dabbed the sweat on his brow with a folded lint free cloth and leaned back in his chair. With a trembling hand, he raised the Eel River Organic Amber Ale to his lips.

I gave him another minute before asking, "What happened to your toothbrush?"

Willie shivered and I thought he might start the whole process again, but he managed to gather himself.

"Every morning—" He paused to clear his throat, almost retching again. "My toothbrush is already wet when I pick it up."

I gasped. Matilda snickered.

"I've only got one toothbrush left from the 10-pack I bought last week," he said sadly. With a sudden wave of his hand he continued, "I can't talk about it. Please! Madame Matilda, can you help me?"

Matilda twitched. (I think she may have drifted off.) She pulled the large black bag from her shoulder and placed it on the table with a thud. What did she have in there (besides the gin)? A crystal ball? Tarot cards? Holy water?

She struggled to pull the long, flat rectangular box out of her black shoulder bag and unceremoniously plopped it on the table. What the heck? The box was white, or used to be white; one corner was gone and old, yellowed tape held the other end together. It had a red cartoonish devil displayed—with a wand! The Sensational Game, the box proclaimed. Entertainment for Everyone!

Matilda tore the lid from the box, removed a flat, wooden board from the bottom and slammed it on the table. Before flinging the box off the table, she took out a triangular piece of wood with a small, round window near the point.

It really wasn't all that surprising "Madame" Matilda intended to ward off Willie's spirits with an Ouija board. My guess is it would work better than a Magic 8 Ball.

"My, that's an old one" was all I could think of to say.

Matilda stroked the wooden board lovingly. "It was the one thing my father gave me before he runned off with the baby sitter. Well, I also got his raging libido."

I shuddered. It was almost impossible to guess Matilda's age after years on a barstool. She could be anywhere from sixty-two to ninety-two. She probably didn't weigh more than ninety-two pounds either.

"Well?" Matilda hollered at Willie. He looked at her dumbstruck.

"The magic sticks! You moron."

Willie hopped up and ran over to the end table, bringing back the three mysterious Q-tips. Magic sticks?

"Okay, my interest is piqued. What are the Q-tips for?" I asked.

"Not," Willie stated emphatically. "For use in the ear canal."

Oh, goody. Willie was feeling better.

Madame Matilda had her eyes closed (had she drifted off again?) and after a few seconds she answered. "Besides my natural abilities, I was taught the art of hoodoo by a witch in Harlem. It was there I learned that cotton can absorb more than earthly matter."

Hmm, chalk up another unusual use for the Q-tip website. (As long as you don't use it to clean a ghost's ear canal.)

"Mr. Big Stuff," I sang. "Hoodoo you think you are?"

Willie and Matilda stared at me blankly. "Daniel," Willie said. "This is no time for a wordplay game. What is wrong with you?"

The number of times I had been in the middle of something, either serious or intense, only to be interrupted by Willie demanding a wordplay match probably numbered in the hundreds. His eyes would light up and there was no turning him away. The first time Willie and Matilda had met at No Egrets, they had locked in a killer game of wordplay revolving around wine and liquor names.

Now they both looked at me as if I was the childish one. "Whatever," I said, rolling my eyes.

Matilda placed the heart-shaped planchette on top of the Ouija board and handed a Q-tip to Willie and me. "Time to get started, before I need another Rose Kennedy Cocktail."

I watched as she and Willie placed the end of their Q-tips on different sides of the planchette. What the heck. "That's not going to work," I claimed. "Without human touch the pointer won't move."

"Au contraire, non croyant," Matilda said.

I looked at Willie. "Did she just call me a croissant?"

"It was French," he said in an exasperated tone. "She called you a nonbeliever."

French? Matilda? Did she learn it from the Harlem Hoodoo Queen? The only French I had heard her mutter at No Egrets was "Merde". I had thought Matilda was only multilingual in "The Seven Words You Can Never Say on Television" as made famous by George Carlin. (She did seem to know that particular word in seven different languages.)

"Please," Willie begged. Feeling somewhat foolish, I picked up the third Q-tip and placed one cotton end on the third side of the planchette.

We sat there motionless for a full minute—the heart-shaped piece of wood did not move. I noticed the color of the wood planchette had faded to a dull gray, reminding me of the color of my spare bathroom. Jaclyn had brought me paint chips from Oak Island Hardware and we planned on painting the bathroom walls soon. I looked at my Q-tip and imagined dipping it in paint, swabbing the faded planchette with a nice buttercream yellow to spruce it up. Or maybe a nice lemon chiffon.

"Someone!" Madame Matilda bellowed. I flinched and my Q-tip

dropped, spinning a little and coming to rest near a word on the Ouija board. "Someone is not concentrating! At least not on the spirits."

As they both glared at me, I started to pick up my Q-tip. "Hey look!" I said excitedly. "My cotton swab is trying to tell us something." My Q-tip was pointing to the word "Goodbye" at the bottom of the board.

Willie actually growled at me. I remembered the last time he had made me so mad that an inhuman "Grrr" escaped my lips. I felt bad for a second, a second and a half maybe, and then I smiled. Chalk one up for Daniel. Score: Daniel-one; Willie-five hundred and fifty-three.

I picked up the Q-tip and placed the end back on the planchette. The other two followed suit.

I tried my best to concentrate on the spirits, wondering what they looked like. The only spirits I had seen recently were on the shelves of the Oak Island ABC Store.

Madame Matilda's head slowly lolled back until she was staring at the ceiling. I had to look away because it reminded me of the day she brought a test tube into No Egrets, leaned back on her barstool and tried to get Pinhead Paul to give her a Zombie shooter (it was Thursday).

When a low moan escaped her lips, I gave sudden thought to fleeing out the cabin door. The last thing on earth I wanted to hear was Matilda moan. That would be the granddaddy of all nightmares.

Her head shot forward again and she called, in a crusty voice, "Spirits of the past move among us. Is there anyone here who wishes to speak with us?"

I almost dropped my Q-tip as the planchette jerked. I eyed Willie to see how he had made the wood jump, but he had a shocked look on his face.

Madame Matilda spoke again. "Is there anyone from the spirit world who wishes to speak with us?"

I had a strange feeling in the pit of my stomach. It seemed to be a mixture of fear and...hunger? Had I eaten breakfast this morning? My stomach let out a weird, prolonged gurgling noise.

Willie gasped. "Yes," he whispered. "I hear the spirits."

I was about to open my mouth to debunk this particular development when the planchette jerked again.

"Is there a spirit present in the Silent Cow who wishes to speak with us?" Madame Matilda cried.

The planchette, which had been in the middle of the board, began moving slowly to the left. Amazed, I watched as it came to rest over the first letter on the top row: "A". Now it was moving again to the right and toward the bottom row. The next letter was "Y". Back to the top row on the left, the planchette stopped on "E". We all waited breathlessly for it to continue moving.

When the planchette didn't move again, I asked, "Aye? Who says aye nowadays?"

"They're here," Madame Matilda proclaimed in a high-pitched voice, staring, for some reason, at Willie's blank television screen in the corner.

"Who?" Willie asked, shivering.

I couldn't contain myself. "Why Captain Ahab and his great, white whale. We're all in here together. In the Silent Cow." Muttering, I pondered again, "Who says aye?"

Willie looked at Madame Matilda. "Can I ask them a question?" As she nodded, the black veil/half-slip fell back over her face.

"Oh, great spirit!" Willie nearly shouted. (I had a sudden image of the Peanuts gang in the pumpkin patch summoning the Great Pumpkin—Willie did look a little like Linus.)

"Oh, great spirit," Willie repeated. "Is it you that has been...um, touching my toothbrush?"

I looked sideways at Willie. One question to ask the netherworld and he chooses that one?

A quick spasm in the planchette and it began to move again. First letter: "C". A quick left to "A" and finally to the right on the second row: "T".

"Cat!" we all three exclaimed, somewhat perplexed.

"That doesn't make any sense," Willie said, shaking his head.

"Sometimes," Madame Matilda offered. "The words are too long and the spirits can't gather enough energy to finish."

We pondered this for a moment, waiting to see if the planchette would move again.

"Maybe they were spelling a name and didn't finish," Madame Matilda finally said, the black veil still hiding her face. "Have you been banging somebody named Cathy and she's been using your toothbrush when you're not looking?"

"What?" Willie screamed. "No. A thousand times no! And even if it were true, if I found out she was using my toothbrush, I would throw her over the stern and into the woods, just like all of the contaminated toothbrushes."

I was only half-listening, thinking about the first spelled word, the beer bottle, Ian Anderson photograph, drinking glass and toothbrush. How could they all be tied to the word "aye"? The logical mind of the pharmacist tried to fit them all together

"I've got it!" I cried. They both looked at me expectantly. "Who says aye?"

"Johnny Depp in those Disney Pirate movies," Willie answered.

I grimaced. "Close. However, I don't think the Silent Cow was built that long ago; I don't know how pirates could be haunting it. But I do think it's seamen."

Willie looked around his home, aghast. "You mean there's seamen—"

His eyes flicked from floor to ceiling. "Seamen all over the Silent Cow?"

I could sense a cackle building deep within Matilda and a lewd comment just around the bend. I waggled my finger at her, saying, "That would be very un-Madame-like." It was all I could do to hold my own tongue with a Monica Lewinsky one-liner on the tip.

I tried to steer the conversation in a different direction. "So, how does the word cat fit into a seaman—er, seafarer's world?"

They both looked at me stupidly (or at least I imagined Matilda did through her veil).

"Seamen were often flogged with a cat o' nine tails!" I said triumphantly.

"Huh-what?" Willie stammered. "I don't get it."

"It's simple," I said slowly, as if explaining to kindergartners. "The Silent Cow is haunted by seamen. They are using…um, some kind of invisible whip, a cat o' nine tails to knock over your beer bottle, move your glass on the table, knock Ian Anderson off the wall—"

"Sacrilege," Willie exclaimed. "But what about the toothbrush?"

I thought about it for a minute, then had an idea. "Easy. I assume your toothbrush is secure in some kind of wall holder?"

"Yes," Willie answered.

"Then the ghost seamen can't knock it off the wall with the invisible cat o' nine tails. But—apparently, they can use the cat o' nine tails to flick it and apply a coat of some kind of ectoplasmic slime to the bristles."

Willie eyes grew wide and he started retching again.

"I might be wrong," I said loudly, over Willie's gagging and coughing. "It's just a theory."

A sudden low, guttural moan silenced us; it sounded inhuman, seeming to reverberate off the walls, building in the room until we had to cover our ears. I glanced at Madame Matilda and her head was tilted back at what seemed a ninety-degree angle, the black veil still covering her face. The sound was coming from her!

The lights flickered. Willie let out a girly scream (or maybe it was me). The Ouija board flipped from the table and landed on the floor. I watched as the planchette pirouetted through the air in slow motion, heading toward Willie's head. Too stunned to move, the point of the planchette struck Willie just below the left eye. His hand went immediately to his cheek and I could see blood leaking down between his fingers. I watched in horror as my Fat Tire bottle moved a little on the table and then fell over. It was three-fourths full!

The lights began flickering so fast I thought I was back in the disco era, dancing my cool white-boy dance ("Do the Hustle!"). The strobe effect finally died and the Silent Cow was immersed in darkness, with only a slim ray of light coming from the other room.

Willie let out a little whimper (or maybe it was me, mourning my spilled

Fat Tire). The inhuman moan from Madame Matilda became louder. I leaned closer to get a better look. Her head was still tilted back and—she seemed to be rising out of her chair. Now when I say rising, I don't mean standing up. She was floating! Her bony behind was at least a foot off her chair.

I was terrified, but I couldn't help wonder how much Glenn and Glenda would pay to have the ghostly technology available to float Matilda off her barstool and out the door of No Egrets on occasion.

I was still looking at Madame Matilda when a fireball of light seemed to shoot from beneath her veil, blinding me. The moaning stopped. The Silent Cow was silent. After a few seconds, I heard the sound of Willie rubbing his eyes (or maybe the table, trying to sanitize it).

My eyes were still adjusting when a deep, masculine voice began spatting an unending string of curses. I could only make out a word here or there, but there was no mistaking the intent. I heard strange words like "quim", "quiffing", "doxie", followed by more familiar words like "feck", "arse" and "shite".

Finally the spots were gone from my eyes and I concentrated on focusing on Madame Matilda's face. Her face was shimmering beneath the veil and it looked like…she had whiskers! A foul smell emanated from her, unlike any I had smelled before (even worse than the time she had eaten cooked cabbage at No Egrets—the rest of the day an olfactory sensation I will never forget).

The floating form of Madame Matilda reached out two bony hands, one grabbing Willie by the throat and the other latching onto my windpipe. She had the strength of ten seamen.

A growling voice came from beneath the veil. "Fecking arses!" My eyes, popping, beheld a sneering, bearded, masculine face shimmering in place of the old woman's.

"Not pirates," the voice growled. "Privateers!"

I tried to break the hold on my neck but Madame Matilda gripped it like she was hanging on to a ship's boom during a storm (or the last Rose Kennedy Cocktail on earth).

"Shite," the voice said, starting to weaken. "A cat—" I could see the shimmering face beginning to fade. With a final burst of energy, the voice shouted, "Is a fecking cat!"

The Silent Cow went dark. Madame Matilda's hands loosened and fell from our throats.

A loud sound, like fingernails scratching the inside of a coffin, filled the interior of the Silent Cow.

CPSIA information can be obtained
at www.ICGtesting.com
Printed in the USA
FSHW011012051020
74469FS

9 781520 395579